D0891724

J.M.G. LE CLÉZIO

THE INTERROGATION

TRANSLATED FROM THE FRENCH BY
DAPHNE WOODWARD

SIMON & SCHUSTER

NEW YORK   LONDON   TORONTO   SYDNEY

 Simon & Schuster
1230 Avenue of the Americas
New York, NY 10020

This Simon & Schuster hardcover edition December 2008

SIMON & SCHUSTER and colophon are registered trademarks
of Simon & Schuster, Inc.

For information about special discounts for bulk purchases,
please contact Simon & Schuster Special Sales at
1-800-456-6798 or business@simonandschuster.com

Manufactured in the United States of America

10 9 8 7 6 5 4 3 2 1

ISBN-13: 978-1-4391-4918-8
ISBN-10:   1-4391-4918-6

'POLL, AS IF HE HAD BEEN MY FAVORITE, WAS THE ONLY PERSON PERMITTED TO TALK TO ME.' Robinson Crusoe

I have two secret ambitions. One of them is to write, one day, a novel of such a kind that if the hero dies in the last chapter—or, at a pinch, develops Parkinson's disease—I shall be swamped beneath a flood of scurrilous anonymous letters.

From this point of view, I know, The Interrogation *is not entirely successful. It is perhaps too serious, too mannered and wordy; its style ranges from para-realistic dialogue to pedantically aphoristical bombast.*

But I don't despair of writing a really effective novel later on: something in the spirit of Conan Doyle, appealing not to the readers' taste for realism—along the broad lines of psychological analysis and illustration—but to their sentimentality.

It seems to me that in this direction there are great untrodden wastes to be explored, vast frozen regions dividing author from reader. Their exploration should employ every kind of sympathetic approach, from the humorous to the naive; it should not be systematic. There comes a moment when between the teller and the listener belief manifests itself, takes shape. This is perhaps the moment attained in the novel of 'action', the essential factor of which may be a species of compulsion. Where the words convey an elusive touch of reminiscence, a domestic quality. Where—just as in a magazine serial or a strip-cartoon in a cheap paper—every girl is expected to heave a sigh of excitement, filling in the gap that yawns between the lines until then.

It seems to me that writing, communicating, implies the ability to make anybody believe anything. And only an uninterrupted sequence of indiscretions can dent the reader's armour of indifference.

The Interrogation *is the story of a man who is not sure whether he has just left the army or a mental home. In other words, I deliberately chose, at the outset, a tenuous, abstract theme. I have made very little attempt at realistic treatment (I have a stronger and stronger impression that there is no such thing as reality); I would like my story to be taken as a complete fiction, interesting only in so far as it produces a kind of repercussion (however briefly) on the reader's mind. This sort of thing is familiar to all readers of detective stories and so forth. A kind of game or jigsaw puzzle in the form of a novel. It couldn't be taken seriously, of course, but for the fact that the method has other advantages—it lightens the style, livens up the dialogue, and avoids dry-as-dust description and stale psychology.*

I apologize for putting forward a few theories in this way; that form of vanity is rather too fashionable nowadays. I also apologize for any slips or typing mistakes there may still be in my manuscript, in spite of several readings. (I had to type it myself, and I can only type with one finger of each hand).

Lastly, I would like to mention that I have begun another and much longer story, telling as simply as possible what happens the day after a girl's death.

Very respectfully yours,
J. M. G. LE CLÉZIO.

A. Once upon a little time, in the dog-days, there was a fellow sitting at an open window; he was an inordinately tall boy with a slight stoop, and his name was Adam; Adam Pollo. He had the air of a beggar in his way of looking everywhere for patches of sunshine and sitting for hours practically motionless in the angle of a wall. He never knew what to do with his arms, he usually left them to dangle at his sides, touching his body as little as possible. He was like one of those sick animals that make a canny retreat into some refuge and watch stealthily for danger, the kind that comes creeping along the ground and hides in its skin, blending right into it. Now he was lying on a deck-chair by the open window, naked to the waist, bare-headed, bare-footed, with the sky slanting overhead. All he had on was a pair of beige linen trousers, shabby and sweat-stained; he had rolled the legs up to his knees.

The yellow sunshine was hitting him full in the face, but without glancing off again: it was immediately absorbed by his damp skin, striking no sparks, not even the faintest little gleam. He guessed as much and made no movement, except that from time to time he lifted a cigarette to his lips and drew in a gulp of smoke.

When the cigarette was finished, when it burnt his thumb and fore-finger and he had to drop it on the floor, he took a

I

handkerchief from his trousers pocket and with great deliberation wiped his chest and forearms, the base of his throat and his armpits. Once rid of the thin film of sweat which had protected it until that moment, his skin began to glow like fire, red with light. Adam got up and walked quickly to the back of the room, into the shade; from the pile of blankets on the floor he pulled out an old shirt made of cotton, flannelette or calico, shook it and slipped it on. When he bent down, the tear in the middle of the back, between his shoulder-blades, opened in a way it had, to the size of a coin, and revealed, at random, three pointed vertebrae which stuck out beneath the taut skin like fingernails under thin rubber.

Without even buttoning his shirt, Adam took from among the blankets a kind of yellow exercise-book, the sort used in schools, in which the first page was headed, like the beginning of a letter:

My dear Michèle,

then he went back to sit in front of the window, protected now from the rays of the sun by the material that clung to his ribs. He opened the exercise-book on his knees, ruffled briefly through the pages covered with closely-written sentences, produced a ball-point pen from his pocket, and read:

'My dear Michèle,

I would so much like this house to stay empty. I hope the owners won't come back for a long time.

This is how I'd dreamt of living for ages: I put up two deck-chairs facing each other, just under the window; like that, about midday, I lie down and sleep in the sun, turned towards the view, which is beautiful, so they say. Or else I turn away a little towards the light, throwing my head into full relief. At four o'clock I stretch out further, provided the sun is lower or shining in more directly; by that time it's about ¾ down the window. I look at the sun, perfectly round; at the sea, that's to say the horizon, right up against the window-rail, perfectly straight. I spend every minute at the window, and I pretend all this is mine, silently, and no one else's. It's funny. I'm like that the whole time, in the sun, almost naked, and sometimes quite naked, looking carefully at the sky and the sea. I'm glad people think everywhere that I'm dead; at first I didn't know this was a deserted house; that kind of luck doesn't come often.

When I decided to live here I took all I needed, as though I were going fishing, I came back in the night, and then I toppled my motorbike into the sea. Like that I gave the impression I was dead, and I didn't need to go on making everyone believe I was alive and had heaps of things to do, to keep myself alive.

The funny thing is that no one took any notice, even at the beginning; luckily I hadn't too many friends, and I didn't know any girls, because they're always the first to come and tell you to stop playing the fool, to get back to the town and begin all over again as though nothing had happened: that's to say cafés, cinemas, railways, etc.

From time to time I go into town to buy stuff to eat, because I eat a lot, and often. Nobody asks me questions, and I don't have to talk too much; that doesn't worry me, because years ago they got me into the habit of keeping my mouth shut, and I could easily pass for deaf, dumb and blind.'

He paused for a few seconds and wiggled his fingers as though to relax them; then he bent over the exercise-book again, so that the little veins in his temples swelled and the egg-shaped, hirsute lump of his skull was exposed to the savage thrusts of the sun. This time he wrote:
'My dear Michèle,

Thanks to you, Michèle—for you exist, I believe you—I

3

have my only possible contact with the world down the hill. You go to work, you're often in the town, at the different street crossings, among the blinking lights and God knows what. You tell heaps of people you know a chap who lives alone in a deserted house, a complete nut; and they ask you why he isn't shut up in a loony-bin. I assure you I've nothing against it, I've no cervical complex and I think that's as good a way as any other to end one's days—in peace, in a comfortable house, with a formal French garden and people to see that you get your meals. The rest doesn't matter, and there's nothing to prevent one from being full of imagination and writing poems—this kind of thing:

> today, day of the rats,
> last day before the sea.

Fortunately I can make you out amidst a mass of memories, like when we used to play hide-and-seek and I would catch sight of your eye, your hand or you hair between clusters of round leaves, and thinking about it all of a sudden I would discard my faith in appearances and cry shrilly: "Seen you!".'

He thought about Michèle, about all the children she'd be having sooner or later, in any case; irrationally, that didn't matter, he could wait. He would tell those children a whole heap of things, when the time came. He'd tell them, for instance, that the earth was not round, that it was the centre of the universe, and that they were the centre of everything, without exception. Then they would no longer be in danger of losing themselves, and (unless they got polio, of course) they would have 99 chances in a hundred of going about like those children he had seen last time he went to the beach—shouting, yelling, chasing rubber balls.

He would tell them, too, that there was only one thing to

be afraid of—that the earth might turn over, so that they would be head downwards with their feet in the air, and that the sun might fall down on the beach, about six o'clock, making the sea boil so that all the little fishes would burst.

Dressed now, he sat in the deck-chair and looked out of the window; to do this he had to raise the cross-bar of the chair to the highest notch. The hill went down to the road in a slope that was half gradual and half steep, jumped four or five yards; and then came the water. Adam couldn't get a complete view; there were lots of pines and other trees and telegraph poles in the way, so he had to imagine parts of it. Sometimes he wasn't sure whether he'd guessed right, so he had to go all the way down. As he walked along he could see the skein of lines and curves unravelling, different things would splinter off and gleam; but the fog gathered again further ahead. One could never be definite about anything in this kind of landscape; one was always more or less a queer unknown quantity, but in an unpleasant way. Call it something like a squint or a slight exophthalmic goitre; the house itself, or the sky, or it might be the curve of the bay, would become obscured from view as Adam walked down. For shrubs and brushwood wove an uninterrupted screen in front of them; at ground-level the air quivered in the heat, and the far horizon seemed to be rising in puffs of light smoke from among the blades of grass.

The sun distorted certain things, too. Beneath its rays the road would liquify in whitish patches; sometimes when a line of cars was going by, the black metal would burst like a bomb for no apparent reason, a spiral of lightning would flash from the bonnet and make the entire hill blaze and bend, shifting the atmosphere by a few millimetres with a thrust of its halo.

5

That was at the beginning, really at the beginning; for afterwards he began to understand what it meant, monstrous solitude. He opened a yellow exercise-book and wrote at the top of the first page, as though beginning a letter:

'My dear Michèle,'

He used to play music as well, like everyone else; once, in the town, he had stolen a plastic pipe from a toy-stall. He had always wanted a pipe and he'd been delighted to have this one. It was a toy pipe, of course, but good quality, it came from the U.S. So when he felt inclined he would sit in the deck-chair at the open window and play gentle little tunes. Rather afraid of attracting people's attention, because there were days when fellows and girls used to come and lie down in the grass, round the house. He played softly, with infinite gentleness, making almost inaudible sounds, blowing hardly at all, pressing the tip of his tongue against the mouthpiece and pulling in his diaphragm. Now and then he would break off and rattle his fingertips along a row of empty tins, arranged in order of size; that made a soft rustling, rather like bongo drums, which went zigzagging away in the air, rather like the howls of a dog.

And that was the life of Adam Pollo. At night he would light the candles at the back of the room and take up his position at the open window in the faint sea-breeze, standing absolutely erect, full of the energy that the dusty noonday takes from a man.

He would wait a long time, without moving, proud of being almost dehumanized, until the first flights of moths arrived, tumbling, hesitating outside the empty hole of the window, pausing in concentration and then, maddened by the yellow blink of the candles, launching a sudden attack. Then he would lie down on the floor, among the blankets, and stare fixedly at the hustling swarm of insects, more and more of them, thronging the ceiling with a multiplicity of shadows and collapsing into the flames, making a wreath of tiny legs round the corolla of boiling wax, sizzling, scraping the air like files against a granite wall, and smothering, one by one, every glimmer of light.

For someone in Adam's circumstances, and who had been trained to meditation by years at a university and a life devoted to reading, there was nothing to do except think of things like this and avoid madness; hence it was probable that only fear (of the sun, to take one example) could help him to remain within the bounds of moderation and, should the occasion arise, to go back to the beach. With this in mind, Adam had now slightly changed his usual position: leaning forward, he had turned his face towards the back of the room and was looking at the wall. Seeing the light dimly across his left shoulder, he was forcing himself to imagine that the sun was an immense golden spider, its rays covering the sky like tentacles, some twisting, others forming a huge W, clinging to projections in the ground, to every escarpment, at fixed points.

All the other tentacles were undulating slowly, lazily, dividing into branches, separating into countless ramifications, splitting open and immediately closing up again, waving to and fro like seaweed.

To make sure, he had drawn it in charcoal on the wall opposite.

So now he was sitting with his back to the window, and could feel terror creeping over him as the minutes went by and he contemplated the tangle of claws, the savage medley that he could no longer understand. Apart from its special aspect of something dry and charred which was shining and sprinkling, it was a kind of horrible, deadly octopus, with its hundred thousand slimy arms like horses' guts. To give himself courage he talked to the drawing, looking at its exact centre, at the anthracite ball from which the tentacles flowed out like roots calcinated in some past age; he addressed it in rather childish words:

'you're a beauty—beautiful beast, beautiful beast, there, you're a nice sun, you know, a beautiful black sun.'

He knew he was on the right track.

And sure enough, he gradually managed to reconstruct a world of childish terrors; seen through the rectangle of the window, the sky seemed ready to break away and crash down on our heads. The sun, ditto. He looked at the ground and saw it suddenly melting, boiling, or flowing beneath his feet. The trees grew excited and gave off poisonous vapours. The sea began to swell, devoured the narrow grey strip of beach and then rose, rose to attack the hill, to drown him, moving towards him, to numb him, to swallow him up in its dirty waves. He could feel the fossilized monsters coming to birth somewhere, prowling round the villa, the joints of their huge feet cracking. His fear grew, invincible, imagination and frenzy could not be checked; even human beings become hostile, barbarous, their limbs sprouted wool, their heads shrank, and they advanced in serried ranks over the countryside, cannibalistic, cowardly or ferocious. The moths flung themselves on him, biting him with their mandibles, wrapping him in the silky veil of their hairy wings. From the pools there rose an armoured nation of parasites or shrimps, of abrupt, mysterious crustaceans, hungering to tear off shreds of his flesh. The beaches were covered with strange creatures who had come there, accompanied by their young, to await no one knew what; animals prowled along the roads, growling and squealing, curious parti-coloured animals whose shells glistened in the sunshine. Everything was suddenly in motion, with an intense, intestinal, concentrated life, heavy and incongruous as a kind of submarine vegetation. While this was going on he drew back into his corner, ready to

8

spring out and defend himself pending the final assault that would leave him the prey of these creatures. He picked up the yellow exercise-book of a little while back, looked again for a moment at the drawing on the wall, the drawing which had once represented the sun; and he wrote to Michèle:

'My dear Michèle,

I must admit I'm a little frightened, here in the house. I think if you were here, in the light, lying naked on the ground, and I could recognize my own flesh in yours, smooth and warm, I shouldn't need all that. While I'm writing you this, just imagine, there happens to be a narrow space, between the deck-chair and the skirting-board, that would fit you like a glove; it's exactly your length, 5 ft. 4, and I don't think its hip measurement is more than yours, $35\frac{1}{2}$. So far as I'm concerned the earth has turned into a sort of chaos, I'm scared of the deinotheria, the pithecanthropes, the Neanderthal man (a cannibal), not to mention the dinosaurs, the labyrinthosaurs, the pterodactyls, etc. I'm afraid the hill may turn into a volcano.

Or that the polar ice may melt, which would raise the level of the sea and drown me. I'm afraid of the people on the beach, BELOW. The sand is changing into quicksands, the sun into a spider and the children into shrimps.'

Adam closed the exercise-book with a snap, raised himself on his forearms, and looked out of the window. There was nobody coming. He reckoned how much time he would need to go down to the sea, bathe and get back. It was too late in the day; he had rather forgotten how long it was since he'd last been out of the house—two days, or more.

It looked as though he had been living entirely on biscuits —cut-price wafers bought at the Prisunic. Now and then he felt a pain in his stomach, and there was a sour taste round his glottis. He leant out of the window and contemplated

9

the small section of the town that could be seen on the right, between two hills.

He lit a cigarette, one of the few remaining from the collection of eight assorted packets bought when he last went out, and said aloud:

'What's the use of going into town? It's not worth while working like I do at these crazy things—getting scared stiff, in fact—believing that if I don't go there, it's they who'll come here and kill me, yes, yes. I understand, my psychological reflexes have gone . . . but before that? Before that I could do one thing or another, and nowadays heaps of things convince me that it's finished. Adam, for God's sake, it's an effort for me to go down among all those buildings, to hear people shouting, grumbling, arguing, etc., listening to them all by myself in a corner of the wall. Sooner or later one has to bring out a word or two, say yes, thank you, excuse me, it's a beautiful evening but of course it's true that yesterday was, I'm fresh from college, and it's only fair, it would be only fair for all that muck to come to an end, and all that useless, idiotic, bloody chatter which is the reason why I'm here this evening, needing fresh air and cigarettes and with malnutrition lying in wait, asking myself why there shouldn't be just a very few more unimaginable things.'

He took a step backwards, blew smoke through his nostrils, and went on, still talking to himself (but luckily he didn't overdo that, no—partly because he had never been talkative).

'Splendid, splendid—that's all very fine, but I must go into town to buy fags, beer, chocolate and stuff to eat."

To make it clearer he wrote on a scrap of paper:

fags
beer

chocolate
stuff to eat
paper
newspapers if
possible take
a look round

Then he sat down on the floor, by the window, in the sun, where he usually waits for dark, and to rest himself he began drawing signs in the dust, aimless patterns of fine lines, scratched with a fingernail. Because of course it's tiring to live all alone like that, in a deserted house at the top of a hill. It means knowing how to look after yourself, enjoying fear, idleness and the unusual, wanting to dig lairs all the time and to hide in them, abasing yourself, keeping well concealed as you used to do when you were a kid, between two ragged pieces of old tarpaulin.

B. He had fetched up on the beach. He was lying on the pebbles at the extreme left, close to the piled-up rocks and the fringe of seaweed, an ideal place for flies to lay their eggs. He had just been swimming and now he was leaning back, propped on his elbows, leaving a small space, conducive to evaporation, between his wet back and the ground. His skin was dark red, not brown, and it clashed with his swimming-trunks, which were painted bright blue. From a distance he looked like an American tourist, but coming nearer one noticed that his face was dirty, his hair too long, and his straggling beard had been hacked off with scissors. His head hung listlessly on his chest.

His elbows were resting side by side on a bath-towel, but from the shoulder-blades downwards his body was in direct contact with the beach, and muddy patches of gravel had stuck to the hairs on his legs. With his head turned this way he could presumably see very little of the water, it would be chiefly the boulders to the left that met his eye; and assuming that these had not been washed for centuries, that for centuries men and animals had been covering them with filth, one could understand his air of vague disgust. Naturally the beach was crowded from end to end (Adam was at the extreme south-east) with people, mostly women and children, walking, sleeping or shouting, all in their different ways.

Adam had dozed for a time, like that, or even dropped right off; in the end he'd thought it would be better to stroll on and find a spot of shade somewhere. He had given himself until two o'clock, and his watch now said half-past one.

In point of fact all this was not unpleasant: it was really very hot, all sounds were dying away, one after another, as though the air were thickening, turning into a cloud. It was almost like being fitted into a hole in the atmosphere, one's very own, under the piled-up land, water and sky.

Adam enjoyed watching the lively crowd on his right; it was many-coloured, humming with voices, and on the whole much less alarming when seen from here. It was rather as though he knew these people's names, as though their mere proximity made them distant relations of the Pollo family; in any case they showed definite signs of common ancestry, the imperceptibly negroid stamp of some vanished Ameranthropus. Some of the women looked attractive in their sleep, with a kind of weighty subsidence of the flesh, a semi-burial amidst the grey pebbles, which gave a corresponding effect of relief, of soft curves, of a kind of vegetable love.

And sometimes they turned over, rolling across their bath-robes with vague movements of the bust, twisting and stretching their necks. Their children did not have this softness. On the contrary they were small, dwarfish, solemn; they gathered at the water's edge and, left to themselves, began systematically to build castles and rake the shingle. Two or three of them, too young to use their hands, uttered regular, piercing cries for no reason, and the rest of the children accepted these as a form of incantation needed for the complete success of their work.

13

Adam watched them absent-mindedly as though they, their noise and movement, had no logical connection with himself; and every sensation of his overwrought body, which magnified details, fashioned his being into a monstrous object, compact of pain, in which consciousness of life was merely consciousness of matter through the nerves. All this, of course, had a legendary past which could be invented a thousand times over without a single mistake.

The air was full of flat flies and microscopic specks of dust, which settled on the heaps of pebbles or moved on a long, horizontal course. As a matter of fact there could be no mistake here either—you could choose to stare at one pebble, selected at random, and give it mental expression by some wish such as:

'I'm going to throw it at the orange peel that's floating out there on the sea.'

Or else you could cast your eyes over the whole stretch of scenery, where everything was enormous and casual, made up of hollows and bulges, headlands and bays, trees and wells, yes and no, water and air. And in that case you must feel yourself to be impressed on the ground, spread out in the sun, the true centre of indefinably more neutral matter.

He was afraid to move too much, though at times he longed almost frantically to do so. He lay still, his spine following the irregular contours of the stones, his neck bent, his stomach muscles strained to breaking-point. A light sweat, caused by fatigue or by the heat, kept gathering in beads on his cheekbones and trickling down like tiny raindrops along his cheeks, neck, ribs and legs. He had the impression of being the only damp spot on the entire beach, as though the clammy patch that was greasing the pebbles beneath his body were intensifying the hardness and the saltish, dusty whiteness of his surroundings.

He knew why. He had a shrewd idea of it. Nobody could have accused him of not knowing what he was about; for as he lay thus motionless he could see more clearly how the world revealed itself, by snatches, in its tranquil, ludicrous, headstrong course, in the thick of action, in aggressive chemical formulae; the sudden to-and-fro movement of pistons, the starting up of mechanical processes, in the trees, carbon cycles, regular lengthening of shadows, and noises, and the cavernous rustling of a fibrous soil which was systematically cracking up, parting its lips with baby-like cries which had seemed hitherto to belong exclusively to fish.

A man went past, calling out in a thin voice. He was a puny creature and his whole sunburnt body appeared to be straining upwards to cope with the weight of a basket of toffee-coated peanuts. He stopped, looked at Adam, made some remark, and then turned back along the beach the way he had come. Adam noticed that he put his feet down quite flat on the stones, and that before throwing the weight of his body onto either foot he moved his big toe in a narrow circle from left to right, no doubt to make sure there was nothing in the way. He walked off quietly like this, moving among the scattered bodies with unexpected dignity and uttering his meaningless cry at frequent intervals.

A dog came quickly by in the shallow water, and Adam followed it. He walked as fast as he could, either hand grasping one end of the towel, which he had rolled round his neck; he made a point of walking with the water half-way up his legs, to imitate the dog. He was savouring two different kinds of fear: first, the fear he would have felt if he had been walking dryshod on the beach, at the risk of cutting his heels on the edges of the stones which, as everyone knows, are sharper when out of the water; and the fear he felt now, because his legs were entering a peculiar

15

element, cooler and thicker than air, and the soles of his feet were sliding, pushing back the layers of sea-water, and finally, after several ice-cold slithers, encountering an unstable, slimy surface covered with rootlets, with microscopic pods of weed that burst under his weight and coloured the liquid, near the bottom, with dark green particles, like a mist of leaves minced up in the process of decomposition.

Fortunately the dog hesitated when it came to concealed hollows, and each time Adam was able to make up the ground he had lost. Feeling that it was being followed, the animal looked round once with a stare that caught Adam on the chin. Then it set off again, towing the man behind it as though on a leash; in a few minutes it had managed to acquire an incredible dignity and now went forward, indefinably steadfast, chest-deep in the sea, exclusively concerned with getting to the right-hand end of the beach and the group of bathing huts that stood there.

They walked like this all the way, one behind the other. As could be surmised from a distance, the bathing huts formed a half-circle, backed up against the concrete jetty with the harbour beyond it. Further down the beach the bathers were lying in a confused mass of brightly-coloured towels and bikinis; they were facing the light and because of the way their bodies were foreshortened when seen from the water's edge, they all seemed to have sloughed their old skins for new, faintly orange-tinted ones on which the sun had dribbled, leaving shiny traces.

The dog halted, began to turn its nose towards Adam, stopped half-way, and jumped ashore. It climbed the ridges of pebbles, skirted past two or three groups of sleepers, and settled itself beside a young woman.

Adam imitated it; but while the dog took up a position on the right, he went to the left. Before sitting down he hastily unfolded the towel he had been carrying round his neck and spread it on the ground; then he squatted there, hugging his knees. For ten or fifteen seconds, a few inches from the woman's stomach, he watched the dog, which was licking its paws; its eyelids were lowered and its nose pointed downwards. Adam looked at his feet and decided to follow the dog's example; oil must have accumulated along the tide line since the last storm, and the soles of his feet were black. He began scraping between his toes with a sliver of driftwood.

Adam quite realized that time was going by in this unexpected way; it was one of the kinds of time you can take to yourself completely, one of the elastic kinds that you need only adjust to the scale of whatever it is you have to do, in order to enjoy it in peace. So Adam told himself in a whisper that he was in control of things; there was no fundamental difference between the two points of the beach that he had occupied in turn. Sitting on the bath-towel, he could let his gaze roam slowly round, carrying it to infinity in concentric circles. Either one was prepared to admit that a pebble, plus a thousand pebbles, plus brambles, plus refuse, plus traces of salt, far from being motionless, lived a life of secretion and moved within a different time-system; or else one must declare that life can only be measured by the evidence of the senses. In that case Adam was undoubtedly the one and only living creature in the world.

'Hadn't you better try this?' the young woman suggested.

Adam smiled his thanks, took the paper handkerchief she held out to him—noticing as he did so that it had left a kind of fluff or snow on the tips of her fingers—and went on wiping away the oil. He thought he ought to say something. He muttered:

'Yes—it is easier like this.'

17

He tried to meet the young woman's eyes, but it was no use: she was wearing the kind of very dark sun-glasses, with thick lenses and frames, that are a speciality of tourists from New York at Portuguese seaside resorts. He was too shy to ask her to take them off, though he felt what a relief it would be to see her eyes. Sentimentally, he could only see his own reflexion in each plastic-rimmed lens; he looked just like a big, fat monkey, bending over and working at his feet. As though, by swaying the body forward, that position set up the concentration needed to produce the intuition that one was living, yes, living all alone in one's corner, isolated from the death of the world.

The young woman suddenly drew up her legs, a little slanting, with her head and shoulders raised just above the ground, sighed voluptuously and sent her fingers groping along her spine, brushing over the white mark on her tanned skin, as she refastened the strap of her bikini. She paused for a moment in this position, a captive figure, arms crossed behind her back, making hollows below the shoulder-blades, as though indicating to some matador the chink in her armour, the point where the sword can be thrust through to the heart. She was sweating very slightly under her arms and between her breasts. She said:

'I must go now.'

Adam followed up with 'Do you come here often?'

'It depends,' she said. 'And you——?'

'I come every day. Haven't you seen me?'

'No.'

He went on:

'I've seen you before, sitting down here—or around here. I mean at this end of the beach. Why do you sit in the same place every day? I mean, is there anything special about it? For instance, is it really cleaner than anywhere else, or cooler, or hotter, or does it smell nice, or what?'

'I don't know,' she said. 'I suppose it's just a habit. Is that what you mean?'

Adam registered this as though it really deserved attention.

'No—no, I don't believe you. Or at least what you say about having habits. It seems to me your dog is the one that has habits. In fact I wouldn't be surprised if he brings you to this part of the beach every time. If you'd watched him you would certainly have noticed how he arrives on the beach, goes in for a bathe, up to the neck in water, with his nose pointing straight ahead, and afterwards sleeps in the sun for a bit, and licks his paws. And then how he trots away, composedly, always stepping on the flat stones so as not to hurt his paws, until he's far enough from the children, so that they won't poke his eye out with their spades and rakes. Isn't that so? And without ever changing his clothes.'

'Listen,' said the young woman, 'you seem to me to be very young.'

Suddenly she had her clothes on, her hair was dry, she lit a Du Maurier cigarette, flashed her sun-glasses darkly two or three times, called her dog, and walked away, up to the road.

C. 'You remember that time in the mountains?' Adam asked. The girl smiled, but her smile was certainly pursuing a different conversation. He had to repeat his question, rather gravely, in a louder, more level tone, in more deliberate words not uninfluenced by a boyish desire to shock.

'Now look, Michèle, surely you remember?'

She shook her head, already beginning to find this tiresome.

'As a matter of fact,' he said, 'every girl has some story like that to tell her mother. When she tells it she says "the time I was raped." You too.'

'Couldn't we talk about something else?' Michèle retorted; but Adam ignored this; he went on telling his story, for other people's benefit, in a cheap parody of uneasy recollections.

'Then you remember, too, that we'd gone off together on the motorbike. First of all I'd taken you to a couple of cafés, because it was in the middle of winter and practically freezing. Couldn't have been more than 1 or 2 degrees above, or perhaps even down to zero. We'd both drunk black coffee, big cups of it. Or rather I'd watched you drinking it; you had a funny way of drinking black coffee, I liked the way you did it, in those days. You used to take the cup in your left hand, like this, put your hand under your chin like a saucer, and stick out your upper lip. You'd dip it daintily into the coffee and before beginning to drink —remember—you'd raise your head slightly, so that one saw the semi-circular shadow the coffee had left round your mouth.'

The waiter brought their order; Michèle extended a hand, chose one of the glasses of beer and swallowed several mouthfuls without pausing for breath. Then she put the glass down, with an abrupt movement of her wrist. The froth round the glass began to evaporate, slowly widening the gaps between the trails of bubbles. Little shafts of effervescence traversed the almost opaque yellow liquid from the surface downwards; to take only one of its aspects, it looked as rich and virile as the sea. Part of it, about a quarter, was now collected in the pit of Michèle's stomach, like a liquid stone, a little petroleum, a suspicion of brilliantine. As for the other three-quarters, waiting in the glass, it might have been an empty goldfish bowl standing at noon on an Empire *guéridon*, its fish having died.

Or even one of those fish-tanks you see in the windows of big restaurants, where solemn gourmets come to have fat carp hauled out for them in a net, each fish leaving a hole in the water between the pilot-light, the oxygen blowpipe and the artificial weeds—departing from behind its emerald-green bulkhead to enter a world of torture, of butter, of parsley in the eyes and tomato in the mouth.

'After the cafés we went off again on the motorbike, along the main road. Then I took that narrow lane that led away into the country, and it got dark and began to drizzle a bit. It's good to remember things so well. Really it is. Does it sound true, anyway? Won't you tell me? Won't you take your turn and tell me a little? Or just say "And then? And what happened next?" Because there's only one way of telling that kind of thing, and that's in the sentimental style—you see what I mean, it gives people confidence and has a certain air of truth about it. I like that.

'D'you know what you said? You said—they were your very words—"It's not worth it." It's not worth it! Not worth what? The extraordinary thing is that I understood, and yet I went ahead all the same. Until we came to a big patch of mud that barred the way. Besides, no—after all, I hadn't understood what you said "It's not worth it". I think I was doing everything without realizing, just anyhow. I propped the bike against a tree and we walked on, through the wet grass; the grass was wet. You said you were cold, or something, and then I said we ought to shelter under a tree till the rain stopped. We found a big umbrella -pine and we stood with our backs to the trunk, one on each side. That was where we got sticky patches on our shoulders. There was a carpet of pine-needles and grass all round, very pretty. That's true. All of a sudden the rain came on harder, and then I sidled round the trunk and put my hand behind your neck and pulled you down on the ground. The raindrops were coming through the leaves, I don't know if you remember, joining together in twos and threes and splashing down on us, as big as your hand. Yes, I tore your clothes, because you were getting frightened and beginning to yell; I slapped you twice, full in the face —not very hard. I remember you had a zip that was absurdly stiff; it kept on sticking; in the end I managed to pull it down by tugging with all my strength. Wait— afterwards you went on struggling, but not too hard. I think you must have been scared stiff, of me or of the consequences. At least I think so. Well, and when all your clothes were off I held you down on the ground with your feet against the trunk of the tree and your head right out in the rain, and I held your wrists in my hands and squeezed

22

your knees between my legs. And in theory I raped you—
like that, easily, you see, as wet with rain as though you'd
been in a bath; listening all the same—if you'll excuse me—
to your cries of rage, the little noises of the storm, and
the shots fired by the sportsmen who were beating the
underwood on the opposite hillside. I say "in theory".
Because in practice it was a flop. But after all, perhaps that
doesn't matter much so far as I'm concerned. Once I'd
managed to get your clothes off. Anyhow—to make a good
story out of it, literary and all that—let's say I saw you
getting gradually covered with wet hair, earth, prickles and
pine-needles and I saw your mouth wide open, you were
breathing hard through it, getting your breath back, and a
trickle of muddy water was coming from an imperceptible
spring somewhere near the roots of your hair. Honestly,
by the time it was all over you looked like a garden. You
wriggled free and sat up with your back against the tree.
For me, you understand, you'd become just a heap of
pinkish earth mixed with grass and raindrops. With some
vestiges of a woman here and there; perhaps because you
were waiting. All the same we stayed there for quite a
while, doing nothing—I couldn't say how long exactly,
ten minutes, perhaps twenty—less than an hour in any
case. That was absolutely ridiculous, considering it was icy
cold, zero degrees above zero in fact. When we—or rather
no, we got dressed without looking at each other, you on
one side of the trunk and I on the other. And as your
clothes were torn I lent you my raincoat. It was still
pouring as hard as ever, but we were tired of waiting, so we
got on the bike again and went away. I left you outside a
café and, without your asking me or anything, I made you
a present of my raincoat. You didn't look too good in it,
did you? I don't know what you told your father, whether
you went to the police or not, but——'

23

'Yes, I did go to the police,' said Michèle. This was pretty incredible.

'You knew what you were about? I mean, you knew what it might lead to?'

'Yes.'

'And then?' said Adam. 'And then?' he repeated.

'Then, nothing . . .'

'What d'you mean, nothing? What did they say?'

Michèle shook her head.

'They didn't say anything. I shan't tell you, so that's that.'

'I didn't see anything in the papers, so far as I know.'

'The papers have other things to talk about—haven't they?'

'Then why did you go to the police?'

'I thought—oh, I don't know; I thought you needed a lesson.'

'And now?'

Michèle swept her hand in a curve, presumably by way of negation.

Adam pretended not to be satisfied with this.

'Now?'

'Now it's over, what the hell does it matter?' she retorted, almost shouting.

It was his turn to be annoyed; he explained:

'You ask me what the hell it matters, do you, when a chap's a deserter into the bargain? You don't realize that a charge like that might land me in the nick? Are you really crazy, or what, Michèle? Can't you see, can't you see that Adam Pollo, a deserter from the army, is at the mercy of the first informer who comes along, and that any day—or rather any hour, any minute—two fellows in uniform may appear on the scene, beat me up, kick me, shove me into a strait-waistcoat, handcuff me—the lot—and not rest content

24

till they've clapped me into the darkest cell in some army barracks, with no food, no heating, no women, no nothing, and even less than that?'

Michèle, after a moment's hesitation, decided to call a halt to the game.

'That'll do, Adam, you're beginning to make me really tired.'

He went on, however.

'Michèle, I can't understand you! Do you really favour the version of life where people always pretend to disbelieve everything? According to you I deserve hanging, or don't I? Answer me!'

'Adam, please, I really have a headache, I——'

'Answer me first.'

'Shut up.'

'Well? Do I deserve hanging?'

'Yes—there—are you satisfied?'

Adam decided to say no more. As for Michèle, she took a mirror out of her handbag and smoothed her eyebrows with a fingertip. Some people going by along the pavement glanced at her furtively. She looked by no means one in a thousand. Defeated by her obstinacy, Adam waited while she combed her hair, powdered her nose and touched up her lipstick; all he had left was to drink his nearly cold coffee.

Then for a few minutes they played a game; it consisted of moving the things on the table by a fraction of an inch; they took turns, attacking and counter-attacking, shifting the beer-mats, the saucer, the cup, the spoon, some scraps of wool, a dead fly, the little square paper the bill was marked on, the white ashtray, a match, their sun-glasses, the butt of a gauloise cigarette, a drop of coffee (spread towards the right), etc.

Adam won in the end, with a big speck of fluff that had

25

fallen off Michèle's sweater; he pushed it forward by a hair's breadth. Immediately after that they got up together and left the café. The waiter called to them as they went past the bar; Adam was the only one who looked round. He paid with small change, glanced at himself in the big mirror on the wall, and went out.

They walked side by side without a word, staring straight ahead; the street ran gently down towards the sea, and they were watching for any glimpses of the horizon that might appear between the square blocks of the houses. On reaching the promenade they paused and almost turned in opposite directions; finally Adam followed Michèle. A bit further on they sat down, on a bench that had lost its back three months previously in a driving accident: a six-ton lorry had knocked over a scooter which had suddenly appeared from the right, and had then lost control and toppled onto the pavement—damaging the bench and causing two deaths.

'I wrote to you,' Adam said. 'I wrote to you and I raped you. Why didn't you do something as well?'

'What did you expect me to do?' asked Michèle wearily.

'I wrote to you, and I put my address.'

'You surely didn't expect me to answer?'

'Of course I did! For heaven's sake!' He enjoyed shouting. 'Of course I did! Or else you should have fetched the cops.'

'I've no use for the cops.'

'You brought a charge, or didn't you?'

'I can't help that . . .'

'I can't help that . . .' she protested several times.

They walked along the seafront for a considerable distance; the wind was blowing in gusts, now cold, now hot. Nobody went past on their pavement. To one side

26

lay the sea, absolutely smooth, dirty with oil in places, the beacon flashing from the sea-wall, and a few street lamps whose vertical reflections seemed to be moving forward. On the other side was the great mass of dry land, systematically covered by the town, by telegraph-poles and trees, exaggerately curved, as though one were looking at it with one's head upside-down. In Adam's mind, they say, the scene was reversed, as though in a convex mirror. So he felt he was balanced on his toes, perched right above the continents, with the round earth like a globe under his feet, imitating the position of Mary and doing the opposite of Atlas's task. It was like the time when (aged twelve or thirteen) he used to throw his whole weight on his rubber beach-ball, forcing it below the surface of the water so that, dilated by the pressure, it slipped up along his calves in little uncoordinated jerks.

As they walked they exchanged a few more remarks.
'Why can't you help it?'
'Because. Because I don't know.'
'Do you know what? You lack concentration.'
'Is that so?'
'And you're too emphatic.'
'Anything else?'
'Wait. You're not persuasive.'
'Really?'
'Yes, really. Not that you care a damn. Because it makes no difference in the long run. I believe just as much in whatever I do; the great thing is always to talk as if it were to be put in writing; that way one feels one's not free. Not free to talk like oneself. And then one mixes better. One's no longer alone. One exists with the coefficient 2, or 3, or 4, instead of that infernal coefficient 1. You understand?'
'I understand. I've got a headache,' said Michèle.
She waited a little for him to reply; then, sensing that

27

he would say nothing more for a long time, she kissed him, said goodbye, and turned back towards the middle of the town. She strode away, with her man's raincoat tightly belted, her hair flattened by the rain, a black spot of oil on her left ankle; her face was set, almost vicious.

D. It almost seemed as though raising artificial problems had become a habit with him. He had four or five tries before making up his mind; asking questions to right and left, consulting old postcards received at Christmas or on New Year's Eve and calendars dating from last year or last month; even asking the advice of grandparents. Several people invited him to have an apéritif, a little glass of Cinzano at the bar; kind of them, but he had his own idea. He refused their invitations and sat down at the far end of the room, with his back to the wall. He dwelt on the fact that by now he must be the oldest of them all, something like twenty-eight to thirty, or thereabouts. That was certainly the age when, if ever, one should be able to understand everything at a hint and capable of action, especially where resolutions of this kind were concerned.

28 August, heat-wave, height of summer; 7.30 p.m.; he stared straight ahead of him, past the customers moving about in the foreground, and saw it was beginning to get dark outside. He had chosen his bar carefully, as one of those where Michèle often went. He sat waiting, with a glass of orangeade in front of him; he was searching his memory.

Three American sailors, probably drunk, came into the bar, singing American songs. Adam watched them as they

29

walked across to lean on the bar, beside the till. One of them left the others and came past Adam's table. He pushed a coin into the slot of the juke-box, bent down to read the titles on the screen, and then suddenly realized that this was unnecessary because every song in the box must be American. He pressed two buttons at random and stepped back, finding it hard to tear his eyes away from the circle of light on the record. Nevertheless he walked off, found his way to the cloakroom door, and was going out just as he heard the first words of the Red River Rock:

> 'Heigho Johnny rockin'
> Rock-a-goose by the river,
> Ho red river rock 'n roll.'

Adam listened to the song right through, beating time with his left hand on the table-top. When the record was over he paid and was leaving the bar as the American sailor came out of the cloakroom and joined his friends.

An hour later Adam ran into them again in a grill-room in the old part of the town. One of them recognized him, heaven knows why, caught him by the arm and muttered into his ear in English. Adam didn't listen; he offered the man a cigarette, lit it for him, and sat down beside him on a stool. He ordered a cheese and salad sandwich and then turned to the American sailor. His mind was empty of thought, he was half-dead. The sailor said his name was John Beaujolais and he came from Portland, Maine. Then he asked 'What's your name?'

'Puget-Théniers,' said Adam, taking a bite of his sandwich and wondering why he had chosen that particular town.

'I used to know a French girl, Mireille her name was,' said the American; he turned to his companions and told

30

them some story, in an undertone; they all burst out laughing. Adam went on eating for a time; he felt a kind of boredom stealing over him, as though he had spent the afternoon among Martians, trying one language after another on them.

'Are you fellows still at war?' he asked Beaujolais, pointing to his uniform with a crust of bread.

'No, not at war,' said Beaujolais, 'but—*le service national*, eh? You too, I guess?'

'No, I'm through with that,' said Adam. He paused to swallow a mouthful of bread and salad and then went on:

'I like American books. I enjoyed reading Wigglesworth, Child, and that poet Robinson Jeffers, who wrote *Tamar*. I enjoyed Stuart Engstrand. You know him?'

'No,' said Beaujolais. 'Me, I'm a jazz musician. Tenor sax. I played with Horace Parlan and Shelly Manne, a couple of years back. Romeo Penque, too. He's a flute-player. I know John Eardley well. He's great. Real great.' He tapped the counter with his finger.

'But I had to quit—yes, quit—so . . .'

'Yes, Stuart Engstrand,' Adam went on. 'He's not well known here, and in America he's looked upon as a guy who rather writes down to the public, isn't he? But personally I think he's good; he writes straightforward stuff. He tells simple stories. Guys who want pretty girls and marry them. And because they're pretty it doesn't go so well. But the fellows are tough, not like over here. So they always win out in the end.'

'French girls are pretty, isn't that so?' said the American. 'I'd like to—marry one.'

'Yes,' said Adam, 'so would I.'

'Listen,' said the American, 'you want to know what Mireille was like? She was like this; like this! In summer she used to wear hats, how d'you call 'em? She had a white dog. He's died since, I believe. I wanted her to go back with me afterwards, to the States. Yes. I said to her, you come; but she said no. I'd have liked her to, no kidding.'

The sailor stared hard at Adam for a moment. Then he said: 'You want a drink?'

'No,' said Adam. He revolved slowly on his stool and leant back with his elbows on the edge of the bar and the middle of his spine pressed against its metal rim. He looked at the three uniformed figures moving about on his right. The peace, thus composed of talk between strangers, tips, parts of evenings joined together without rhyme or reason, could easily be transformed into hostilities, stale bread, scraps of terror by night, and then, all of a sudden, into war, with code language, passwords, blood, trails of black smoke. He could sense wars going on all over the world; in his brain there was a peculiar region that encroached upon the others, a jungle site where nature was truly strange; the vegetation consisted of barbed wire like hard, stiff lianas, with small, spiky knots every six inches instead of leaves.

But the great thing was to know what one would do when the war was over. One might go into business, take up teaching or spend the rest of one's life writing novels about the army. Failing that, one might become a jazz musician, like John Beaujolais of Portland, Maine. Or join up again, pick up one's kitbag and make off into the North African mountains, carrying a big machine-gun—wastelands, pylons, expeditions at 6 in the morning, with a heavy mist clinging to the contours of the ground so that the flights of ducks are half-concealed—just enough for purposes of slaughter. But after that, on leaving the army, would one be able to climb a hill and live all alone in a big, empty house, put two deck-chairs face to face and lie sweating in the sun for days on end, almost naked and sometimes quite naked? To believe that one needn't make money in order to keep alive, but that one does need to defend oneself against all those (and there are plenty of them) who'd like to murder one?

Adam was trying to recapture some link with the past ten years; some phrase, some army habit, the name of some place; anything that would make clear to him how he had spent his time and finally, finally, later on, where he had been before this.

A French soldier came into the restaurant; he wore the uniform of the Alpine regiment and seemed to be looking for somebody; he had the alert, forceful expression customary to those who disregard the petty details of life. Adam felt irresistibly drawn towards him; he could not prevent himself from getting up, walking over to the man and speaking to him without more ado; sweat broke out on his chest as he did so.

'You're a soldier, are you?' he asked.

'Yes. Why?' replied the other.

'What company?'

'Twenty-second *Chasseurs alpins.*'

'Do you know a place called Msila?' Adam demanded.

The other stared at him, surprised.

'No . . . Where is it?'

'In Algeria.'

'I've never been over there,' said the other man. 'Besides . . .'

'Wait a minute!' Adam continued, 'I'm trying to think— I know the map, you see. It's near Bordj-Bou-Arreridj.'

'I daresay,' said the soldier. 'But excuse me, I haven't got time . . . I'm waiting for a girl . . .'

He turned away as if to sit down at a table; Adam followed him, pressing his point:

'Msila, in Bibania. In the foothills of the Hodna mountains. The nearest town is Setif. You must have heard of Setif?'

33

'But I tell you,' the man interrupted, 'I've never set foot in your damned sector . . .'

'How many months have you been in the army?'

'Three!' he shouted, 'Three, and I——'

'Then it's possible,' said Adam, 'it's possible I've never been there. You understand, I'm trying to remember—anyway, what does it matter? I'm sure to find out one day. You won't have a drink while you wait for your girl?'

'No thanks, I'm not thirsty,' said the soldier. He added 'Good night,' and walked quickly to an unoccupied table. When Adam got back to his stool he found the three American sailors had gone. He lit a cigarette and tried to think things out. But his attention was constantly distracted by a host of small happenings he had scarcely noticed before, but which now swelled to huge proportions and clung to his sensory structure like iron filings to a magnet, accumulating and getting in the way.

A handsome auburn-haired girl came into the restaurant, holding herself very straight but wriggling her hips in a slightly ridiculous manner, and walked across to the French soldier's table. The man reddened, stood up and pulled out a chair for her, smearing the edge of his khaki jacket with ash from a cigarette he had dropped on the table and forgotten; it now rolled jerkily to the opposite corner and fell to the ground by its own impetus, not making the slightest sound when it hit the floor; when Adam, in imitation, pushed a cigarette across the metal top of the bar until it fell off, the noise it made was at least a thousand times louder.

Adam huddled on his stool; shut in by a strange old age, he was quietly resuming his place in the sun, in the deserted house at the top of the hill, taking no interest in the countryside, in the town or the sea, no interest in the aircraft that flew along the horizon, sometimes noisy, sometimes silent, no interest in ocean cruises or in the fine, realistic books people occasionally write after their military service, recording in meticulous detail that on a certain day in a certain month of June they were told to swill out the latrines directly after being made to peel forty pounds of potatoes; no interest in the many who are incapable of dying for love of a diadem spider, for the languors of nature, who cannot be brought to the verge of tears when the silence is rent by a drop of water falling into the waste-pipe of a washbasin. Those who refuse to live in the bosom of the earth, in the warm bosom, the bosom full of scents, rustlings and haloes, of the earth; of our microbial earth.

Step by step he was taking up his withdrawn position at the open window, crouching on the ground between the two empty deck-chairs, and he was becoming aware that he did not understand anything at all. There was nothing in the actual structure of these horrible things to show him definitely whether he had just come out of a mental home or out of the army.

E. Michèle had an awful job finding Adam's house. The bus put her down on the road at the first turn after the beach. She looked round at the houses and gardens and the hills rolling softly into the distance, covered with thicker vegetation; but recognized nothing that could guide her in all this. She walked slowly along the bank that bordered the road, stepping cautiously on the gravel as though intent on bending either sandal in turn to the exact point—an angle of about 30°—where the instep stretched the leather straps absolutely taut, making them squeak, just once, a sharp squeak that kept time with her steps.

From her jacket pocket she took a plan Adam had drawn one day on the underneath of a beer-mat. Both sides of the card bore a printed slogan, something like:

'*Drink Slavia, it's different . . . your very good health!*'

but she did not look at that; she studied the plan, a rough pencil-sketch running across the words of the advertisement. A curved line represented the bay beyond the harbour. Two parallel lines marked the road, the one she was on now. To either side of the road and below the S of Slavia a number of little circles or squares had been hastily scrawled, and Michèle remembered what Adam had said:

'There are some shanties there, up and down the hillside. I won't mark them all, because it would take the whole blessed day—there are so many of them. I'm telling you that so you won't think I've under-estimated the landscape. Look, I'll write it for you—there: shanties.'

Further on there were two more parallel lines, closer together this time; that was the path. To left and right of the path the cardboard was covered with a very light network of crisscross lines; a word had been written on top of the cross-hatching, but it was too rubbed to be legible. Some distance up the path, on the left, there was a square which was perfectly clear; it had obviously been drawn with care and was much larger than the others. It was marked in the middle with a kind of St. Andrew's cross. That was where Adam lived—the little, insignificant spot on the earth's surface that one underlines, that one marks in perpetuity somewhere or other, just as one scribbles an indecent drawing on a lavatory door so that, for once at any rate, all the lavatories in the world shall have their centre of gravity.

On reaching the top of the parallel lines of the path, Michèle looked to the left. But the rectangle indicated by the cross could not be seen, owing to the uneven ground, the houses and shrubs. She had to set off at a venture, through a tangle of brambles, at the risk of emerging too high up or too low down, or trespassing on private property. Below her stretched the rounded sea, pricked here and there with white sails. The sun's reflection swung over its surface, flashing like a crystal chandelier, and the waves lay motionless like furrows. The sky was twice its proper size, and in places, particularly in the vicinity of the line of mountains that cut off the horizon beyond the bay, the land was badly put together; its colours clashed and its planes were often heaped one upon another, with a curious disregard for the most elementary notions of balance and perspective; one felt that this landscape would seize any

37

opportunity—a red sunset or a purple eclipse, to take only two examples—of being cheaply melodramatic.

Michèle kept coming upon what might be clearings or uneven patches, craters like shell-holes, inhabited by snakes and ant-lions, or great beds of prickly plants. She caught sight of Adam's house some distance away and realized she must have misread the map, for she was well below the marked point.

She began climbing the hill again, her shirt drenched with sweat and the hook at the top of her check swim-suit digging into her back as the bra was stretched by her bowed shoulders. This time the sun was behind, throwing her shadow directly ahead and painting the front of the house a sickly white.

Adam, at the window, had seen her approaching; he drew back for a moment, uncertain, wondering who the intruder could be; at less than fifty yards he recognized Michèle. Thus reassured, he left his observation post and sat down again in the deck-chair. A voice, hoarse with heat or fatigue, hailed him by his first name:

'Adam! Hi, Adam!'

In this arid terrain the cry sounded so unpleasant that for fear it should be repeated he climbed out of the window and stood at the edge of a flower-bed. Without noticing it, he trod on and squashed two red and black ants, one of which was carrying the remains of a dung-beetle. He waited till Michèle was only a few yards away, and then said, with a perfect imitation of naturalness:

'That you, Michèle? Come on up.'

He took her hand and helped her over the last lumps of earth; he watched her when she stopped, out of breath, her face glistening and her damp clothes clinging to her body.

'You gave me a fright,' he said. 'For a moment I wondered who it could be.'

'What? Who did you think it might be?' Michèle panted.

'I don't know—one never knows . . .'

He cast a glance of concern at his naked stomach.

'I'm terribly sunburnt there, round my navel,' he said.

'Why—why do you always have to be talking about your navel, your nose, your hands or your ears, or something of that kind?' asked Michèle.

He ignored the remark.

'I ought to get dressed,' he muttered. 'Just feel that—no, not there, my stomach.'

She touched his skin and flapped her hand as though she had burnt herself.

'Go and get dressed, then.'

Adam nodded and went indoors by the route he had taken to come out; Michèle followed him, but in a way he didn't care. After putting on his shirt he lit a cigarette and turned to look at her. He saw she had a parcel in her left hand.

'You've brought me something?' he enquired.

'Yes, some newspapers.'

She undid the parcel and spread out its contents on the floor.

'About a dozen daily papers, a *Match* and a movie magazine.'

'A magazine? Which one? Show me . . .'

She held it out to him, Adam turned over a few pages, sniffed them near the cover, and dropped the magazine on the floor.

'Interesting?'

'I took what I could find.'

'Yes, of course,' he said. 'Anything to eat?'

Michèle shook her head.

'No—but you told me you didn't need anything.'

'I know,' said Adam. 'And money? Can you lend me some?'

'Not more than a thousand,' said Michèle. 'Want it now?'

'Yes, if possible.'

Michèle held out a note; he thanked her and thrust it into his trousers pocket. Then he pulled one of the deck-chairs into the shade and sat down.

'Would you like a drink? I've got two and half bottles of beer left.'

She said 'Yes.' Adam fetched the bottles, took a penknife from somewhere near the heap of blankets, and prised the cap off a full bottle. He offered it to Michèle.

'No, give me the half that's left over, it'll be enough for me.'

They drank straight out of the bottles, several good gulps without a pause. Adam was the first to put down his bottle; he wiped his mouth and began to talk, as though continuing some old story:

'Apart from that, what's the news?' he asked. 'I mean, what's the news on the wireless, the TV and so on?'

'The same as in the newspapers, you know, Adam . . .'

He persisted, frowning:

'All right, then, let's put it another way: what news is there that isn't in the papers? I don't know, but for anyone who lives among other people, like you do, it's not the same, is it? There must be things the papers and the radio don't mention, but that everybody knows? Aren't there?'

Michèle reflected.

'But things like that aren't news. Otherwise they'd be in the papers. They're people's opinions, and so forth——'

'Call it what you like—people's opinions, rumours going around—What's the latest? Is there going to be—at least, do they think there's going to be an atomic war, soon?'

'Atomic?'

'Yes, atomic.'

She shrugged.

'I haven't the faintest idea—how should I know? No, I don't believe they think that. I don't think they believe there'll be an atomic war. As a matter of fact I don't believe they give a damn.'

'They don't give a damn, eh?'

'I think, perhaps . . .'

Adam sneered.

'Okay, okay,' he said, with a shade of absolutely unjustifiable bitterness, 'so they don't give a damn—Neither do I. The war's over. I didn't finish it, nor did you, but that's beside the point. It's behind us. You're right. Only one day, it's a hopeless business, you see funny cast-iron animals, painted khaki, the camouflage colour, real tanks, appearing from all directions and swooping down on the town. You see little black dots spreading over the whole district. You wake up, pull back the curtains, and there they are, down in the street; they're coming and going, you wonder why, they're very like ants, you might mistake them for ants. They have kind of hose-pipes that they drag after them everywhere; and with a very soft sound, puff! puff!, they spout jets of napalm onto the buildings. Where can I have seen that, I wonder? The tongue of flame that comes out of the pipe—it goes on through the air by itself, in a slight curve, and then it stretches out longer and longer, it goes in at a window, and suddenly, without your really noticing, the house is on fire, it's erupting like a volcano, the walls are collapsing all in one piece, slowed down by the air, which is incandescent, with big curls of sooty smoke, and the fire pouring out in all directions like sea-water. And the guns and the bazookas, the dum-dum bullets, the trench-mortars, the hand-grenades, etc., and the bomb that drops

41

on the harbour when I'm eight years old and I tremble and the air trembles and the whole earth trembles and sways under the black sky? When a big gun goes off, I tell you, it jerks back with a graceful, agile movement, just like a shrimp if you stretch out your hand towards it, with your fingers all swollen and red because the water's cold. Yes, when a big gun goes off it makes a graceful movement like a well-oiled machine, a graceful mechanical twitch. It growls, it springs back like a piston and it makes splendid holes three hundred yards away, holes that aren't too messy and that turn into pools afterwards, when it rains. But one gets used to it—there's nothing one gets used to as easily as war. There's no such thing as war. People die every day, and so what? War is all or nothing. War is total and permanent. I, Adam, I'm still in it, come to that. I don't want to get out of it.'

'Stop it for a second, will you, Adam? In the first place, what war are you talking about?'

She had taken advantage of Adam's speech to finish her bottle of beer quietly; she liked to drink beer unhurriedly, taking big mouthfuls and letting them filter down slowly between her tongue and her uvula—all but counting the thousands of bubbles that fizzed through her mouth, that searched every tiny crevice and spot of decay in her teeth, took possession of her entire palate and went up into the back of her nose. Now she had finished, and as what Adam was saying did not interest her she thought this would be a good way of stopping him.

'Well, what war are you talking about?' she repeated, 'The atomic one? It hasn't happened yet. The 1940 war? You didn't even fight in that one, you must have been twelve or thirteen years old at the time . . .'

So that's it, said Adam to himself; so that's it. The atomic war hasn't happened yet. And of course I didn't fight in the

42

1940 one, I must have been twelve or thirteen years old at the time. And even if I did fight in it, I'd have been far too young to remember about it now. There had been no wars since then, otherwise they would have been mentioned in the modern history textbooks. And Adam knew, from having read these comparatively recently, that they did not report any war, anywhere, since the one against Hitler.

Perplexed, he fell silent; and suddenly, by pure chance, he realized that the whole universe was redolent of peace. Here, as no doubt elsewhere, there was a wonderful silence. As though they were both coming up from a dive into the sea and breaking surface, both carrying deep inside their ears, against the ear-drum, a ball of warm liquid setting up an imperceptibly rhythmic palpitation, pressing against the brain as a no-man's land of sibillant sounds, warblings, kindly whistles, single notes and the splash of waterfalls, where the worst rages, the most horrible ecstasies, sound like flowing brooks and seaweed.

They spent the rest of the day listening to this peace, to the few sounds that came from outside or the imperceptible displacement of objects inside the house. In any case the silence was not absolute; he had referred to sibillant sounds and whistles; to these must be added other sounds, grating noises, friction between layers of air, specks of dust brushing past one another and falling on flat surfaces; all amplified 1,500 times.

In case of need they huddled together in a corner of the first-floor room and made love mentally, thinking all the time 'We're spiders or slugs.' And much other childishness of the same kind.

Towards evening they arrived at a kind of imperfect state of themselves, as though everything they were doing was off-beat, even their slightest gesture, their faintest breath, and they had become mere halves of people. In this upstairs room, immediately above the one Adam lived in, there was a large billiard-table with a threadbare cloth. They had lain down on this, side by side, gazing up at the ceiling. Adam's face had kept its bored, yet somehow pleased expression; his left hand was lying horizontally across the billiard table with the open palm upturned. Michèle lit a cigarette for the satisfaction of dropping the ash into the pockets of the table; without moving her head, she looked sidelong at Adam's profile; she felt a few seconds' irritation because it had something fastidious about it, an air of satiety; she said she found all this horrible, that she had the impression of waiting for God knows what—the Strasbourg train, or her turn at the hairdresser's.

Adam held his pose perfectly, but one felt that for a fleeting instant he had considered moving his legs or raising his eyebrows. He said something through motionless lips, and Michèle had to get him to repeat it.

'I said,' he repeated, 'that that's what I can't stand about women.' He was still scrutinizing the ceiling; for he had discovered that if one looked straight at the middle of it, owing to the fact that there were no rough patches in the pale green paint that was spread evenly over the plaster, the eye was not arrested by any protuberance. One saw no walls or corners, and there was thus nothing left to indicate that this was a plane surface, theoretically parallel to the horizon, characterized by its pale green colour, smooth to the touch, vaguely sandy, and at all events a man-made affair. Aiming right at the centre, with half-puckered eyelids, one was suddenly faced by a new type of communication which ignored relief, the force of gravity, colour, the sense of touch, distance and time, and drained all genetic desire from you; the effect of which was to atrophy, to mechanize; which was the first stage of anti-existence.

'That's what I dislike—their need to express all their

44

sensations. With no decent restraint. And they're nearly always inaccurate. As though it mattered in the least to other people, anyhow . . .'

He sniggered:

'We're stuffed with sensations, all of us! In my opinion it's more serious to reflect that we all have the same ones. But no—people want to describe them and then go on to analyse them, and then construct arguments on them—which have no more than a documentary value, if that.'

Adam drove his argument home:

'So one gets metaphysics at a café table, or in bed with a woman, or at the sight of a dog that's been run over in the street, because its eyes are popping out and its belly has split open, letting out a tumble of guts and a froth of blood and bile.'

Finally he propped himself up on his elbows, determined to convince Michèle:

'You feel as though you were waiting for something, don't you? Something unpleasant—unpleasant rather than dangerous?—Isn't that right? You feel as though you were waiting for something unpleasant. Well, listen to me. I'll tell you. It's the same with me. I have the same impression of waiting. But you must realize one thing: I personally shouldn't worry about this impression of waiting, except that I'm positive that it's bound to happen—that this unpleasant something-or-other will inevitably happen to me sooner or later. So that now, in point of fact, it's no longer something unpleasant that I'm expecting, it's something *dangerous*. You understand? It's simply a way of keeping one's feet on the ground. If you'd told me what you haven't told me, for instance that you have the impression of waiting for something and that you know, you understand, you *know* that it must be death, then okay. I understand you. Because there always comes a day when

45

one proves to be right in waiting for death. But you understand, don't you, that what matters is not your unpleasant
impression, but the fact that not a moment goes by without
our consciously or unconsciously waiting for death. That's
the point. You know what that means? It means that in a
certain system of life, which one puts into application by the
mere fact of existing, you're leaving a negative element—
which, as it were, perfectly rounds off the human unit. It
reminds me of Parmenides. You know, what he says, I
think: "How, then, can what *is* be going to be in the
future? Or how could it come into being? If it came into
being, it is not; nor is it if it is going to be in the future.
Thus is *becoming* extinguished and passing away not to be
heard of." That's the way to talk. One must have an
inkling of it. Otherwise, Michèle, it's not worth being able
to think. Talking's no use, you know, Michèle, no use at all.'

It suddenly occurred to him, for no reason, that he had
hurt Michèle's feelings, and he was sorry about that, in
a way.

'You know, Michèle,' he said, to make up for it, 'you
may be right. You may tell me—why not—that the whole
involves the whole—in the long run that might perhaps be
truest of all to Parmenides . . .'

In his turn he looked sideways, watching the girl's profile
with eyes that were nevertheless not so perceptive; it
brought him the satisfaction of a connection that suddenly
became possible, a real link between the two halves of his
speech.

'I mean, in the dialectical system of reasoning—rhetorical
seems to me to be a more accurate term from this point of
view—yes, in this system of reasoning that isn't concerned
with experience, you only have to say to me: "What time
is it?" and I interpret your question like this: *What*,
interrogative pronoun, belongs to a fallacious conception

46

of the universe, in which everything is listed and classified and where one can pick out of a drawer, as it were, a suitable adjective for every subject. *Time*—an abstract idea, is divisible into minutes and seconds which, added together in infinite number, produce another abstract idea which we call eternity. In other words, time includes both the finite and the infinite, the measurable and the incommensurable; which is a contradiction and therefore a logical absurdity.

Is? Existence—just another word, an abstract anthropomorphism, existence being the sum of the individual's associations of ideas. *It?* Same thing. *It* has no existence. *It* is the general extension of the male concept to an abstract idea, that of time, in addition to which it contributes to an aberrant grammatical form, the impersonal, bringing us back to the business of *Is*. Wait. And the whole sentence relates to a matter of time. There you are. What time is it? If you knew how that little sentence tortures me! Or rather, no. It's I who suffer through it. I'm crushed by the weight of my consciousness. *I'm dying of it*, that's a fact, Michèle. It's killing me. But fortunately one doesn't live logically. Life isn't logical, perhaps it's a kind of disorder of the consciousness. A disease of the cells. Anyhow, it doesn't matter, that's no reason. One has to talk, I agree, one has to live. But Michèle, isn't it just as well to say only what's really useful? It's better to keep the other things to oneself until one forgets them, until one comes to live solely for one's own body, seldom moving one's legs, huddled in a corner, more or less hunch-backed, more or less subject to the crazy impulses of the species.'

Michèle still said nothing; she was not vexed, but her whole being was concentrated on the discomfort built up, over what would soon be a period of hours, by movements one is hardly certain of having made, disconnected words, and all the rare or microacoustical sounds in the house and

47

outside; she was perhaps discovering—who knows?—that we have in our ears a kind of amplifier which needs to be constantly regulated and which we must not turn up beyond a certain point, or we shall never understand anything again.

'What time is it?' Michèle asked, yawning.

'After all I've been saying to you, you still keep it up?' said Adam.

'Yes, what time is it?'

'The time when, *bright in the darkness, wandering around the earth, a light from elsewhere . . .*'

'No, listen, seriously, Adam—I bet it's past five o'clock.' Adam looked at his watch:

'You've lost your bet,' he said, 'it's ten to five.'

Michèle sat up, got off the billiard table and walked across the darkened room. She looked through the chinks in the shutters.

'It's still sunny outside,' she announced—and added, as though suddenly suspecting the fact that the back of her shirt was drenched with sweat:

'It's really hot today.'

'We're right in the summer,' said Adam.

She buttoned up her blouse (in actual fact it was a man's shirt altered to fit), never for a moment taking her eyes off the slit in the shutter and the little bit of landscape to be seen through it; she was black all over, except for a white streak that cut across her face at eyebrow level. It was as though someone had taken control of their bodies, depositing them in a furrow and only letting them see parts of things. She, whose view was restricted by the size of the slit in the shutter, measuring about ¾ inch by 12 inches; he, still lying on the table, only half-aware that she was looking out.

'I'm thirsty,' said Michèle, 'you haven't got a bottle of beer left?'

'No, but there's a tap in the garden, on the other side of the house . . . The only one the Water Board hasn't cut off . . .'

'Why do you never have anything to drink in the place? It seems to me you could easily buy a bottle of grenadine or something, now and again.'

'I can't afford it, little girl,' replied Adam. He had still not moved. 'I expect you'd like us to go into town for a drink?' Michèle swung round on her heel. She peered into the depths of the room and the shadows were mirrored in her eyes, as black dots against a background of dazzle.

'No, let's go down to the beach,' she said decidedly.

They agreed to go for a walk on the rocks, along the headland. There was a kind of smugglers' path starting from the beach, and they followed this, side by side, in almost total silence. They passed groups of anglers going home as though from work, with their rods over their shoulders. They went soberly along the path, which followed the line of the shore at a convenient height, not too near the water or too far up the hill. Clumps of aloes had been planted at regular intervals, to rest the eyes and the mind. In the same way, the surface of the sea was decorated with an almost geometrical design of sharp crests, imitating waves. The whole thing looked as carefully done as a piece of cloth in hounds-tooth check or a huge allotment laid out to suit the tastes of beetles or snails.

There were at least a dozen houses on this stretch of the hill; one could see faint traces of their drain-pipes, winding along just below the ground, like roots. A few yards further on the path ran below a concrete pill-box; a steep flight of steps went down a shaft and came up again bringing with it a hot smell of excrement. Adam and Michèle skirted round the building without realizing it was a pill-box. He simply thought it was one of those modern-styled villas, and wondered how the owners could bear to live in the vicinity of such a stench.

When they reached the tip of the headland the sun had quite disappeared. All signs of the track petered out here; they had to leap from rock to rock, almost at sea-level, with only half of the sky overhead, the other half being cut off by the overhang of the hillside. Jumping from a bit too high up, Michèle twisted her ankle, and they both sat down on a flat rock, to rest. They smoked—he had two cigarettes, she one.

About a hundred yards from the shore a big fish was swimming along, its black, cylindrical body half out of the water. Adam said it was a shark, but they couldn't be certain because, in the gathering dusk, they could not make out if it had fins or not.

For half an hour the big fish swam round and round in the bay, widening its circle each time. The spiral it traced was by no means perfect; it was more in the nature of a lunatic figure, the practical illustration of a species of delirium in which the dark creature was losing its way, endlessly and blindly running its nose against superimposed layers of hot and cold currents. Hunger, death or old age was perhaps gnawing its belly, and it was prowling aimlessly, almost a ship in its desires, almost a sandbank in its imperfection, its almost invisible negative eternity.

As Michèle and Adam stood up it appeared for the last time, its menacing torpedo shape gliding between the waves; then it moved out to sea and was obliterated. Michèle said very softly, pressing close to Adam:

'I'm cold . . . I'm cold, I'm very cold . . .'

Adam did not shrink from the touch of the girl's body; indeed, he even took her hand—a soft, slender, warm hand —and repeated, as they walked on:

'You're cold? You're cold?'

To which Michèle replied:
'Yes.'

After that came the holes in the rocks; there were all sizes of them, large and small; they chose an average-sized one, a one-person hole, and sprawled in it at full length. Especially Adam: not a day went by without his achieving the miracle that consisted of whipping up his mythological sense to a frenzy, surrounding himself with stones and rubble; he would have liked to have all the rubbish and refuse in the world and bury himself under it. He surrounded himself on all sides with matter, ashes, pebbles, and gradually turned into a statue. Not like one of those Carrara marbles or mediaeval Christs which always sparkle to some extent with an imitation of life and pain; but like those pieces of cast-iron, a thousand years old or twelve, which are not dug up but are occasionally identified by the dull sound the spade gives back when it encounters them between two crumbling lumps of earth. Like a seed—just like the seed of a tree—he lay concealed in the cracks in the ground and waited in beatitude for the water that would germinate him.

He moved his hand a little towards the right, gently, already knowing what he would touch. In a second's infinite pleasure he felt his knowledge vacillating, a tremendous doubt overwhelming his mind; while a certain logical, memorable experience tried to make him recognize the feel of Michèle's skin (the bare arm lying beside him), his fingers groped blindly to left and right and met only the soil, granulous to the touch, hard and crumbling.

Adam seemed to be alone in this ability to die whenever he wanted, a private, hidden death; the only living creature in the world who was passing insensibly away, his flesh not decaying and putrefying, but freezing into a mineral.

Hard as a diamond, angular, brittle, at the heart of the

crystal, held in position by a geometrical pattern, confined within his resolute purity, with none of the weaknesses characteristic of the shoals of codfish which, in their collective refrigeration, never lose the little drop of moisture that glitters at the junction of their fins, or the glazed eye, two evidences of a painful death.

Michèle got up, dusted her clothes with her hands, and said plaintively:

'Adam—Adam, shall we go?'

She continued:

'Adam, you frighten me when you're like that—not moving, not breathing, you might be a corpse . . .'

'Idiot!' Adam retorted, 'you've disturbed my meditations! That's finished it, I should have to begin all over again.'

'Begin what?'

'Nothing, nothing . . . I can't explain. I'd already got to the vegetable stage . . . To mosses and lichens. I was just coming to the bacteria and the fossils. I can't explain.'

It was over. He knew now that the danger had been averted for the rest of the day. He got to his feet, seized Michèle by the shoulders and the waist, threw her to the ground and undressed her. Then he took her, with his mind far away, concentrated, for instance, on the leaden-hued body of the shark which must be describing wider and wider circles in the world as it sought for the Straits of Gibraltar.

Later on, with a shout of HAOH, he ran off by himself over the rocks and along the path that led back to the beach, through bushes and thorns from one slab of rock to the next, peering into dark hollows, divining the host of obstacles that might have tripped him up, barked his shins or snapped him in two with a sharp crack down there on some flat stone, leaving him still quivering, to be devoured by those disgusting parasites. The night had achieved a sort of black perfection; each object was a fresh disturbance on the map of the district. The earth's surface was striped black and white like a zebra's hide; the concentric circles of the mountains were like fingerprints laid one beside another, sometimes one above another, with no pause for rest. The tips of the cacti had piled arms in anticipation of a mysterious battle.

The liquid mass on the left had ceased its headlong rush and become a sea of ice; all slumber and all steel, it had turned into a metallic carapace.

Adam was now running through a vista of iron, by no means dead, but living in depth, an enigmatic life of enclosed animation which no doubt found expression in currents or bubbles a hundred yards underground; the polished crust of the world was like a knight asleep in his armour, motionless but possessed of potential life so that the icy gleam indicates blood, resolution, arteries or brain. A smokeless fire, an electric fire, was smouldering under the black soil. And the earth's surface was drawing off the whole strength of that fire, to such an extent that the rocks, waters, trees and air seemed to burn still more fiercely, *to be* the flames of petrified nature. The path, widening already, brought Adam to the bottom of a shaft beside the pill-box, steeped him in foul odours and sent him hurtling up the flight of steps. This was the culminating point of the road. The only place along the coast where the view was multiplied thousands of times over the three expanses of sea, land and sky. At the apex of this ascent Adam suddenly realized that running had become unnecessary and he stopped, petrified.

Coming from the vista that lay before him, the chilly wind covered him from head to foot, transformed his paralysis into pain. He stood there, prominent as a lighthouse, contemplating his own intelligence in the universe,

53

certain now that he would be occupying its centre to all eternity, without intermission; nothing could break this embrace, drag him out of the circle, not even death which, on a certain day in a certain year, would photograph his human form between two thin planks, at the centre of his geological Age.

He took a few steps forward, against the breeze.

He was almost hobbling as he walked, as though facing up to a tremendous blaze; coming to a rock below the level of the path, he sat down, with an indifferent glance towards the horizon. His body was completely insignificant, as puny as a nerve against the blood-red background of a kind of dream.

A sailing boat, half hidden from the other side of the sea, was crawling imperceptibly forward. After a quarter of an hour Adam began to feel cold; he shivered and looked in the direction of the pill-box, wishing more and more that Michèle would come along at last, out of breath from running after him and discomfited by having lost the race.

F. The sun went on blazing in the naked sky, and the countryside shrank back into itself, little by little, under the heat; the soil cracked in places, the grass turned a dirty yellow, sand heaped up in holes in the walls, and the trees were weighed down by dust. It seemed as though the summer would never end. Now the fields and terraced hillsides were occupied by cruel hordes of grasshoppers and wasps. The rutted lanes ran through the tumult of their wings, cut like razor-blades through these excrescences of the air, these hot bubbles full of spicy scents, which jostled one another at stubble height. The atmosphere made unremitting efforts.

Men cycled across the fields, emerged on to the main road and mingled with the flood of cars.

In the distance, all round the great amphitheatre of mountains, the houses flashed back the sunlight from their windows, and it was not difficult to assimilate them mentally to the stretches of cultivated land along the roadside. One could defy perspective and make a deliberate mistake about them, likening them to the splinters of mica that lay among the clods of earth. The boiling countryside looked pretty much like a black blanket thrown over red-hot coals; the holes sparkled violently, the material was blown into folds by subterranean gusts, and here and

55

there columns of smoke rose as though from hidden cigarettes.

A sort of cast-iron grating encircled the park. On the south side it bordered the main road, parallel to the sea, and there was a big gate half-way along; on either side of the gate stood a kind of wooden sentry-box, keeping the sun off a pair of women in their fifties who sat knitting or reading thrillers. In front of each of the women, on a board that stuck out from the window of the sentry-box, lay a roll of pink tickets traversed at regular intervals by rows of perforations so that they could be easily torn off. A man in a blue uniform and cap lounged beside a stand of geraniums, taking the tickets bought at the sentry-box and tearing them with the tips of his fingers; little pink crumbs were clinging to the rough cloth of his jacket, at about stomach-level. The man did not so much as cast a bored glance behind him at the area under his charge, where he would have seen a crowd of people walking away, their faces inquisitive yet apathetic, and vanishing behind the barred cages. He didn't speak to the women in the sentry-boxes either, and he barely replied to questions from the visitors; when he did, he spoke absent-mindedly, not looking at the questioners' faces but staring at the roof of a restaurant on the beach—Le Bodo—all decked with flags and streamers. Occasionally, of course, he couldn't avoid saying 'thank you', 'yes', 'go ahead', or something of the kind. And there were a few people who knew nothing, hadn't a clue; as he took their tickets, tore them gently with a double twist of the wrists and dropped the useless scraps into a basket on his left, he would bring out a whole sentence:

'Yes, Madame, I know. But we close at half-past five, Madame.'

'You have plenty of time. At half-past five, yes, Madame.'

56

Adam set out at random past the cages, listening with half an ear to the talk going on around him, and sniffing a bit at the variety of smells emanating from dung and wild beasts; the yellowish smell, laden with urine, had the special faculty of bringing things—particularly animals—into sensuous relief. He stopped in front of a lioness's cage; for a long time he stared through the bars at the supple body, full of vague muscles, reflecting that the lioness might have been a woman, an elastic woman moulded of rubber, and this acrid smell might have come from a mouth accustomed to Virginia tobacco, mixed with a suspicion of lipstick, a smell of peppermint tablets from the teeth, and all the faint, indefinable shadows, downy growths and chapped skin that leave a halo round the lips.

He leant on the railing that kept people away from the cage, and surrendered to an invading torpor dominated by a longing to touch the beast's fur, to thrust his hand into the thick, silky pelt, to fasten his claws like iron nails at the back of the creature's neck and overlay the long, sun-hot body with his own body, now sheathed in a leonine hide and covered with a mane, extraordinarily powerful, extraordinarily typical of the species.

An old woman went past the cage, leading a child, a little girl, by the hand; she went past, and as she walked on, against the light, her shadow blinking across each bar in turn, the lioness raised her head. Two flashes passed in opposite directions; at some point above the sand the black shaft, heavy with human experience, encountered the strange, greenish steely flare from the lioness and it seemed for an instant that the old woman's white, almost naked body was mated with the beast's tawny coat; both of them reeled, then sketched an advancing and receding movement of the loins, as though in this barbarous understanding they were performing an erotic dance-step. But a split second

57

later they drew apart and their gestures were separate again, leaving beside the cage only an immaculate white patch like a pool in the sunshine, a kind of peculiar corpse, a phantom where the wind stirred twigs and leaves. Adam, in his turn, looked at the woman and the child and felt himself gripped by an unfamiliar nostalgia, a quaint need to eat; unlike most of the people who went by he had no wish to speak to the lioness, to tell her she was beautiful, that she was big or that she was like a great cat.

He spent the rest of his afternoon walking all over the zoo, mingling with the tiniest races that lived in its cages, at one with the lizards, mice, beetles or pelicans. He had discovered that the best way to mix with a species is to make oneself desire a female member of it. So he concentrated, round-eyed, stooping, elbows propped on all the railings. His searching gaze penetrated the smallest concavities, the folds of skin or plumage, the scales, the fluffy hairs that sheltered the visibly ignoble slumbers of balls of black hair, masses of flabby cartilage, dusty membranes, red annulations, skin that was cracked and split like a square of earth. He stripped the gardens of their grass, dived head-first into mud, devoured humus voraciously, crawled along burrows at a depth of twelve yards, pawed a new, kindred body born from the putrified corpse of a field-mouse. With his mouth drawn down between his shoulders he pushed forward his eyes, his two big, round eyes, gently, with a thousand precautions, waiting for a kind of electric shock that would contract his skin, activate the ganglions that propelled him, and throw the rings of his body against one another like copper bracelets, with a faint tinkle, when once he had become subterranean, coiled, gelatinous—yes, the one and only real, tenebrous earthworm.

At the panthers' cage, this is what he did: he leant

forward slightly, over the railing, and suddenly waved his hand at the bars. The animal—a dark-furred female—flung herself towards him with a roar; and while the terrified bystanders fell back a step and the beast, mad with fury, tore the ground with her claws, Adam, paralysed with fear, trembling in every limb, heard the voice of the keeper, which set up a delicious vibration somewhere in the back of his head.

'That's a clever thing to do, that is! That's clever! That's a clever thing to do! Clever! Clever, eh?'

Thus divided again from the panther, Adam retreated a little way and muttered, without looking at the keeper:

'I didn't know . . . I'm sorry . . .'

'You didn't know what?' said the man in uniform, trying at the same time to quieten the animal with words such as 'Ho there! Ho there! Ho! Ho! Rama! Rama! Quiet! Quiet! Rama!' 'You didn't know what? You didn't know that there's no sense in teasing wild animals? It's clever, yes, clever, to play tricks like that!'

Adam did not try to make excuses; he muttered again, in embarrassment:

'No . . . I didn't know . . . I wanted . . .'

'Yes, I know,' the man interrupted, 'It's amusing to play tricks on the animals when they're shut up in cages! It's fun; but it wouldn't be such fun if the cage happened to come open, would it, eh? That wouldn't be such fun. And it would be fun if you were the one who was inside, don't you think?'

He turned away in disgust and appealed to a woman bystander:

'Some people just don't seem to have a clue. That there beast hasn't eaten for three days and as if that wasn't enough, there are people who think it's a joke to come and jeer at the creatures in their cages. Yes, I sometimes

59

wish the cage would open a crack and let one of those devilish brutes out. Then you'd see 'em running—oh yes, they'd understand fast enough then, they'd know fast enough.'

Adam moved away without waiting for the end of the sentence. He did not shrug his shoulders, but walked slowly, dragging his feet. He went past the mammals' cages; the last of these, the smallest and lowest, held three gaunt wolves. A kind of wooden kennel had been set up in the middle of the cage, and the wolves were circling round and round this, tirelessly, incessantly, their slanting eyes stubbornly fixed on the bars that rushed past at top speed, level with one's knees.

They circled in opposite directions, two one way and one the other; after a certain number of turns, let's say ten or eleven, for some sudden, queer, unaccountable reason, as though at the snap of someone's fingers, they wheeled about and went on again in the other direction. They were mangy beasts, grey with dust, mauve round the jaws; but they never stopped circling their den and the steely glint of their eyes was reflected all over their bodies—they looked as though they were covered with metal plates, violent, full to vomiting with hatred and ferocity. The circular movement they were making inside the cage became, owing to its regularity, the one really mobile point in the surrounding space. All the rest of the park, with its human beings and its other cages, sank into a kind of motionless ecstasy. One was suddenly frozen, fixed in an unbearable rigidity that spread all round as far as that bell-shaped structure of iron and wood, the wolves' cage; one was like a luminous circle seen through a microscope and containing, stained in bright colours, the basic elements of life, such as chromosomes, globules, trypanozomes, hexagonal molecules, microbes and fragments of bacteria. A structural geometry of the microcosmic universe, photographed through dozens of lenses; you know, that white disc, dazzling as a moon, coloured by chemical products, which is true life, without movement, without duration, so far away in the second infinity that nothing is animal any longer, nothing is apparent; nothing remains but silence, fixity, eternity; for all is slow, slow, slow.

They, the wolves, were in the middle of this desiccated landscape, its only sign of movement; movement that, seen from above, perhaps from an aircraft, would have resembled some strange palpitation or the ant-like stirring that sets up on the surface of the sea, diametrically below the plane. The sea is round, whitish, crested, and hardened like a block of stone, it lies 6,000 feet below; yet if you look carefully there is something independent of the climbing sun, a sort of little knot in the substance, a flaw that glints, advances, has a scrabbling centre. That's it; for if I suddenly turn away from the electric light I see it, that tiny star that looks like a white spider; it struggles, swims, makes no progress, it lives on the black landscape of the world, and it falls, to all eternity, past millions of windows, millions of engravings, millions of chasings, milliards of flutings, lonely as a star, never to die of its perpetual suicides because it is long since dead in itself and buried at the back of a sombre bronze.

When Adam left the wolves' cage he went to another enclosure; an artificial glade in the middle of the park, with several ornamental basins to left and right where a few big pelicans, their wings clipped, could come to drink. The pink flamingoes, the ducks and penguins, were the same kind of life too; the discovery that Adam had made little by little, since a certain day that summer on the beach, then in two or three cafés, then in an empty house, a train, a motor coach, a newspaper, he was now making again, a little more completely each time, as he watched the lions, the wolves and the puffins.

It was so simple that it stared you in the face and made you crazy, or at any rate most unusual. That was it, he'd got it, he grasped it and let it escape at the same moment; he felt sure, and yet he no longer even knew what he was doing, what he was going to do, whether he had escaped from a lunatic asylum or deserted from the army. That was what was happening, what was going to happen to him; by dint of *seeing* the world, the world had gone right out of his eyes; things had been so thoroughly seen, smelt, felt, millions of times, with millions of eyes, noses, ears, tongues, skins, that he had become like a faceted mirror. Now, the facets were innumerable, he had been transformed into memory, and the blind spots where the facets met were so few that his consciousness was virtually spherical. This was the point, verging upon total vision, where one sometimes becomes unable to live, ever to live again. Where sometimes, lying on a sickening bed on a hot summer afternoon, one sometimes empties a whole bottle of Parsidol into a glass of cold water and drinks and drinks and drinks, as though there were never to be another fountain on the face of the earth. People had been waiting centuries for that moment, and he, Adam Pollo, had reached it, had suddenly got there and appropriated all things to himself; he was no doubt the last of his race, and this was true, because the race was approaching its end. After that one need only let oneself expire gently, imperceptibly, let oneself be stifled, invaded ravished, no longer by milliards of worlds but by one single, solitary world; he had effected the junction of all times and all spaces, and now, covered with ocelli, huger than a fly's head, he was waiting, solitary at the tip of his slender body, for the strange accident that would flatten him on the ground and encrust him, once more among the *living*, in the bloody pulp of his own flesh, his shattered bones, his open mouth and blind eyes.

Towards the end of the afternoon, just before the zoo's closing-time, Adam went into the snack-bar, found himself a table in the shade, and ordered a bottle of Coca-Cola. To his left was an olive-tree in which someone had thought fit to set up a kind of wooden platform with a chain; and at the end of the chain there was a lively black and white marmoset, evidently put there to amuse the children and cut down the animals' food bill; children were never satisfied until they had bought a banana or a bag of sweets from a toothless old woman who was there for the purpose, and offered them to the monkey.

Adam leant back in his chair, lit a cigarette, took a sip out of the bottle, and waited. He waited without knowing exactly for what, settling down vaguely between two layers of warm air and watching the monkey. A man and woman went slowly past his table, loitering along with their eyes fixed on the small, furry animal.

'Pretty things, marmosets,' said the man.

'Yes, but bad-tempered,' said the woman. 'I remember my grandmother had one for a time; she was always giving it titbits. But do you suppose it was grateful? Not at all, it would bite her ear till it bled, the nasty brute.'

'That may have been a sign of affection,' said the man.

Adam was suddenly seized by a ridiculous impulse to get things straight. He turned to the couple and explained.

'It's neither pretty nor bad-tempered,' he said, 'it's just a marmoset.'

The man burst out laughing, but the woman looked at him as though he were a complete imbecile and she had always known it. Then she shrugged and walked away.

The sun was quite low by this time; the visitors were beginning to leave, emptying the space round the cages and the café tables of a multitude of legs, shouts, laughter and colours. As dusk came on the animals emerged from their artificial lairs and stretched themselves; barking was heard on all sides, with the whistling of parrots and the growling of the carnivores impatient for their food. There were still a few minutes left before closing time; Adam got up, went across to the old woman and bought a banana and some sweets; while he was paying she said crossly:

'Do you want to feed the monkey?'

He shook his head.

'No I don't—why?'

'Because time's up. It's too late now to feed the animals. It's forbidden after five o'clock, otherwise they'd have no appetite left and they'd get ill.'

Adam shook his head again.

'It's not for the monkey, it's for me.'

'Oh well, if it's for yourself it's not the same thing.'

'Yes, it's for me,' said Adam, and began to peel the banana.

'You understand,' the old woman went on, 'After the time-limit it would upset the creatures.'

Adam nodded; he ate the banana, standing in front of the woman but with his eyes fixed, as though abstractedly, on the marmoset. When he had finished he opened the bag of sweets.

'Will you have one?' he asked; he noticed she was staring inquisitively at him.

'Thank you,' she said, taking one.

They shared the rest of the sweets, leaning on the counter and watching the monkey all the time. Then Adam crumpled the empty bag into a ball and put it in an ashtray. The sun was level with the tree-tops by this time. After that Adam put a great many questions to the old woman, asking how long she had been working in the snack-bar, whether she was married, how old she was, how many children she had, whether she enjoyed life, whether she liked going to the cinema. Leaning closer and closer, he gazed at her with growing affection, just as, a few hours earlier, he had gazed at the lioness, the crocodiles and the duck-billed platypus.

In the long run, however, she grew suspicious. While Adam continued to ply her with questions and badgered her for her Christian name, she seized a damp cloth and began rubbing the zinc top of the counter, with vigorous movements that made the fat of her arms quiver. When Adam tried to take her hand as it went by, she blushed and threatened to call the police. A bell rang somewhere on the far side of the park, to announce closing-time. At this, Adam decided to leave; he said goodbye politely to the old woman; but she, standing with her back to the light, made no reply. He added that he would certainly come to see her again one of these days, before winter.

Then he left the café and made for the gate at the other end of the zoo. Men in blue uniforms were swilling buckets of water over the floors of the cages. A kind of purple shadow filled the hollows of the landscape and savage cries rose to the surface in waves, witnessing to the presence on all sides of stifling heat that smelt of viscera. The sentry-boxes on either side of the entrance were closed. But as far as the road, almost as far as the sea, despite the general withdrawal of men and beasts, there hovered here and there a vague odour of she-monkey, gently insinuating itself into you till you began to doubt your own species.

65

G. After that I know he went to wait for the dog, every day at the same time, on that kind of breakwater to the right of the beach. He didn't go and sit on the pebbles, among the bathers, although he could have waited more comfortably there; partly because it was hot and partly because he liked to feel he could move more freely in a more open space, where the wind would all the same bring a gust of fresh air from time to time, he used to sit on the edge of the breakwater, with his feet dangling over the side. The entire beach lay before his eyes, the stones, the little heaps of greasy paper, and of course the bathers, always the same people, always in the same places. He used to spend quite a time watching like this: his shoulders propped against a block of concrete brought there by the Germans in 1942, his body sprawling full length in the sun, one hand in his trousers pocket, ready to fish out of the packet one of the two cigarettes he allowed himself per hour. With the other hand he would be scratching his chin, fumbling in his hair, or raking through the stones on the breakwater to find dust and different kinds of sand. He kept an eye on the whole beach, the people coming and going, the imperceptible rolling of the pebbles. But above all he watched for the black dog to emerge from the unknown mass of bathers and trot towards the road, sniff the clumps of grass, and leap and run and throw itself headlong into the little adventure on the pavements.

Then, as though lassoed out of his torpor, he would set off once more to follow the animal, with no suspicion of where he was being led, without hope; yes, with the strange sort of pleasure that makes one continue a movement automatically or imitate everything that moves because, being a sign of life, it justifies all possible suppositions. One always likes to carry on a movement, even when it is trotting briskly on its four paws with their damp, brushing sound, propelling along the tarmac a light fleece of black hairs, two pricked-up ears and a pair of glassy eyes and is called, called once and for all, a dog.

At ten minutes to two, the dog left the beach; he had splashed about in the water for a bit before he set off, and the hair on his chest was still matted into little fluffy locks. He scrambled up the embanked pebbles, panting with the effort, went past Adam at a distance of a few yards and stopped at the roadside. The sun made him blink and threw a white patch on his cold muzzle.

He paused, as though waiting for someone; this gave Adam time to jump off the breakwater and get ready to leave. For a moment Adam was tempted to whistle or snap his fingers or just to call to him as most people do with most dogs— something like 'Come on, dog!' or 'Hi, Fido!' But the words were cut short in his head before he had even begun to utter them.

Adam merely stopped and looked at the animal from behind; seen from this angle he was curiously fore-shortened, standing foursquare on his pawns with arched back and the hair thinning out along his spine; and his neck looked bulgy, thickset and muscular, the kind of neck dogs never have.

He looked at the top of the dog's head, with the furrow

67

down the middle of the skull and the ears cocked. A train made a noise as it entered a tunnel—a long way off, of course, far up in the mountains. The dog's right ear moved forward a fraction of an inch to catch the rattle of the engine; then twitched smartly back, as a child down on the shore began to yell and went on and on at the full pitch of its lungs—smitten by some grief, a burst ball or a sharp stone.

Adam waited, motionless, for the starting signal; but the dog took him by surprise—darted forward, ran round a car, and went on up the road. He trotted rapidly, keeping close to the bank, rarely glancing to right or left. He stopped twice before reaching the crossing where the main road runs through the village: once beside the back wheel of a parked Oldsmobile; although there was nothing special about that car, he didn't look at it, or sniff it, or lift his leg quietly against the metal hub-cap. The second time was when that elderly woman was coming down to the beach with a boxer bitch on a lead; she glanced in his direction, gave a slight tug at her dog's leash, and then looked at Adam. She felt entitled to remark, as she went by:

'You should keep your dog on the lead, young man.'

Adam and the dog both followed the bitch with their eyes—their bodies turned the way they were walking, but their heads twisted back over their shoulders. They went on like this for a few seconds' silence, with little yellow flecks at the back of their eyes. Then the dog barked and Adam growled wordlessly, deep down in his throat: rrrrrrrrrrrrrrrroa, rrrrrrrrrrrrroaa, oaarrrrrrrrr, rrrrrrrro.

At the fork in the road Adam hoped the dog would turn right, because a bit further along was the hill where he lived, the path you've heard about and the big house—still empty—that he occupied. But as usual the dog unhesitatingly turned left, making for the town. And as usual Adam followed him, merely regretting, in a particular

68

corner of his memory, that such an imperative reason should draw the quadruped towards the crowds and the houses.

After the road along the sea-front there came a sort of avenue, with plane-trees set at regular intervals along the pavements, casting dense black shadows. The dog made a point of walking through these shady patches, and at such moments, because of his curly coat, he disappeared among the black ringlets and discs of the leaf-shadows.

Once this business of shade and sunshine began, hesitation became more frequent; the dog would veer abruptly from left to right and then back from right to left; he was weaving his way among the pedestrians, whose numbers were increasing all the time because by now they were well into the town: open shops, hot or cool smells coming in waves, colours everywhere, faded canvas umbrellas—all this clamped between walls, together with posters, shreds of posters bearing snatches of print that announced events over and done with three months ago:

'Squa   id ATCH
Bar de Band and James W. Brown
Fem in
MARTI
    ritive'

The dog had slowed down considerably, partly because the crowd was growing thicker and thicker and partly, no doubt, because he must be approaching his goal. So Adam was able to relax and smoke a cigarette. He even took advantage of a moment the dog spent in sniffing at an old patch of urine, to buy a chocolate-filled roll from the stall outside a confectioner's shop; he had eaten nothing since morning, and felt weak. He nibbled at the warm roll while he followed the dog along the main street. Coming to a red light, the animal stopped, and Adam came and stood beside him; he was still holding a small piece of roll in the grease-spotted paper from the shop, and he thought of giving part of it to the dog. But he reflected that if he did that the animal might take a liking to him, which would be risky; afterwards it would be the dog that would follow him, and he didn't know where to go, he didn't want the responsibility of leadership. And besides he was hungry and would rather not give away what little food he had left. So he finished the chocolate roll and looked down at the dark, hairy body panting beside his feet, sniffing, with back legs tense, and waiting obediently for the traffic policeman to wave people across the road.

The town was curiously empty of dogs; except for the boxer bitch they had passed just now on the way up from the beach, led on a leash by the old woman, they had only met people. Yet the streets bore the stigmata of a secret animal life; such as smells, patches of dried urine, excrement, tufts of hair left on the kerb where a sudden, compelling coitus had taken place in the full flood of the sunshine, among the hurrying feet and growling buses.

The signs of canine life thus to be found—by looking carefully, as one went along, at the pattern of the pavement —made a cryptic record of comings and goings through the labyrinth of the town. They all helped to build up a concept of space and time with nothing human about it, and to bring hundreds of dogs home to their usual lairs every evening, safe and sound and sure of being themselves.

He, Adam, was well and truly lost; not being a dog (or not yet, perhaps) he could not steer himself by all these notes inscribed on the ground, these smells, these microscopic details that rose up from the resonant tarmac and automatically enveloped the rachidian bulb via the muzzle, the eyes, the ears or even the mere contact of padding

paws or scratching toe nails. And being in any case no
longer human—never again—he passed, unseeing, right
through the town, and nothing meant anything to him any
more.

He did not see 'Studio 13', 'Gordon's Furniture',
'Frigidaire', 'High Class Grocers', 'Standard Oil', 'Café La
Tour', 'Williams Hotel', 'Postcards and Souvenirs',
'Ambre Solaire', 'Galeries Muterse', 'Bar and Tobacconist',
'Place Your Bets', 'National Lottery'.

Who had drawn lines on the pavement? Who had carefully laid sheets of glass over the showcases? Who—yes,
who—had written 'Pyjamas and Matching Striped Sheets'?
or 'Today's Menu'? Who had said one day 'Wireless Sets
and Spare Parts', 'Come In and Look Round', 'Great Sale
of Bikinis', 'Autumn Fashions', 'Wholesale and Retail
Wine-merchants', etc., etc.?

Yet there it all was, put there so that in the summer people
like Adam could find their way about, be reminded that
they were greedy or that they longed to sleep naked in
striped pyjamas with matching striped sheets and striped
pillows, perhaps with striped wallpaper on the bedroom
walls, and striped moths bumping into striped lampshades
during the striped nights streaked with neon lighting and
days striped with railway-lines and cars. So when people
saw Adam, round-shouldered, his hands thrust into the
pockets of his grubby-kneed trousers, following just ONE
dog, not even on a leash, a dog covered with blackish wool,
the least they murmured under their breath was 'there are
some weird types along this coast', even if they didn't go
as far as 'some people would be just as well in a loony-bin'.

A dog is certainly much easier to follow than most
people suppose. In the first place it depends on the angle of
vision, the level of one's eyes; one has to search among the
swarms of legs to find the black patch living, palpitating,

running below knee-height. Adam managed this without much difficulty, for two reasons: the first was that his slight stoop gave him a natural tendency to look down at the ground, and thus at the quadrupeds that live there; the other reason was that for a long time he had been training himself to follow something. They say that from the age of twelve or fifteen, when he came out of school, he would spend half an hour at a time following people—often teenage girls—through the crowded streets. He didn't do it with any purpose, but because he enjoyed being led to a lot of different places without bothering about street-names or any serious considerations. It was at this period that it had been revealed to him that the majority of people, with their stiff bearing and self-willed expressions, spend their time doing nothing. At the age of fifteen he was already aware that people are vague and unscrupulous and that, apart from the three or four genetic functions they carry out every day, they go about the town with no inkling of the millions of cabins they could have had built for themselves out in the country, to be ill, or pensive, or nonchalant in.

There was, after all, another dog, just across the street, accompanying a man and woman who were both about forty; this was a very beautiful bitch, slender and silky-haired, poised confidently on long legs; and Adam and the other immediately wanted a closer look at her. She had gone with her owners into a department store, packed with people, which was engorging and disgorging every second through its glass doors a flood of visitors, mostly women, laden with parcels and paper bags. The dog kept its nose to the ground, following some kind of trail, and Adam followed the dog. They entered the shop almost together. As they went through the door a neon sign flashed above their heads, reflecting downwards between people's feet, on the dog's woolly back and on bits of the linoleum-covered floor, in reversed letters, 'Prisunic', 'Prisunic', 'Prisunic'.

At once they were surrounded by people, women or children, or by walls, ceilings and displays of goods. Overhead was a kind of yellow slab from which there hung at intervals, between two strips of lighting, cards bearing inscriptions such as 'Bargain prices', 'Hardware', 'Wines', or 'Household Goods'. People's heads were right up among these cardboard rectangles and sometimes knocked into one, making it twirl round on its string for a long time. The counters were set at right-angles, with gaps for the customers to pass through. The whole place shone with a multitude of bright colours, jostling you to left and right, calling 'Buy! Buy!', displaying goods for sale, smiles, the click of women's heels on the plastic floor, and then putting records on the record-player at the back of the shop, between the bar and the photomaton booth. The whole thing was covered by the generalized strains of piano and violin music, except now and again when the low, placid voice of a woman, speaking with her mouth close against the microphone, was heard to say: 'Beware of pickpockets, ladies and gentlemen.'

'Section 3 Supervisor is wanted in the Manager's Office . . . Section 3 Supervisor is wanted in the Manager's Office. . . .'

'Hello! Hello! We recommend our snag-proof seamless nylon stockings, all sizes, three different shades—pearl, flesh or bronze—now on sale in the lingerie department on the ground floor. . . .'

The dog found the bitch again in the basement, at the electrical goods counter. He had been obliged to search the entire ground floor, slipping past hundreds of human legs, before he saw her. When he caught sight of her she was beginning to go down the stairs that led to the basement;

73

Adam hoped for a moment that the dog would not venture to follow her to the bottom. Not that he himself was not eager to get closer to the female—on the contrary; but he would willingly have foregone that pleasure so as to escape from this horrible shop; he was dazed by the noise and the lights and felt somehow caught up in the human swarm; it was rather as though he were moving in reverse, and a hesitant nausea lingered in his throat; he sensed that the canine species was eluding him in this stuffy place, all formica and electricity; he couldn't resist reading the price-tags all round him; a sort of commercial instinct was trying to put things to rights in his consciousness. He did some half-hearted mental arithmetic. An ancestral attachment to all this material that man had taken a million years to conquer was stealthily awakening, defeating his will-power, flooding right through him, translated into diminutive shufflings, tiny movements of the eyelids and the zygomatic muscles, shivers passing down the spine, dilations and contractions of the pupils as they adjusted themselves; the dog's black spine was bobbing up and down, ahead of him, and he was almost beginning to *see* it again, to weigh it in the depths of his brain in a native tremolo of unborn judgments.

The dog did indeed pause at the top of the stairs, intimidated by this dimly-lighted pit that kept swallowing up the crowd. But a little girl tried to pull his tail as she went by and babbled 'D-doggy, . . . want doggy . . .' and he had to go down. Adam followed him.

Down below there were fewer people. This was where records, stationery, hammers and nails, espadrilles, etc., were on sale. It was very hot. The man, the woman and the bitch were standing at the electrical goods counter, inspecting lamps and lengths of flex. The bitch had sat down under a lamp-shade with her tongue hanging out. When she saw

74

Adam and the dog she got up; her leash was trailing on the ground. Her owners were apparently too busy shopping to notice anything at all. Adam sensed that something funny was going to happen; so he stayed where he was, at the record counter. He pretended to be looking at the shiny cardboard sleeves; but he turned his head slightly to the left and watched the animals.

And all of a sudden it happened. There was a kind of flurry in the crowd, with the sound of a guitar and the click of stiletto heels. The little blue light in the photomaton machine went on and off, a livid hand drew the curtains and he saw himself reflected, snow-white, in the metal structure. At his feet now, right against his feet, the black dog's woolly body was covering the bitch's yellow coat; minutes went by, while men and women still walked past and round them, pounding the linoleum with metal-tipped shoes. The bitch was now the colour of old gold, and beneath her sprawling, outstretched paws the floor undulated gently, flecked with highlights, with hundreds of overlaid, spectral shadows; in this vault of the shop, sunk below ground-level, people were talking louder, laughing more boisterously, buying and selling hand over fist. There was a constant clicking of photographs, and every time the magnesium flashed it shattered something in the middle of a white circle where the dogs seemed to be wrestling, open-mouthed, their eyes wide in a kind of avid terror. Adam's forehead was damp with sweat; full of hatred and jubilation he stood motionless, whirling his brain round at high speed; a siren was shrieking in the middle of his skull; no one else could hear it, but it cried: 'Warning, warning!' as though war would break out at any moment.

Then the pace slackened, the bitch began to moan, almost in pain. A child came into the trampled space, pointed at the animals and laughed. Everything had rushed past. As though a film had been speeded up for a few minutes there were still a few spasms of frenzy; but Adam had already turned his eyes away from the pile of dogs and was breathing again, as he pressed his fingerprints on the record-sleeves. The sound of the guitars died away and the cool lips that had spoken not long ago came again to the rim of the microphone and announced:

'The last models from our summer collection are being offered at reduced prices on the lingerie counter . . . Fancy petticoats, cardigans, English blouses, swim-suits and light jerseys, ladies . . .'

Then Adam turned round and, with an almost straight back, began to climb the stairs to the ground-floor, preceded by the black, wool-clad hero; behind them, in the midst of the shaded labyrinth, close beside the electrical goods counter, in the bitch's orange-coloured belly, they left a nothing, an emptiness—it was funny—which in a few months' time would be filled with half-a-dozen little mongrel puppies.

They went on together up the high-street. It was getting late; the sun was already going down. That meant that yet another day was over, one more to be added to thousands of others. They walked at a leisurely pace on the sunny side of the road.

There were more cars than pedestrians, and at a pinch one could feel almost alone on the pavement.

They passed two or three cafés, because it was one of those southern towns with at least one café to every building. Not one single man suspected that the dog wasn't with Adam, that it was Adam who was with the dog. Adam sauntered along, glancing now and again at the people who went by. Most of the men and all the women wore dark glasses. They didn't know him, or the dog either. And it was quite a time since they'd last seen this tall, ungainly fellow slouching along the street, hands in the pockets of his dirty old linen trousers. He must have been living for quite a while all alone in the deserted house at the top of the hill. Adam looked at their dark glasses and reflected that instead of going to live all by himself in a corner he might have done something else; such as buying a parrot that he could have carried on his shoulder wherever he went; so that if anyone stopped him he could have left the parrot to speak for him:

'Morning, how are you?'

'Morning, how are you?'

and people would have realized he had nothing to say to them. Or he might have got himself up like a blind man, with a white walking-stick and thick, opaque spectacles; then other people would have been shy of coming near him, except occasionally, to help him across the street; and he would have let them do it, without saying thank you or anything, so that in the long run they'd have left him in peace. Another thing would have been to apply for a little kiosk where he could have sat all day selling tickets for the National Lottery. People would have bought as many tickets as they wanted, and he would have prevented anyone from talking to him by calling out at regular intervals, in a falsetto voice:

'Tonight's last winning tickets,

Try your luck!'

Anyhow, the dog served the purpose well enough, for the few people who went by in the opposite direction scarcely glanced at him through their smoked glasses and showed not the faintest wish to exchange greetings. That proved that he was no longer quite a full member of their detestable race and that like his friend Dog he could go about the streets and nose round the shops without being seen. Soon, perhaps, he too would be able to urinate placidly against the hubs of American cars or the 'No Parking' signs and make love in the open air, on the dusty footpath, between two plane-trees.

At the far end of the high-street there was a sort of fountain, a greenish bronze affair such as one used to see all over the place in the old days. Set firmly in the pavement, with a handle to pump up the water and an iron-barred drain through which it ran away. The dog was thirsty, and stopped in front of this post-cum-fountain; he waited for a moment, doubtfully, sniffed at the grooved flagstone and then began to lick the grating, where faint traces of moss were clinging and empty cigarette-packets lay about, crumpled into balls. Adam came up silently behind him, hesitated, and then turned the handle. After a few gurgles the water came gushing out, falling on the dog's head and splashing the toes of Adam's shoes. The water flowed on as though the movement of the handle were manufacturing it, and the dog lapped up several mouthfuls with his jaws wide open; when he had finished he moved away from the fountain, shook his head, and trotted off. Adam scarcely had time to swallow two or three gulps of the water that goes on falling even after one stops turning the handle. He wiped his mouth as he walked away, and took a cigarette from his pocket.

Some rough-and-ready signal must have gone off somewhere in the town—a flight of pigeons perhaps, or else the fact that the sun was vanishing behind the five-storey houses; for the dog was now walking straighter and faster. He had adopted a gait that, without being hurried, indicated frank indifference to all that was happening around him; his ears were pricking forward and his paws only touched the ground very briefly, as though he knew he was drawing a straight line that could not possibly be deflected.

78

He trotted along, right in the middle of the pavement, doing five miles an hour in the opposite direction from the hooting cars and the red and green streaks of the buses. All this, no doubt, in order to reach a house somewhere in the town, where a plump woman, whom he could see only as far up as below the breasts, would set before him, down on the kitchen floor, a plastic plate of finely chopped meat and vegetables. Perhaps a red-and-white bone, bleeding like a scratched elbow.

Behind the dog came Adam, almost at the double, as they crossed a succession of identical streets, past gardens, park gates that were just closing, quiet squares; a succession of big doorways, brown benches where tramps were already asleep with their heads leaning on the back of the seat; men and women were getting into cars; two or three old men were hobbling nonchalantly along, all in black; red workmen were putting oil lamps round the crater-like holes where they had been working all day under the open sky. A man of indeterminate age was going down the road too, on the opposite pavement, carrying on his back a wooden box full of panes of glass; every now and then he turned his head towards the house-fronts with a strange, melancholy cry that sounded like 'Olivier! . . . Olivier! . . .' but which must have been 'On the way! On the way!'

That was what the dog was trotting among; along the streets, past the houses, below the roofs that bristled with television aerials and brick chimneys; through the maze of drain-pipes and glinting windows, right out in the grey street down below, at a jog-trot, his body hard as a sword.

That was how he scampered by without looking at the stretches of house-wall or the shrubs in the little gardens, notwithstanding the thousands of caverns that could have been disclosed by tearing away what was concealing them,

79

the thousands of caverns in the depths of which people were nestling, ready to live among oak tables heavy-laden with flowers and baskets of fruit, velvet curtains, double beds and reproductions of impressionist paintings.

What the dog was doing was walking quickly, going home; it was, crossing a final street in the village which would soon be asleep, trotting the length of a final wall covered with posters, pushing with his muzzle to open one side of a wrought-iron gate, and vanishing from sight close by, somewhere between the house-front and the orange-grove—all his, all theirs, not Adam's.

What the dog had done now was to desert Adam at the entrance to the house, leave him standing with his back against the concrete gate-post with its engraved name and number—Villa Belle, 9—where he could stare through the gate's twenty-six bars, gaze at a shaggy garden as pink and green as in a child's picture-book, and wonder if it had been hot there that day or if it would rain there during the night.

H. There was something new in the empty house on the hill. This was a rat, of a handsome size, not black like most sewer-rats, but on the white side—between grey and white —with pink nose, tail and paws and two piercing blue, lidless eyes which gave him a courageous expression. He must have been there a long time already, but Adam hadn't noticed him before. Adam had gone up to the living-room on the first floor, where he had once lain on the billiard table with Michèle. He had not been back there since, presumably because it hadn't occurred to him; unless it was because he couldn't be bothered to climb the little wooden staircase to the upper floor.

Then he had remembered the billiard table and reflected that he might while away a few hours by playing billiards. That was why he had come back there.

So he opened the window and pushed back one of the shutters, so as to see properly. He hunted everywhere for the billiard balls; he thought the owners had hidden them away in a drawer and he broke open all the furniture with a knife. But there was nothing in the chest of drawers or in the sideboard or in the cupboard or in the little lemon-wood table, except old newspapers and dust.

Adam stacked the newspapers on the floor, intending to read them later on, and went back to the billiard table; he now found, on the right-hand side of the table, a kind of drawer, which was locked, where it seemed the balls must drop after falling into the pockets round the table. With his knife, Adam dug a groove round the lock. It took him a good twenty minutes to force the drawer. Inside, sure enough, he found nine or ten ivory balls, some red and some white.

Adam took the balls and laid them on the table. He still needed a cue to play with. But these the owners must have hidden carefully, perhaps in another room; perhaps they'd even taken them away with them, God knows where.

Adam suddenly felt tired of searching. He looked round him, hoping to find a substitute for the cues. There was really nothing except the legs of a Louis XV armchair; it would have meant taking them off, and besides they were twisted and gilded and Adam didn't want to dirty his hands with gold.

He now remembered that in the little front garden of the house he had seen two or three rose-trees, tied to bamboo props. He went down to the flower-bed, pulled up one of the rose-trees, and wrenched the bamboo shaft out of the ground.

Before going upstairs again he took his knife and cut one of the roses off the tree; it was not very large but it was a nice, round shape, with sweet-scented pale yellow petals. He put it into an empty beer-bottle, on the floor in his room, beside the heap of blankets. Then, without even looking at it, he went back upstairs.

He played billiards by himself for a few minutes; he sent the balls one against another without paying much attention to their colour. Once he managed to send four into the pockets at one stroke. But except for that once, which seemed to be more or less of a fluke, he had to admit he was not much good. Either he missed the balls he was aiming at, or he failed to hit the right spot: the cue struck the ivory surface a little to one side instead of in the middle, and the ball went off in all directions, spinning madly on its own axis. In the end Adam gave up playing billiards; he took the balls, dropped them on the floor and tried to play bowls. He was no better at this, please note, but as the balls fell on the floor they made a certain noise and set up certain movements, so that one could take more interest in the thing, even get some satisfaction out of it.

Anyhow it was while he was amusing himself like this, that he saw the rat. It was fine, muscular rat, standing on its four pink paws at the far end of the room and staring at him insolently. When Adam caught sight of it he lost his temper at once; he tried to hit the rat with a billiard ball, meaning to kill it or at least to hurt it badly; but he missed it. He tried again several times. The rat didn't seem to be frightened. It looked Adam straight in the eye, its pallid head stretched forward, its brow furrowed. When Adam threw his ivory ball the rat sprang to one side, with a kind of plaintive squeak. When he had thrown all the balls, Adam squatted down on his heels, so as to be more or less level with the beast's eyes. He reflected that it must be living in the house, like himself, though perhaps it hadn't been there so long. It must come out at night from a hole in some piece of furniture, and trot upstairs and downstairs, hunting for food.

Adam did not know exactly what rats ate; he couldn't remember whether they were carnivorous or not. If it was true what the dictionaries said: 'Rat: s. Species of small mammiferous rodent with a long annulated tail.'

He could only remember the two or three legends related to the subject of rats, in connection with sinking ships, sacks of corn and plague. To tell the truth he had not even realized until today that there were such things as white rats.

83

Adam stared at this one, listened hard; and discovered in the rat something akin to himself. He reflected that he too might have gone to ground in the daytime between two worm-eaten boards and roamed about at night, searching for crumbs between the floor-boards and being lucky enough now and again, in some recess in a cellar, to come across a litter of white cockroaches that would have made a fine treat for him.

The rat still stood motionless, its blue eyes fixed on him; there were rolls of fat, or of muscle, round its neck. In view of its size, which was slightly above average, and of the above-mentioned rolls of flabby muscle, it must be a rat of advanced age. Adam didn't know how long a rat lives, either, but he would easily have put this one at eighty years old. Perhaps it was already half dead, half blind, and past realizing that Adam wished it ill.

Slowly, quietly, imperceptibly, Adam forgot that he was Adam, that he had heaps of things of his own downstairs, in the sunny room; heaps of deck-chairs, newspaper, all sorts of scribbles, and blankets that smelt of him, and scraps of paper on which he had written 'My dear Michèle' as though beginning a letter. Beer-bottles with their necks broken, and a sort of tea-rose that was spreading the ramifications of its hot-flower perfume, minute by minute, between four walls. The yellow scent of a yellow rose in a yellow room.

Adam was turning into a white rat, but by a strange kind of metamorphosis; he still kept his own body, his hands and feet did not turn pink nor his front teeth lengthen into fangs; no, his fingers still smelt of tobacco and his armpits of sweat, and his back was still bent forward in a crouching position, close to the floor, regulated by the S-shaped bend in his spine.

But he was turning into a white rat because he was

thinking of himself as one; because all of a sudden he had formed an idea of the danger that the human race represented for this breed of small, myopic, delicate animals. He knew that he could squeak, run, gnaw, stare with his two little round, blue, brave, lidless eyes; but it would all be in vain. A man like himself would always be sufficient; he need only resolve to take a few steps forward and lift his foot a few inches, and the rat would be killed, crushed, its ribs broken, its oblong head lolling on the floor-boards in a tiny pool of mucus and lymph.

And suddenly he stood up; he had turned into fear itself, been transformed into danger-for-white rats; his head was full, now, of something that was no longer anger or disgust or any form of cruelty, but a kind of obligation to kill.

He decided to set about it rationally. First of all he shut the doors and windows so that the creature should not run away. Then he went and picked up the billiard balls; as he came closer the rat drew back a little, pricking its short ears. Adam laid the balls on the billiard table and began to talk to the rat in a low voice, making strange, hoarse, throaty sounds.

'You're afraid of me, eh, white rat?' he muttered. 'You're afraid. You're trying to behave as though you weren't afraid . . . With those round eyes of yours . . . Are you looking at me? I admit you're a brave chap, white rat. But you know what's ahead of you. They all know, all the members of your species. The other white rats. And the grey ones and the black ones. You've been waiting a long time for what I'm going to do to you. White rat, the world is no place for you. You're doubly disqualified for living: in the first place you're a rat in a man's world, among men's houses and traps and guns and rat-poison. And in the second place you're a white rat in a country where rats are generally black. So you're absurd, and that's an extra reason . . .'

He counted the balls; there was one missing. It must have rolled under the cupboard. Adam scraped about with the bamboo stick and brought out the sphere of ivory. It was a red one, and cold, and held in the palm of the hand it felt bigger than the others. And consequently more lethal.

When everything was ready, Adam took up his stance beside the billiard table, resolute; all at once he felt himself becoming a giant, a very tall fellow, ten feet or thereabouts, bursting with life and strength. At a little distance, against the back wall, close beside the square of pale light falling from the window, the animal stood, planted on its four pink paws, displaying great patience.

'Dirty rat!' said Adam.

'Dirty rat!'

And he threw the first ball, with all his strength behind it. It crashed against the top of the skirting-board, an inch or two to the left of the animal, with a noise like thunder. A split second later the white rat squealed and leapt aside.

'You see!' exclaimed Adam triumphantly, 'I'm going to kill you! You're too old, you don't react any more, you beastly white rat! I'm going to kill you!'

And then he let himself go. He threw five or six balls one after another; some of them broke against the wall, others bounced on the floor and rolled back to his feet. One of the balls, as it broke, fired a splinter at the rat's head, just behind the left ear, and drew blood. The rodent began to run along by the wall, with a kind of whistling draught emerging from its open mouth. It rushed towards the cupboard, to hide there, and in its haste it bumped its nose against the corner of the piece of furniture. With a yelp it vanished into the hiding-place.

Adam was beside himself at this.

'Come out of there, you filthy brute! Filthy rat! rat! filthy rat! Come out of there!'

He sent a few billiard balls under the cupboard, but the white rat didn't budge. So he shuffled across on his knees and poked his bamboo stick about in the darkness. It hit something soft, close to the wall. Finally the rat emerged and ran to the far end of the room. Adam crawled towards it, holding his kitchen knife. With his eyes he thrust the animal back against the wall; he noticed that the stiff fur was slightly bloodstained towards the top of the head. The thin body was quivering, the ribs rising and falling spasmodically, the pale blue eyes bulging with terror. In the two black rings set in their limpid centres Adam could read an inkling of doom, the anticipation of an outcome heavy with death and anguish, a moist, melancholy gleam; this fear was mingled with a secret nostalgia relating to many happy years, to pounds and pounds of grains of corn and slices of cheese devoured with quiet relish in the cool dusk of men's cellars.

And Adam knew he embodied this fear. He was a colossal danger, rippling with muscles—a kind of gigantic white rat, if you like, ravenously craving to devour its own species. Whereas the rat, the real one, was being transformed by its hatred and terror into a man. The little animal kept twitching nervously, as though about to burst into tears or fall on its knees and begin to pray. Adam, moving stiffly on all fours, advanced towards it, shrieking, growling, muttering insults. There were no such things as words any longer; they were neither uttered nor received; from the intermediate stage they reissued eternal, veritable, negative; they were perfectly geometrical, sketched against a background of the unimaginable, with a touch of the mythical, something like constellations. Everything was written round the central theme of Betelgeuse or Upsilon Aurigae.

Adam was lost amid the abstract; he was living, neither more nor less; occasionally he even *squeaked*.

He grabbed some of the balls and hurled them at the beast, hitting the target this time, breaking bones, making the flesh clap together under the hide, while he yelled disconnected words such as 'Rat!' 'Crime! Crime!' 'Foul white rat!' 'Yes, yeh, arrah!' 'Crush! . . .' 'I kill', 'Rat, rat, rat!'

He threw the knife, blade foremost, and drowned the white rat's words by shouting one of the greatest insults that can possibly be flung at that species of animal:

'Filthy, filthy cat!'

It was by no means over yet; the myopic little beast, maimed though it was, bounded out of Adam's reach. It had already ceased to exist.

At the conclusion of a life full of concentrated memories it was a kind of pale phantom in ghostly outline, like a dingy patch of snow; it was leaking away over the brown floor, evasive and persistent. It was a lobular cloud, or a fleck of soft foam, dissociated from blood and terror, sailing on the surface of dirty water. It was what remains from an instant of linen-washing, what floats, what turns blue, what traverses the thick of the air and bursts before ever it can be polluted, before ever it can be killed.

Adam saw it gliding first left, then right, in front of him; a kind of fatigue added to his determination, sobering him.

Then he stopped talking. He stood upright again and decided to finish the fight. He took a billiard ball in each hand—nearly all the others were broken by now. And he began to walk towards the rat. As he moved along beside the skirting-board he saw the famous spot—he would mark it later on with a charcoal cross—where the white rat had begun to lose its life. Nothing remained on the parquet floor to testify to the beginning of the massacre except a few tufts of light-coloured hair, some scraps of ivory like splinters of bone, and a pool. A pool of thick, purple blood, dulled already, which the dirty boards were swallowing drop by drop. In an hour or two, the time required to penetrate bodily into eternity, it would all over. The blood would look like a stain caused by no matter what liquid—wine, for instance. As it coagulated it would harden or become powdery and one could scratch it with a finger-nail, put flies there and they wouldn't be drowned or be able to feed on it.

With a veil of moisture in front of his eyes, Adam walked up to the rat. He saw it as though he were trying to look through a shower-curtain, a nylon hanging with little drops of water trickling down it and a naked, flesh-coloured woman concealed behind, amid the dripping of rain and the smell of soap-bubbles.

The white rat was lying on its stomach, as though asleep at the bottom of an aquarium. Everything had drifted out of its ken, leaving a naked, motionless space: now very close to bliss, the rat was awaiting the ultimate moment when a half-sigh would die away on its stiff whiskers, propelling it for ever and ever into a sort of double life, at the exact meeting-point of philosophy's accumulated chiaroscuri. Adam listened to its calm breathing; fear had left the animal's body. It was far away now, scarcely even in the death-agony; with its two pale eyes it was waiting for the last ivory balls to come thundering down on its bones and despatch it to the white rats' paradise.

It would go down there, partly swimming, partly flying through the air, full of mystical rapture. It would leave its naked body lying on the ground so that all its blood could drain out, drop by drop, marking for a long time the sacred spot on the floor that had been the scene of its martyrdom.

So that Adam, patient, should stoop down and pick up its dislocated body.

So that he should swing it to and fro for a moment and then, weeping, fling it in a wide curve from the first-floor window to the ground on the hill-top. A thorny bush would receive the body and leave it to ripen in the open air, in the blazing sunshine.

I. Question:
'My dear Michèle,

I do wish you'd come up to the house again one of these days, I haven't seen you since we had that race, you remember, down below, along the headland. It's ridiculous how much time I waste doing nothing in particular; perhaps because it's so hot that I wonder if summer will ever come to an end. I found a dead white rat in an arbutus bush just under the wall of the house. It must have been dead for a good time, it was quite yellow except for some spots of blood, which looked like dust. And it had little concentric wrinkles round its eyes; the closed lids made an X shape; and it had fallen into a lot of thorny bushes; the arbutus berries or bilberries were ripe, and made hundreds of scarlet dots round its head. The thorns had torn it to pieces, unless it was the sun that had reduced it to that condition; I suppose a dead body decays more rapidly in the sun.

As well as this, someone has cut with a penknife on a cactus leaf, You say Cécile J.'s a Shit.

Cécile J. says Shit on you.

I wonder who on earth can have written that. Some little girl who happened to go past, or perhaps one of the idiots I sometimes see in the grass on Sunday afternoons, with fellows who have moustaches. She must have been angry

because her moustached fellow had gone out with some other
girl; so she took her penknife, and instead of doing the
usual thing, carving a heart with compartments and putting
Cécile   Eric
on either side, she put
Cécile J. says Shit on you.
And I say it back to her.

What's fun sometimes is to sit at home, in the house,
with my feet in the sun; I remember this kind of thing too.
It happened a long time ago, but I remember it to this day;
there was some sort of big Girls' School not far from my
home. Four times a day they went past where I lived—at
8 in the morning, at noon, at 2 o'clock in the afternoon and
at half-past 5. I was always there when they went by. They
usually came along in groups of ten or twelve; they were all
stupid, and most of them were ugly. But I'd picked out
four or five who were vaguely pretty, and it amused me to
see them go by like that, four times a day. I felt as if it
gave me some kind of steady dates; I could do whatever I
wanted, go fishing, go away for a week, be ill in bed—I'd
know they were coming past regularly, just the same; it
was nice, because it gave me the impression of having
something to fill in my time. Like going home and seeing
the four walls still there, and the table and the chair and
the ashtrays just as you'd left them.

It's fun to remember that, here in a house that isn't my
own—where the deck-chairs are deck-chairs stolen from
the beach, and the candles are candles stolen from the
chapel on the port. The newspapers taken out of dustbins
in the town. The scraps of meat and potatoes, the tins of
pineapple, the odds and ends of string, the charred wood,
the sticks of chalk and all these three-quarter objects that

prove I'm alive and that I steal things. I'm glad I found this house; I can have peace at last, even if I don't know how to fill in the twenty-four hours. Twenty-four hours of peace and silence, I'm caught up in the strip-cartoon I chose for myself. . . .'

Reply:

'I can't answer you, Adam, I can't answer your question about the girl who wrote those words on the cactus leaf; but I've thought of a whole lot of stories; it's rather as if I were afraid to tell them to myself and had to start writing so as to bring all these queer things out of the confusion they're in as a rule. In any case it's not disagreeable, because when they're all strung together—all the little happenings one sees everywhere, the bits of paper with three words written on them, the leaves on which somebody has carved a phrase with a penknife, the insults one sometimes hears while crossing the street, etc.—they amuse me and I believe I'm fond of them.

Yesterday I went to the cinema; it was a curious film, but it's made me feel talkative; I think you're wasting your time on things of no importance; you're wasting yourself; it won't get you anywhere; you're afraid of everything that's sentimental; I'd like to tell you a story. No matter what. No matter what.'

Reply:

'All right. Let's tell stories. They've not much connection with bloody reality; but one enjoys them; let's tell the most delicate stories imaginable, like the story of a garden we'll suppose to be covered in snow and at the same time bathed in sunshine. There'd be cherry-trees all over the place. Except at the far end of the garden, where there'd be a high wall, very white. The snow would have settled on the branches of the cherry-trees and along the top of the wall. But because of the sun it would be slowly melting and it would fall on the grass, making a sound like drops of water, plop-plop.

And one of the trees would grumble: "Quiet! quiet! I can't get to sleep!" it would groan, creaking its boughs.

But the drops would go on falling, making even more noise. The sun would say:

"Sleep! Who's talking about sleep? Nobody is to sleep when I'm here on the watch!"

And the pear-trees would have plump, ripe pears on them, with scars for mouths. The scars would have been made by birds, but they might look very like lips all the same. And the pears would roar with laughter.

Then one of the cherry-trees, the oldest, would begin to grumble again:

"Be quiet! I must get some sleep! I must get some sleep! Or I shall never be able to flower!"

The drops would take no notice. Just before falling, while still hanging by their tails from the branches, they would call out in shrill voices:

"*Silence, silence! La queue du chat balance!*"

Just to tease.

It would be like that all over the garden. The little flakes of snow would be falling on the grass, softly, placidly, and the effect would be funny, because it would sound like rain although the sun would be blazing away. And everybody would be grumbling. The grass, because it's green and would like to change colour. The dead twigs, because they're dead. The roots because they would so much like to see the sky; the lumps of soil because they've had an overdose of phosphates; the blades of grass because they can't breathe. And the strawberry leaves because they're covered with soft, whitish hairs and it's somehow ridiculous, for a leaf, to be covered with soft, whitish hairs. Then the garden would change, little by little; there would be hardly any snow left on the cherry-trees and none at all along the top of the wall. And there would be hardly any sun left, either, to melt it. The noises would begin to be different. For instance the cherry-tree would creak its boughs, to get its own back. The pears would suddenly become too ripe and fall; some of them would go squash, making a mushy patch of over-ripeness on the grass. The others would manage to escape, and would crawl away, dribbling juice through their scars. But the wall would still stand straight and calm and silent. All white. It wouldn't move. And the result would be that seeing the wall so handsome, so noble, all the rest of the garden would feel ashamed of its noisy excitability.

And then we should see the garden gradually becoming gentle and icy again. There would only be a spiritless turbulence here and there, microscopic in every respect. Another few hours and it would be all white, green and pink, like a beautiful iced cake, all tranquil; and sleep would descend, with nightfall, just at the right moment—yes, really just at the right moment—on all those leaves, eh.'
Reply:
'My dear Michèle,

Again today I've been thinking that summer's bound to finish one of these days, and wondering what I should do when summer's over, when it'll be less hot, without the sun, and we shall see the water seeping in everywhere, rain-water, all the time, drop by drop.

There'll be autumn, and then winter. They say it will be cold when summer's over. I've been thinking that I shan't know where to go then. I've been thinking that the people who live in this house will come back one evening, by car. They'll bang the car doors and climb up the path that cuts across the hill, and invade the house again. Then it occurred to me that they'll throw me out—kick me out, perhaps. Unless they send for the police. And I shall be dragged off somewhere; it's sure to be some place where I shan't want to stay. That's as far as I can look ahead. After that it's all vague again, I don't know what will happen to me.

They'll certainly be angry with me for a whole lot of things. For sleeping here, on the floor, for days and days; for messing up the house, drawing squids on the walls and playing billiards. They'll accuse me of opening beer-bottles by smashing the necks against the window-sill: there's practically no yellow paint left on the wooden edge. I imagine I shall have to appear before long in a law-court full of men; I'm leaving them this filth as my testament; I'm not proud, but I hope they'll sentence me to some kind of punishment, so that I can pay with my whole body for the crime of being alive; if they humiliate me, whip me, spit in my face, I shall at last have a destiny, I shall at last believe in God. Perhaps they'll tell me I live in some other century, the 26th, for example, and you'll see how far I shall last into the future.

But I prefer to think of what I shall be able to do if they leave me free to go away.

It's hard to say, because I have masses of plans in my mind already. And that's funny, because I've not really given it much thought; I've had ideas, naturally, like every-one has, when I was strolling round the town by myself, or with you, Michèle, or wool-gathering in my own room, lying in my deck-chair.

For instance, I might go into mourning, a grey suit with a black band. I'd walk about the streets and people would think I'd lost a near relation, one of my parents, my mother. I'd attend every burial service and when the ceremony was over some people would shake hands with me and others would kiss me, whispering expressions of regret. In that case my chief occupation would be reading the "Deaths" column in the newspapers. I'd go to all funerals, handsome or shabby. And little by little I should get used to the life. I should discover what one's supposed to say, and the proper way to walk very softly, with downcast eyes.

I should like going to cemeteries, and I should enjoy touching dead people on the brow, seeing their pale, bulging eyes and empty jaws, and the marble slabs on the tombs; and I'd read what was written in the middle of the wreaths, on the ribbon that's hooked to the plaster violets:

"Regrets"

If necessary I could drone out:

"Nigher still and still more nigh
Draws the day of prophecy
Doomed to melt the Earth and Sky.
O, what trembling there shall be
When the world its Judge shall see."

Or I might travel; I'd go to a lot of towns I don't know, and make a friend in each of them. Then, later, I'd go back to the same towns: but I'd deliberately choose a day when I was sure not to meet my friend. For instance I'd go to Rio during the Carnival. I'd ring the bell at my friend's house—let's call him Pablo—and of course he'd be out. So then I could take a piece of paper and write him a note:

"My dear Pablo,

I came to Rio today to see you. But you weren't at home. I suppose you were at the Carnival, like everyone else. I'm sorry not to have been able to see you. We could have had a drink and a chat. Perhaps I shall be back this way next year. 'Bye for now.

Adam Pollo."

97

Or I'd go to Paris on the Fourteenth of July, or to Moscow for the procession in the Red Square, to Rome for the Council or to Newport the day of the Jazz Festival.

The real difficulty would be to choose my friends properly; I should need to be certain they'd be away when I came back to see them.

Otherwise my little game would go wrong, and I might not have the heart to carry on with it. I should muddle up my dates, and when I rang the bell their doors would be flung open and they'd exclaim, with beaming smiles of welcome:

"Adam Pollo? You here? What a delightful surprise! If you'd come tomorrow you'd have missed me, it's the Bull Fight . . ."

Yes, it would be just as well to plan that sort of amusement methodically. I must think about it often; perhaps I'll buy a diary where I can jot down the dates of festivals and important events in towns all over the world. Of course there'll always be the risk that one of my friends has been taken ill or turned eccentric and not gone to the fiesta. But risks like that give a spice of adventure to the thing.

These ideas I've been telling you about are only two among any number of others; I've thought up a whole heap of different schemes for fitting into the world. I might suffer from elephantiasis; I've noticed that always disgusts most people and keeps them at a distance. Or I might have a prognathous jaw; that makes people sorry for you and they never want to see how your bottom teeth jut out when you open your mouth. To limp because of eczema in one leg, to be a scoundrel, or to pick one's teeth with a little red celluloid spoon, the kind that's given away in packets of soap-powder—those aren't bad methods either. Or one can spend whole days trying to pick out decayed

98

places in one's teeth with the point of a knife. Generally speaking, anything in the nature of disease, madness or physical infirmity will do the trick.

But there are convenient situations in social life where people tend to leave you in peace; jobs like water-divining, pimping or gardening are particularly advantageous.

I've often thought I'd like to be a cinema operator, up in the projection-room. For one thing, you're shut up in a small room, all alone with the projector. There are no openings except the door and the slits that let the beam of light through. All you have to do is to put the reel on the spindle, and while it's running off, with a pleasant humming sound, you can smoke cigarettes and drink beer straight out of the bottle, keeping an eye on the blueish electric light bulb and saying to yourself that this is like being on board a liner during a cruise, one of the few people who aren't fooled by what's going on.'

Reply:

'My dear Michèle,

Now that it seems it's going to rain soon

Now that it seems the sun will be getting weaker, from day to day, from ray to ray, until it dies through being changed into a snowball, and that I shall be obliged to follow the cooling process, huddled up in my deck-chair,

Now that I have the impression that the triumph of the infirm and the crippled is about to begin,

Now that I am abandoning the earth to the termites, I think you ought to come.

Don't you really want, as I do, to come and sleep in the last remains of the light?

Do you really not want to come and tell me a quiet story while we drink beer or tea and hear sounds go past the window? And then we'd be naked, and we'd look at our bodies, we'd count something on our fingers, and we'd relive the same day a thousand times.

We'd read the newspaper.

When are the people of the house coming back? I'd so much like you to tell me sometime who carved those things on the cactus leaf and who killed that animal, the white rat that died by being impaled perhaps with two blue eyes glazed with its courage in the tangle of arbutus-bushes and didn't rot but became embalmed and by now must be pierced through and through with the heat.'

J. It was raining. So the dog would not be on the beach today. Where would he be? Nobody knew. At home, no doubt; unless he decided to roam the streets all the same, hunching his broad woolly back under the raindrops.

Adam went to the beach to have a look, though with no great hopes. The beach was ugly in the rain. The wet stones were not like stones any longer, the concrete like concrete or the sea like sea. They had all run on top of one another and mixed into mud. Nothing to be seen of the sun, naturally. In its place in the sky there was a funny little knot of seagulls, and at the spot it usually shone down on there was another little knot, of black seaweed.

In the town, Adam found it was almost cold. He was uncertain where to go; he didn't know whether he liked the rain or not. If he hadn't liked it at all he would not have hesitated to go into a café and drink beer, quietly bored. But he wasn't sufficiently sure of not liking it, to take on that expense. Letting himself drift, he arrived in a kind of department store. Because of the rain there were three times as many people as usual inside. Adam edged his way between the counters, telling himself he wouldn't stay there very long.

Then he found himself stuck behind a fat woman who was looking at socks. Adam looked too, and saw there were all sizes. Blue dominated except in the children's socks, where it was white. The fat woman was principally interested in that category. She handled most of them, at random, stretching them between her big red hands. Lifting the hem of her pinafore-dress with the toe of his shoe, Adam saw she had varicose veins; they ran in a series of purplish lumps just under the skin and that made him want to look higher up, to see what happened on her thighs. But Adam was drawn away by a movement in the crowd, and left the woman before he could find out any more. He stopped at the record counter, waited a moment for his turn, and then asked the assistant:

'Have you got MacKinsley Morganfield?"

Adam looked at the girl before she answered, reflecting that she was pretty; she had the soft cheeks of a little girl in quite good health, nut-brown hair, and her best feature was a pair of full lips, not made up but very red, which were now parting silently so that a pearly drop sparkled in the middle of the warm cavity of her mouth; her voice would certainly flow from deep down in her throat and, with four vibrations of the upper vocal cords, put an end to that faint quivering at the corners of her mouth, complete the most recent of human apotheoses, half desire, half habit.

'What did you say?' she asked.

'MacKinsley Morganfield,' said Adam. 'A fellow who sings.'

'What does he sing?' said the salesgirl; her eyes hovered blank and evasive, round the circum-ocular part of Adam's face.

'He's an American singer,' said Adam, 'a Negro who sings blues.' The girl went to the other end of the counter, opened a drawer and began searching through some lined-up records.

Adam watched her from behind, looking particularly

at the back of her neck; it was bent and the nape was rounded and white, with thousands of little curly hairs growing up from it. He still didn't understand how an imaginary name, such as 'MacKinsley Morganfield' or 'Gallaher's Blues' or 'Ricardo Impres' could have power to bend, at will, the round necks of the little girls who sold records in multiple stores.

After a time she turned to him and said no, she hadn't got that record.

Adam wanted to see the nape of her neck again, so he threw out another name, at random.

'And Jack Crivine?'

But the girl seemed to have understood. With a faint smile, she replied:

'No, I don't know that name.'

Disappointed, Adam thanked her and went away. And yet, as he fled he could feel her eye, a big green eye, staring at his back.

There were books there, hooked onto a kind of wire turnstile; Adam reflected that he might come to the shop every day at the same time, for example, and read one page from a selected book. If the book had 251 pages it would take him 251 days to read it. Probably a bit longer, allowing for the covers, foreword and list of contents, and for days when he couldn't come. Adam took a book from the turnstile, at random, opened it towards the middle, and read:

114   *A HIGH WIND IN JAMAICA*

back into the bows for a fresh run: but at each charge his run grew shorter and shorter. The pig was hemming him in. Suddenly the pig gave a frightful squeal, chiefly in surprise at his own temerity, and pounced. He had got the goat cornered against the windlass: and for a few flashing seconds bit and trampled. It was a very chastened goat which was presently led off to his own quarters: but the children were prepared to love him for ever, for the heroic bangs he had given the old tyrant.

But he was not entirely inhuman, that pig. That same afternoon, he was lying on the hatch eating a banana. The ship's monkey was swinging on a loose tail of rope; and spotting the prize, swung further and further till at last he was able to snatch it from between his very trotters. You would never have thought that the immobile mask of a pig could wear a look of such astonishment, such dismay, such piteous injury.

Adam closed the book; strictly speaking there was nothing so very touching about that page; and yet as he hooked the volume back onto the wire turnstile, Adam smiled tenderly. He felt he would discover little by little, within his enclosed world, heaps of unknown things, battles between wild animals, decks of ships overloaded with coal and sunshine. With buckets of water and coils of tarred rope. He resolved to come back tomorrow, or later on, to read another page.

He was happy to be living in a scale model of the universe, all his own, a gentle place with a thousand different ploys to occupy it.

K. Adam left the shop abruptly. He put a cigarette between his lips; by squinting he could see it getting spotted with raindrops. When the paper was thoroughly soaked he lit the cigarette and listened to the tobacco sizzling as it struggled against the damp.

He went down several streets and emerged on the promenade.

Until today there had been no rain for a long, long time. You could tell that just from the smell of the rain as it mingled with the dust on the pavements.

Adam set out along the sea-front; the fresh water was trickling in streams over his temples, through his hair and down inside his shirt-collar. It was making its way in little rills through the layer of salt that months of sunshine and sea-bathing had deposited on his skin. The promenade was a funny place, a widish, tarred road running below the public gardens; at first it bordered the harbour with its quays; then it went round a succession of small inlets, used as beaches for the tourists. There was only one footpath, on the side nearest the sea. So going past on a fine day, you could gaze in wonder at a crowd of pensive sadists, backs bent, elbows resting on the handrail as they gazed at another crowd consisting this time of masochists, slumbering, naked, on the beach below.

You made your choice; sometimes you'd stay up above with the sadists, your goggle-eyes rivetted on somebody's stomach which was usually dented by a navel.

Sometimes you went down below, staggering over the scorching pebbles, and then stripped and lay on your back, arms outstretched, under the avalanche of heat and staring eyes. The proof is that on a day like this no one was leaning on the railings because there was no one crazy enough to be lying naked on the beach in the rain. Unless it was the other way about.

Anyhow, there was nobody there. Adam strolled along with his hands in his pockets. The rain had put out his cigarette; he threw it over the parapet and watched it drop to the quay below. When he raised his eyes he noticed two cranes and a boat, a good distance away.

Their black ironwork was absolutely motionless. The cranes stood with arms extended, frozen in a kind of sinister cramp; the ship was framed between them, hardly smoking at all. It was a dark red colour all over, and the rain was driving against its portholes. Half of a name could be seen curving round the stern in capital letters, thus:

'DERMY'
and
'SEILLE'

The part one couldn't see must be 'Commander' or 'Admiral' or 'Captain' or perhaps 'City of'. It could have been 'Pachy' or 'Epi' or any old thing. As for the other word, below, one could easily have betted ten million that it was 'Marseille' if one had had the ten million, or if it had been worth while.

But that was not all; the rain was still falling, and the rustle of dead leaves could be heard on all sides; the dirty landscape was ringing with this monotonous sound, the only one. Adam felt a disastrous listlessness creeping over him; he bent down slightly and leant on the iron balustrade. He closed his fingers round it and allowed the water to flow down his arms like blood onto the wet railings. He was also thinking, no doubt, of his approaching death, his drained body lying full length on the concrete of a rain-washed, nocturnal quay, his acquiescent corpse, white as morning, which would still be shining with a thin trickle of blood, a hair's breadth of daily life, the last root thrusting down into the bowels of the earth. He listened to the noise that came zooming out of the sea like a waterfall; everything ahead of him, right to the far end of the docks, was quiet and calm, yet quivering with menace and hatred. He could feel his heart beating harder and harder, faster and faster; and he crumpled up, with his chest against the iron rail. The deserted wharves were cluttered with abandoned merchandise, some of it covered with tarpaulins, some not.

Standing at the water's edge or floating on its surface, two cranes and a boat had been left about. They were sharpened ruins, collections of broken razor-blades that made a grating sound as they clove the raindrops in two. Everything had been deserted, owing to a bit of a storm; some object or other, the pale shadow of something left over from a murder, the scattered materials. There was no more work, and that meant death.

Perhaps, one never knows, there was still a faint breath of life here and there, hidden behind the rubbish. Not in the shell-holes, anyhow; nor down there, you can be sure. A tuft of grass, drunk with rain, bent double with the weight of coal-dust and still thrusting up through the veneer of asphalt. Perhaps a pair of ants, perhaps a cat, perhaps some kind of seaman, smoking his pipe in a vacated shanty-town. But those didn't count; they were merely Phantoms and Co.

You must understand that what was happening to Adam

on this particular rainy day might equally well have happened to him on any other day. On a very windy day, for instance. Or on a day during the equinox, or on one of those much-vaunted sunny days. With great patches of light spreading over the ground, there would have been an enormous crowd on the promenade, lots of women and children. The cars would have kept up a continuous roar behind him; he would have met groups of boys and girls in sweaters, T-shirts and blue jeans, passing him on their way to the beach; they'd have set their transistors yelling as they went by. This way:

> 'But darling darling
> Keep in touch
> Keep-in-touch
> Keep-in-touch-with-me.'

And down there, on the docks, the cranes would have been set turning and the boat's funnel smoking, the men shouting, the barrels of oil rolling and the big rounds of cork would have been stowed; the ground would have been made to smell of coal and diesel oil and the air to ring with hammer-blows banging on the rusty hulls of the cargo-boats. That's it, everything would have been done that is done on a sunny day. But Adam would have guessed, all the same; he would have sat down, quite dumbfounded, on a bench on the promenade and seen space being peopled with ghosts. He would have felt death invading all his movements, only instead of being grey and unoccupied death would have been red and white and industrious.

But one particular noise would have come spurting out of everything, drowning all other sounds—a noise bordering on rain, very close to the tumult of waterfalls or the hissing of steam-engines. This was a kind of fate; Adam had gone beyond the evidence of his senses, and for him, henceforth, nothing seemed to move. He reconciled all measures of time and motion, from the butterfly to the rock. Time, having become universal, was destroying itself through its own complexity. In the world as he now understood it, everything was explicitly alive or dead.

After that it didn't matter so much that he should have stood up and walked on again beside the hand-rail, whistling a waltz tune through his teeth. That he should walk the length of a big puddle of yellow water that was boiling under the rain. That with the toe of his shoe he should crush an empty matchbox that had (I 25 A) written on its underside. Nor did it matter that as he went along he should try to catch a glimpse of the little stucco temple an old bourgeois family had erected at the far end of their garden in more prosperous days. Or that he should happen to pass a group of seminarists, shivering in their long, black cassocks and whispering:

'At Castelnaudry, didn't you know?'

'And yet he told me it was better not to' and laughing.

No, it didn't matter much, because the breath of real life was no longer in them; they were no longer bright and victorious, they were nothing but lean spectres who brought forewarning of a great void that would open up some day. They predicted all possible causes of death—the burst of machine-gun fire from a passing car, the chopper of the guillotine, smotherings under pillows, stranglings, poisonings, murders by axe, embolisms, or just simple runnings-over in the street by four vulcanised rubber tyres.

Adam expected some such violent end whenever he put a foot forward. It wasn't difficult to imagine. He might be struck by lightning; they would bring him down from the top of the hill on a stretcher, black and charred, amid the rumbling of the storm. He might be bitten by a mad dog. Poisoned by water. Or else, drenched as he was by the rain, he might very easily get pneumonia. Trailing his hand along the balustrade, he might scratch himself on a jagged piece of metal and develop lockjaw.

An aerolite might fall on his head. Or an aeroplane. The rain might cause a landslide so that the promenade would collapse, burying him under tons of earth. A volcano might erupt beneath his feet—there—at any moment. Or he might simply slip on the wet asphalt, or on a banana skin, why not, and fall backwards, fracturing his cervical vertebrae. A terrorist or a lunatic might choose him for a target and send a bullet into his liver. A leopard might escape from a menagerie and tear him to pieces at a street-corner. He might murder somebody and be sent to the guillotine. He might choke himself on a sugared almond. Or war, sudden war, might touch off some gigantic calamity, some kind of bomb, send up a mushroom of smoke surrounded by flashes of lightning, and annihilate him, vaporize him— Adam, poor, puny Adam—in a microscopic contraction of the atmosphere. His heart would stop beating and silence would spread through his body; in a chain reaction, the cold would creep slowly along his limbs until with tremendous stupefaction he would vaguely recognize that his furthest recesses of red flesh, which used to be warm, now had something corpse-like about them.

At every step he faced some new peril: that a beetle would fly into his open mouth and block his windpipe; that a wheel would come hurtling off a passing lorry and decapitate him, or that the sun would be extinguished; or that he himself would be gripped all at once by a suicidal impulse.

He suddenly felt tired; tired of living, perhaps, tired of constantly having to defend himself against all these dangers. It wasn't his actual end that mattered, so much as the moment when he would decide he was ready to die. He had a horror of that bizarre transformation, which would certainly take place one day or another and prevent him from thinking about anything any more.

Adam sat down on the back of a bench; he had got beyond the docks some time ago, to where the promenade ran round the rocky inlets. A man came past on a bicycle; he wore oilskins and seaman's boots. In his right hand he was carrying a dismantled fishing-rod, its sections held together by three sock-garters. The saddle-bags on his bicycle seemed to be full—of rags, or fish, or a wool jersey; as he pedalled along the road, his tyres making a sticky noise on the tarmac, he turned his head to look at Adam. Then he pointed over his shoulder and called out, sounding as though he had a cold:

'Hey! There's a drowned man back there!'

Adam followed him with his eyes. Thinking he had not understood, the man—a long way off already—looked round and shouted again:

'A drowned man!'

Adam said to himself that the man was right; as everyone knows, a drowned body is the choicest possible entertainment for anyone who is wandering aimlessly along the sea-front, soaked to the skin and sometimes sitting on the back of a bench. As he got to his feet he reflected that all over the place there must be one such case of drowning every day. To show others how to set about it, summoning them, likewise, to meet their end.

Adam walked on again, faster; the road was bending round a sort of cape, and one could see nothing. The drowning must have occurred on the other side; perhaps at the Roc-plage, or along by the German blockhouse, opposite the Seminary. He was ready to bet that in spite of the rain there would be a lot of people staring down at the sea, a lot of people, all enjoying themselves, despite the faint contraction of their nostrils and hearts, where shamelessness would pause for an instant, just long enough to become tinged with embarrassment, before hurtling ahead, mingled with the thick breath of meals and wines, towards *this*, towards the *object*. And indeed, as soon as Adam got round the corner, he saw a gathering of people, still some distance along the road. It was a group of men, mostly fishermen in oilskins. There was a firemen's van as well, with its back doors open. As he drew nearer, Adam noticed another car, but this was a private one, and foreign, Dutch or German or some such. A couple of tourists had emerged from it and were standing on tiptoe, trying to see.

The closer Adam came, the more activity he seemed to perceive. He leant over the parapet and saw down below, on the beach, a yellow plastic inflatable raft and two frogmen taking off their diving gear.

It couldn't have been long since they fished the body out, for on the short flight of steps leading up to the road there were still some puddles of sea-water, not yet washed away by the rain. One of them had shreds of seaweed in it. When Adam arrived they let him through to the front row without comment, perhaps because after being out in the rain so long he looked like a drowned man himself.

And Adam saw that in the middle of the ring of bystanders, laid flat on the gravel like a heap of rags, there was that insubstantial, ridiculous thing which had nothing terrestrial about it any more, and nothing aquatic either. This amphibious monster was a man of no particular age, just a man like any other. His only peculiarity—and it made you want to laugh, a deep, throaty laugh—was the quantity of water he represented, what with his flesh and his clothes, in the middle of this wet scene; it was the fact of being a drowned man out in the rain. The sea had already ravaged his body. A few hours more and he would have looked like a fish, one felt. His hands were blue and swollen and on his feet—one bare, the other shod—there were tufts of weed. From the depths of his clothes, which were twisted round him, soaked and saturated with brine, his head and neck hung out limply. His face, though dead, was curiously mobile, crawling with a kind of movement quite alien to life, because of the water that puffed out his cheeks, eyes and nostrils, and rippled beneath the skin with every drop that fell from the sky. Within a few hours this man of about forty, honest and hard-working, had become a liquid man. Everything had melted, in the sea. His bones must be jelly now, his hair seaweed, his teeth tiny stones, his mouth an anemone; and his eyes, which were wide open, staring straight up to where the rain came from, were veiled by a kind of glaze. Air mingled with vapour must be bubbling invisibly between his gill-shaped ribs. The bare foot, screwed into the trouser-leg like an artificial limb, had emerged from the depths of the sea with the skin greasy or grey and a suggestion of embryonic webbing between the toes. He was a giant tadpole, floated down accidentally from the mountains, where lonely pools of water lay in the hollows of the peaty ground and shivered beneath the wind.

When one of the firemen turned the man's head over, the mouth opened and vomited. 'Oh!' said one of the lookers-on.

The idlers had lost their excitement and now stood rooted to the spot like stone images, while the rain poured down on their heads. Only the firemen were still active, slapping the corpse with the flat of their hands, talking together in undertones, manipulating little bottles of spirits.

But the drowned man lay alone, huddled on the ground, muddy-eyed, ready for some imaginary reflex action, perhaps for a leap that would carry him back towards the element in which resurrection must find him. And the heavy rain was still falling on his blue flesh, splashing louder than ever, as though hitting the surface of a pond.

Then things began to happen very quickly; a white stretcher was brought; the firemen pushed back the ring of spectators; there was a brief glimpse of a strange, grey, confused body retreating towards the ambulance. The doors banged. There was a noise, the crowd took a step forward; and the ambulance drove off townwards with its dripping burden. In the middle of the road, where just for a few hours people would still avoid treading, a strong smell of seawater now hovered, despite the rain. The wheel-shaped pool was slowly absorbed by the gravel, and everyone's heart shrank at the strange passing—for now the dead man's body was quietly shedding its ludicrous memory. It was flowing down at the back of their minds, they were no longer even trying to hold it, to imagine it tossed from mortuary to pauper's grave. He had become a queer archangel, white or clad in armour. He was at last the victor, single and eternal. His blue-gloved hand pointed imperiously, showing us the sea where he had been born. And the sea's edge, the fringe of waves washed up with refuse, invited us to approach. Sirens disguised as empty hair-oil bottles, headless sardines, jerrycans and half-peeled leeks, chanted their hoarse-voiced summons; we were to go down the steps, still puddled with salt water, and without undressing, entrust our bodies to the waves. We should cross the edge, with its floating orange-peel, corks and patches of oil, and go straight to the bottom. In a little mud, stabbed with pangs of osmosis, tiny fish swimming into our mouths, we should be motionless and gentle.

Until a group of men dressed like monsters came to look for us, thrust hooks into the back of our necks, dragged us to the surface and drove us away in ambulances towards the mortuary and paradise.

L. When you've seen a drowned body, only just taken from the water, still lying on the road, you don't find much to say. Especially when you have understood why some people drown themselves, one day or another. The rest doesn't matter. Whether it's raining or fine, whether it's a child or a man, or a naked woman with a diamond necklace, etc., makes no difference. Those are the particular settings of an unchanging tragedy.

But when people haven't understood, well . . . When they allow their attention to be distracted by the details that seem to justify the event, give it a certain reality, but which in fact are merely stage effects; then there is a great deal to say. They pull up, get out of their cars, and join in the game. Instead of seeing, they compose. They lament. They take sides. They cerebrate and write poems.

He asks whence comes this subterranean dust
to take its place on things. Reigning gently.
all amidst the cogwheels granite in crumbs.
it petrifies the level surfaces, he says.
he wishes for yet more tedium and taste: ashes.
he listens. then one must leave him thus
await his pleasure, the high priest.
he looks to every form to remind him
of a forgotten wish: one would think he waits for war.

true, he may be mistaken
War may Be no longer the Giver of Courage
but the Breaker of Stones
It may Be War that Grinds the Granite to crumbs
It may Be War that Fabricates the Hardest Dust
The millimetric Abrasions

He asks
He wishes He waits
He counts on his fingers
and gathers himself to leap

he—yes—LOVES
the hard dust
that is why he does not know
that there is the sand,
what is called sand
what is called ashes
and the yellow leaves and the bird-droppings
and the rainy soil
the lavas and other seeds
yes, all that.
which is called gentle dust.

And of course (since he who writes is shaping a destiny for
himself) they little by little become one with those who
drowned the chap.

One of them, his name's Christberg, says:
'But what happened?'
'There was an accident' says his wife, Julia.
'You saw how swollen he was? He must have been a
hell of a time in the water. It seems it was two days . . .'
says a fisherman called Simonin.
'Do they know who he is?' Christberg enquires.
They all stayed where they were, though. In a circle

round the patch of sea-water with bits floating in it. As though the-man-just-now, the drowned man, had begun to shrink until he was only a tiny insect, almost invisible, still swimming in the middle of the pool.

'Was it a man or a woman?' asked Julia.

'I saw one like that last year. At much the same place. A bit further along, though. Beyond the restaurant over there. I was on the beach and there was a woman going up to people and asking, "You haven't seen Guillaume?" Asking everybody, like that. They all said no. She—she went on doing that for quite a time. Afterwards something was seen floating a little way out, not so very far from the shore. There was a fellow who was a good swimmer and he went in after him. It was Guillaume. It was the—— He was just a kid, about, about twelve, I remember. When the chap brought him to land he wasn't a pretty sight, I can tell you. They, they laid him down on the shingle and he was all purple. They wanted to prevent his mother seeing him, but they couldn't, it was too late, she got through all the same. She saw him and she began turning him over and over on the shingle, crying, and calling out, like this:

"Guillaume, oh, Guillaume!"

Well, she turned him over so often that you know, everything came out of his mouth. Bile, and milky stuff, the lot. And gallons of sea-water. But a funny thing, eh, he was dead all the same', said the narrator, whose name was Guéraud.

'But what exactly happened?' Christberg asked again.

'It seemed he was drowned,' his wife whispered.

'D'you suppose he's dead?' asked Bosio.

'After two days I don't see how he could still be alive,' said Joseph Jacquineau.

'They always vomit when they're turned over. They've swallowed such a lot of water, you understand, the least

117

jerk makes them throw it up. Not a pretty thing, death,' said Hozniacks.

'Even with all the things, the injections they give them in the heart, and everything? They say they can be saved even when they've been dead for days,' said Bosio.

'Do you believe all that stuff?' asked Simone Frère.

'Dunno,' said Bosio.

'How can one tell,' said Hozniacks, 'I . . .'

'I saw a fellow once, but it wasn't the same thing. He was a fellow who'd been knocked down by a car. Without exaggeration, the two lots of wheels had run right over him, one across his neck and the other across his legs. Funny thing, that kind of car leaves the marks of the tyres on the skin. Well, I tell you for sure, they could have given that chap all the injections they wanted to. It wouldn't have brought him round. There was blood everywhere, even in the gutters. And both eyes had popped out of his head. Like a squashed cat, exactly like a squashed cat,' explained a man leaning on a walking-stick, who was known as M. Antonin.

'It took them three hours to find him,' said Véran. 'They looked everywhere along the coast. And here, they hunted for three hours. Three whole hours, they hunted. I saw them right from the start, because I was walking along the seafront. I just happened to see them.'

'So they knew he was missing?' said Guéraud.

'Must have,' replied Véran.

'Perhaps he committed suicide. Left a letter at home and they found it,' said Hozniacks.

Some people were going away already, walking beside the parapet. They were getting into cars and slamming the doors, and groups of idlers were calling to one another:

'Hey, Jeannot! You coming?'

'Yes, wait for me!'

'Hurry up!'

'Paul! Paul!'

'Hey, Jeannot! Well, then?'

'It's all over, there's no point in staying here, come along!'

The rain drove them away, one by one; a few new arrivals slowed down, in cars or on foot, but went on again at once, slightly bothered by not discovering what had happened; those who remained had broken up the circle. Now they had turned away from the last traces of the puddle of salt water and were looking out to sea. The horizon was veiled, uncertain, because of the grey mist. There were few gulls flying, and the earth looked as though it were round.

'Was he in a boat?' asked Hozniacks.

'Unless he was fishing from a rock and fell in,' said Olivain.

'No, no, it must have been a boat that capsized, he was too far from the shore,' said Véran.

'Perhaps he fainted? It does happen,' said the spectacled woman, Simone Frère.

'Yes, but two days ago the sea was very rough,' said Bosio.

'And in two—in two days, he may have drifted a long way. There are strong currents round here,' said Olivain.

'That's true—must be why they've been looking all over for him,' said Hozniacks.

'I saw one drowned man last summer. Young chap. He'd dived in, fully dressed, from one of those cycles on floats. Showing off, probably. And he'd gone down like a stone. They fished him out and tried everything, artificial respiration, massage, injections, the works. But he never came round,' said Jacquineau.

'Yes, I remember seeing about it in the papers,' said Véran.

'But this one wasn't a young man, was he?' said Hozniacks.

119

'A lot of people get drowned along this coast,' said Simone Frère.

The rain was trickling down their chins and plastering their hair to their heads; if they'd only known, or seen, how they were getting to look more and more drowned. There was only one group left now, with five people, viz.:

Hozniacks	– –	– fisherman
Bosio –	–	– fisherman
Joseph Jacquineau	–	pensioner
Simone Frère		– wife and mother
Véran –	–	– no occupation

They couldn't tear themselves away. The last memory of the man who had lain dead before their eyes and who still haunted the spot a little, was keeping them together, exposed to the rain. It was their human memory that gave them a fellow-feeling even without love, and made them dread the long, lonely journey over the abyss even more then death or pain. This would go on until the day when— in a month, a week, or less—one of them would refer to the incident for the very last time.

Let's say it would be Hozniacks. In the café, on his way home, he'd tell the story just once more:

'The other evening I was walking along by the sea, coming in from fishing because it was raining. I saw a drowned man. He was all swollen with water, quite blue, and no one could bring him round. There was something in the paper about it next day.

Tired of Life

M. Jean-François Gourre, 54, travelling salesman for a toilet-soap firm, was found drowned yesterday. Accident seems to be ruled out, and a verdict of suicide was returned at the inquest. The unfortunate man is believed to have taken his life by throwing himself from a hired boat. When the body was found it had been in the water for three days. M. Gourre, who was much esteemed in the trade, seems to have given way to a fit of depression. We offer our sincerest sympathy to his family and friends.

'Yes, I felt sure it was suicide. I said so to the others. The chap looked like a suicide; I felt sure from the start that he hadn't been drowned naturally.'

Swathed in black, M. Gourre's widow and her daughter Andrée, aged fifteen and a half, will make their way along the corridors in the Mortuary, following a little bent, white-overalled man who jingles bunches of keys in his pocket as he leads them to the big cold-storage room. He will open the door, turn his bald or pallid skull towards the women and say to them softly:

'This way, please.'

They will follow him; they will watch him scanning the numbers on the drawers; he will pull aside a kind of very clean white sheet from drawer No. 2103 V, and whisper:

'This is the one.'

After identifying the fresh, pink corpse, the little corpse of M. Jean-Françoise Gourre, husband of one and father of the other, they will go away without a word. The subject will never be mentioned again, not at table, not in the living-room, among relatives and friends, nor even to the tradespeople when they do their shopping. At the very most somebody, now and then, may venture to say to one or other of them: 'My deepest sympathy . . .' without even shaking hands.

Between them and him, all will be over; he was not a good man; he often told lies, deceived his wife, used to peer at his daughter through the bathroom keyhole when she was getting into the bath, quite naked. He was a good man. He was a good father. He never went to cafés and was not believed to go often to a brothel. He went to church sometimes on Sundays; and above all he earned an honest, regular living.

He had even promised to buy a television set. He had never existed.

Her husband had been killed in the war, dying a hero's death during the attack on a Japanese stronghold. Andrée's father had been killed in a car or plane crash when she was only three. He was handsome, rich and affectionate. Too bad that fate should have carried him off so soon!

That was pretty much what must have happened, apart from Adam, among a few people, the day that chap was found drowned and then dragged to the roadside, when it was raining and everything was drenched.

So now, as a result, there is a kind of God dwelling in each of them by turns and calling them to Himself, at the hour of His choice, that they may live in what they had never seen before, dead men.

M. They would be forgotten. They would be left to lead their own lives, go home, do what they had to do, all those others, Hozniacks, Guéraud, Bosio, Simone Frère, Olivain, Véran, Joseph Jacquineau, Christberg and little Guillaume. Adam allowed them to pass him on the road. He had been one of the first to leave, but because he was tired, fearfully tired, he had dragged along the seafront. He had stopped for a minute under a plane-tree, to shelter from the rain. But the leaves were heavy with water and the shower easily came through. So he had trailed on again, soaking, his pockets full of rain. He wanted a cigarette, but the packet was wet and the cigarettes spoilt: the paper and tobacco had dissolved into a lumpy paste that lined his pocket.

The idlers were going home in little groups; one could still hear vague snatches of conversation, not all connected with the accident. There was talk of drowning, avalanches, fainting-fits, fly-fishing and politics.

Adam had a stitch in his side. He did not feel at all alone now. He had even stopped trying to understand. He was beginning to remember that he must very often have been mistaken.

When he got to the harbour he paused under the awning of a Bar-Tabac. He looked at the postcards on the revolving stand; there were coloured ones and black-and-white ones.

There was a batch of several showing a young woman with a rather plain face but a lovely figure, wearing a bikini. Adam went into the bar and bought this, together with a packet of cigarettes. Then he came outside again and stood under the awning, sheltering from the rain and looking at the photo. It was in five colours and showed the young woman kneeling on a kind of pebble beach and smiling very hard. With her right hand she was pulling down the bottom half of her biniki, disclosing a patch of plump brown hip. With the other hand she was hiding the tips of her breasts. To make it quite clear that they were bare, her bra was lying on the ground beside her. And to make it quite clear that it was a bra, it had been laid out flat on the pebbles, with the cups sticking up. The whole thing was pretty ridiculous; the card was good quality, shiny, rich in texture, creamy, translucent as sugar, gleaming all over. Running his eyes over it and scratching it with the nail of his middle finger, Adam reflected that it was about a thousand times more erotic than the half-naked woman in the photograph. When you came think of it, the communicative power of this commonplace object was completely separate from its pornographic intentions; the collective message was feeble and not likely to call forth more than laughter or melancholy; but its true essence lay far beyond, it rose to the heights of geometry or technique; sawdust and cellulose formed a halo that sanctified the girl, proclaiming her to all eternity virgin and martyr, blessed among women. She seemed to reign over the world like a madonna, remote from blasphemy, onanism and giggles; the glossy surface of the photo could preserve her for centuries, as safely as a glass case in a museum. A large drop of water, blown by the wind, fell off the edge of the awning, splash into the middle of the postcard. Here it spread out, suddenly, somewhere between the Venus's navel and her left breast.

Adam turned the card over; all it said on the back was:

'Photo Duc' 'A genuine photograph, all rights reserved.' '10, Rue des Polinaires, Toulouse.'

For Adam, who had been betting he would find 'Pretty girl on the beach', or else something vulgar, 'Come down and see me sometime'—that kind of thing—this was a disappointment.

Adam tramped the streets until nightfall. About eight o'clock he ate a piece of bread; he sat on a bench in the bus station. He watched people going past, sharing an umbrella or belted tight into raincoats.

On the other side of the square, behind two or three parked buses, there was a cinema. The front was lit up and a small queue had formed in the rain, waiting for the doors to open. The cinema was called the Rex; the name was written in red neon lighting, which blinked now and then. Under the name 'Rex' there was a big poster, showing some man in a raincoat kissing some woman in a raincoat on a kind of breakwater. They both had red faces and yellow hair, as though they had stayed too long on the beach. The background of the poster was a black blur, except for a big yellow globe just beside them, which looked like a street lamp. But the weird, sinister thing was that this man and woman had such crudely coloured faces, frozen into clumsy stiffness; their eyes were ugly, rolling skywards, their eye lashes were broken, and their gaping mouths looked like wounds bleeding side by side.

The film was called 'Pick-up on South Street', or something like that; Adam thought Samuel Fuller would have been glad to see the poster that had been designed for his film. For a moment he was tempted to go into the cinema. But he remembered he hadn't enough money left. He ate the rest of his bread, and lit a cigarette.

125

A little further along, under the arches, two or three girls were waiting for their bus. They were decked out in flowered dresses, shawls, flesh-coloured stockings, umbrellas, imitation leather handbags, and probably scent if one had gone close enough to smell it. Adam wondered whether it was Saturday. He tried to work it out, but in vain. In the end he decided it must be Saturday, Saturday the dance-hall night, etc. He thought of going to one of the places where he used to spend evenings in the old days, the Pergola, the Shooting Star or the Mammouth Club. To drink a glass of beer and have a girl for a few hours. What stopped him was that he had never enjoyed dancing. He not only danced badly, but everyone knew he danced badly. So, he said to himself, what would be the use? No one would learn anything new. Besides, he hadn't enough money left.

A bus arrived and carried off the girls; a few minutes later they were replaced by other girls, curiously similar in appearance. Near by, watching them and smoking, were two Algerian workmen. They said nothing, just smoked their cigars, and while they smoked they stared at the girls' legs.

There were three buses like this, one after another, and each one took away a little group of girls and workmen. It really must be Saturday. A short time before the fourth bus arrived, a ragged man came in under the arches, dragging a bundle of old cardboard boxes and discarded newspapers, which he must have found in a dustbin. He propped his burden against one of the pillars, right opposite Adam's bench, and sat down on it to wait for the bus. In this position he looked more like a tramp or a beggar than anything else. Adam noticed he wore spectacles.

Adam suddenly got up and walked over to the man, determined to speak to him. After some mutual hesitation they exchanged a few brief remarks, almost in whispers. The spectacled tramp did not look at Adam. His head was bent slightly sideways, slightly forward, and he was staring at the toes of his shoes. Now and then he scratched himself, on the leg, under the arms, or on the head. He did not seem surprised or nervous, only a bit contemptuous, and bored. With his left hand he was steadying the bundle of cardboard and newspapers on which he sat, to keep it from toppling over. He was dirty, unshaven, and he stank. He made no gestures, except that once he pointed vaguely in the direction where the buses came from. He said he didn't smoke, but asked Adam for money all the same; Adam wouldn't give him any.

When the bus arrived the man rose unhurriedly, picked up his bundle of newspapers and cardboard, and got in without so much as a glance at Adam. Following him with his eyes, Adam watched him through the window of the bus as he rummaged in the pockets of his overcoat, which was too big for him, and found the money for his ticket. His bony head was tilted forward, and with his left hand he steadied his glasses because of the jolts, which sent them sliding down his nose a millimetre at a time.

Adam hadn't the courage to wait for the fifth bus. Men were eternal and God was death. Men were eternal and God was death. Men were eternal and God was death. Men were eternal and God was death.

Going into the 'Magellan', you found the cloakrooms and the telephone on your left, at the far end. When you had finished with the cloakroom and opened the door marked 'Gentlemen', while the water gurgled and splashed out of the tank, you looked on a shelf below the telephone to find the directory. To make a call, you had to give the number to the barman. He wrote it on a scrap of paper— 84.10.10—dialled it on the telephone that stood on the counter, and then put the call through to the other telephone, under its sound-proof hood at the far end of the bar. As he did so he waved to you, saying:

'Your number!'

Whereupon you pressed a little red button in the base of the telephone, and heard a nasal voice replying:

'Hello? Hello?'

'Hello? Michèle?'

'This isn't Michèle, it's her sister. Who . . .'

'Oh, I see. Tell me, Germaine, isn't Michèle there?'

'No.'

'Is she out?'

'This isn't Michèle, it's her sister. Who . . .'

'Listen, you don't happen to know where she is?'

'But who's that speaking?'

'A friend of Michèle's, Adam.'

'Adam—oh, Adam Pollo?'

'Yes, that's right.'

'Yes—you've got something important to say to her?'

'Well, yes, rather . . . That's to say—I just wanted to know what, what's become of Michèle. I've not seen her for quite a time, and you understand . . .'

'Yes.'

'You don't know where she's likely to be now?'

'Michèle?'

'Yes, Michèle.'

'Listen, I don't know—she went out about two o'clock, taking the car. She didn't say anything special as she left.'

'And . . . about what time do you think she'll be back?'

'It all depends, you know. It all depends where she's gone.'

'But in the ordinary way?'

'Oh, in the ordinary way she's always home by—by eleven or thereabouts . . .

'Do you mean you don't know whether she's coming back this evening?'

128

'This evening?'

'Yes, all night.'

'Oh, I shouldn't think—I shouldn't think she'd be out all night. It does happen sometimes, of course; she has a girl friend with whom she sometimes spends the night. But I shouldn't think so, all the same. When she's not coming home she usually lets us know, either by ringing up or as she's going off. So as she said nothing to me, I imagine she'll be back before long.'

'I see. And—you think after eleven o'clock?'

'Oh, before that, I think. I don't know.'

'Yes.'

'Listen, the best thing—if you have a message for her, would be to leave it with me, and I'll tell her as soon as she gets home.'

'The thing is, I've no message. I wanted, I wanted just to ask how she was getting on.'

'I know. But if you want to arrange to meet her, or something. Or if you'd like her to ring you back when she gets in. Have you a telephone number or something?'

'No, I haven't got a telephone. I'm in a bar.'

'Then the best thing would be for you to ring back in an hour or two. Before midnight, of course.'

'Before midnight?'

'Yes, about eleven.'

'Yes—the trouble is, I can't. You see I have a train to catch an hour from now. I have to get the boat for Senegal. I'd have liked to say goodbye to her before leaving.'

'Ah—you have to catch a boat for Senegal?'

'Yes, I——'

'Oh, I see . . .'

'Listen: do you think Michèle may be with that girl friend now?'

'I don't know at all.'

129

'You don't know at all. And—you couldn't give me her friend's name? What is it?'

'Sonia. Sonia Amadouny.'

'Has she got a telephone?'

'Yes, she's got one. Would you like me to go and find you the number?'

'If you would, yes.'

'Half a minute, I'll go and see.'

Adam was sweating beneath the sound-proof hood. All sorts of strange noises were going on close to his ear: footsteps, incomprehensible phrases, and then a kind of far-off explanation, between the living-room and the stairs to the first floor: 'Who was that, Germaine?' 'A friend of Michèle's, Mummy, he's going off to Senegal and he wants to say goodbye to her.' 'To Senegal?' 'Yes, and he wants Sonia's telephone number—what is it, exactly, 88.07.54 or 88.07.44?' 'Whose number?' 'Sonia's—you know, Sonia Amadouny.' 'Oh, Sonia Amadouny—88.07.54.' '88.07.54 —you're sure that's it?' 'Yes . . . Are you going to give it to him?' 'Yes.'

'Hello?'

'Yes?'

'88.07.54.'

'88.07.54?'

'Yes, 88.07.54. That's right. Sonia Amadouny, 88.07.54.'

'Thank you very much.'

'Not at all.'

'Good, then I'll give her a ring. Anyway, if Michèle did happen—did happen to come in before eleven . . .'

'Yes?'

'No, never mind, it doesn't matter. I'll try to get hold of her like that, otherwise it doesn't matter. Just tell her I rang up.'

'Right.'

'Right, thank you. Excuse me, and thank you.'
'Goodbye.'
'Goodbye, Mademoiselle.'

Once you begin playing about with the telephone there must be no hesitation; you must never stop to think, not even for a few seconds. What can I say to Amadouny? Isn't it too late to ring her up? Michèle probably won't be there; and so forth. You must go right ahead, call the barman, shout '88.07.54', add 'Please, it's very urgent!' rush over to the other telephone, press the red button, and let yourself slip into that spectral language where the words seem to rise up towards invisible clouds, like a mystic's cries of pain. You must cast aside all misgivings, all fear of being laughed at, confer humanity upon the swarthy instrument that skids about in your damp clutch, presses its filter-shaped mouth to your ear and, while waiting to establish some nasal communication, murmurs its mechanical chant. You must wait, with your head almost invisible between the bakelite shells, warmed by their electricity, until the hissing stops, the sparks begin to click, and from the depths of an abyss there rises a treacherous voice whose falsehood will enfold you, lead you on to a point at which, whether you believe in it or not, you will be obliged to say —hearing your own voice as it passes along the wires and mingles with those distant hellos:

'Hello—Monsieur Amadouny? Could I speak to Sonia, please?'

If she's not there you must stick to it, explain you're leaving for Senegal in half an hour and absolutely must get hold of Michèle. You then learn that Michèle and Sonia have gone out together in Michèle's car. That you missed them by two minutes. That they may have gone into town to dance; but that in any case they've certainly not gone to

131

the cinema, because they talked about that at dinner and said there was nothing worth seeing. They went off together, apparently, not more than two or three minutes ago. They probably won't have gone to dance at the Pergola or the Hi-Fi or the Mammouth, because those are too crowded on Saturday evenings. That leaves the Staréo and the Whisky. Sonia wouldn't mind which, but if Michèle's a snob she'll no doubt have chosen the Staréo. Michèle is 67 per cent snob.

Sixty-seven chances out of a hundred that she'd have dragged Sonia Amadouny to that pretentious night-club, with its fake indirect lighting, its fake easy-chairs upholstered in fake red satin, and its fake gigolos dancing with the fake daughters of fake tycoons. Luckily no one was taken in by it.

There was nobody at the Staréo; the regulars avoided it on Saturday evenings, preferring to come on Mondays, when it was crowded. Adam made his way through the darkened room, looking for Michèle or for Sonia Amadouny; they were not there. He went up to the bar and asked loudly:

'Do you know Sonia Amadouny?'

The barman turned a bored face towards Adam. He had grey temples and a silk tie. He shook his head. Soft music was coming from a pick-up. Leaning on the bar beside Adam there were two smiling, fair-haired pansies.

Adam stared at them and at everything else; it was all really very quiet, very gentle, very nauseating. It was the first time for ages that one had breathed such pure air; one felt like staying here, in this species of oblivion, and waiting for anything or nothing; drinking a little whisky out of a big, cold glass, and standing next to these two handsome, effeminate boys; next to their soft-hued, short-lived suede jackets, next to their over-red lips, their over-white skin, their long, over-blond hair; with their bursts of laughter, their hands, their black, faintly dark-ringed eyes.

But before that, one must walk as far as the Whisky, about a hundred yards away; it was on the first floor, and was probably the most popular night-club in the town. Two adjoining rooms, one with a bar, the other surrounded by leather benches. Adam put his head in at the door. Here the air was tense, packed with noises; the lamps were blood-red, everyone was dancing and shouting. To a jazz record by Coleman, Chet Baker, Blakey. A woman standing behind the cash-desk bent forward and said something to him. Adam couldn't hear. She beckoned to him to come closer. Finally he caught a few words: he took a step towards her and shouted:

'What?'

'I said—come in!'

Adam stood motionless for ten seconds, without thought or speech; he felt he had burst in all directions, was spread out over at least ten square yards of noise and movement. The woman at the cash-desk yelled again:

'Come in—come in!'

Adam made a trumpet of his hands and shouted back:

'No. Do you know Sonia Amadouny?'

'Who?'

'Sonia Amadouny?'

'No.'

The woman added something, but Adam had already stepped back and didn't hear her; what with the darkness, the red lights, the convulsively jerking legs and hips, the two rooms were roaring like engines. It was like being suddenly flung into a steel shell, the cylinder of a motor-cycle, for instance, and imprisoned in four metal walls, with thickness, violence, explosions, petrol, and flames, smuts, coal, explosions, and the smell of gas, thick oil, as

133

viscous as melting butter, bits of black and red, flashes of light, explosions, a great heavy, powerful gust of air that tears you limb from limb, kneads you and crushes you against four cast-iron walls, splashings, metal filings, clicks, forward-reverse, forward-reverse, forward-reverse: *heat*.

Adam shouted again: 'No, I want . . .'

And then, louder: 'Sonia Amadouny!'

'. . . Sonia Amadouny!'

The woman said something in reply and then, as Adam still couldn't hear, shrugged her shoulders and grimaced 'No!'

The rain had almost stopped; just a few drops from time to time. The town was drenched. Adam walked the streets all night. From 9.30 in the evening till 5 in the morning. It was as though there had been a huge sun burning everything along its path, reducing it all to heaps of ashes.

While he walked, Adam was thinking:

(I took the wrong line. I was too off-hand about things. I went wrong. Idiot. What I wanted to do was to trail that girl Michèle. Like I did the dog. I wanted to play a game, like one, two, three, four five, six, seven, eight, nine, ten, eleven, twelve—are you ready?—thirteen, fourteen, fifteen, sixteen, seventeen, eighteen—are you ready?—nineteen, twenty, twenty-one, twenty-two, twenty-three, twenty-four —I'll count up to thirty—twenty-five, twenty-six, twenty-seven, twenty-eight, twenty-nine, twenty-nine-and-a-half, twenty-nine-and-three-quarters—and, and—thirty! and then hunt everywhere in the town. In the angles of walls, in doorways, in night-clubs, on beaches, in bars, in cinemas, in churches, in the parks. I wanted to look for you until at last I'd find you, dancing the tango with a medical student, or sitting in a deck-chair by the sea. You'd have left clues, of course, to help me find you; that would have been in the rules of the game. A name or two, Amadouny Sonia-Nadine, Germaine, a handkerchief on the ground with a streak of pinky orange lipstick on it, a hairpin in a deserted avenue. A conversation between two boys in a self-service restaurant. Some sly hint left under the blue plastic table-cloth at an all-night cake-shop. Or two initials—M.D.—stamped with the tip of a fingernail on a horsehair bench in a No. 9 trolleybus. And gradually I'd have begun to tell myself *'I'm getting warm!'*

And then, at twenty-five past six in the morning, when I was absolutely whacked, I'd have found you at last, belted into your man's raincoat, your lips firm, your hair wet with dew, your wool dress a bit creased; your eyes tired from staying open all night. Alone, nobody with you, cuddled up in a deck-chair on the promenade, looking towards the grey sunrise.

But nobody waits for anybody; there are more important things in the world, of course. The world is over-populated and starving, with tensions on all sides. One ought to search that real world, investigate its minutest details; the lives of individual men and women don't matter.

Much more serious was the universe as a whole. Two thousand million men and women getting together to build things, cities, to prepare bombs, to conquer space.

The newspapers announce: 'The space-ship Liberty II has made seven circuits of the earth.'

'The 100 megaton H Bomb has burst in Nevada.'

And really it was as though a big sun had been shining everywhere, all the time. A pear-shaped sun that could be measured by the Beaufort scale, a sun with down-geared dawns. They were weaving an impenetrable net all round the planet. They were ruling it systematically into squares by extending lines xx', yy', zz'. And inspecting every square.

Society was arranging itself in groups of specialists:

That's to say the army, the Civil Service, the doctors, the butchers, the grocers, the metal-workers, the electronic engineers, the Merchant Navy captains, the Post Office clerks.

People were putting up buildings twenty-two storeys high and then planting television aerials on the roofs. Underground they were putting drainpipes, electrical cables, metropolitan railways. They were making the earlier chaos bristle with posts and dykes. They were digging, sinking, burning or blasting. Dynamos were starting up with a soft purring sound and throwing their magnetic fields to every corner of the sky. Aircraft were taking off, with a noise like tearing paper. So were rockets, in saffron-yellow clouds, making straight for the unknown spot in the middle of outer space. And then dissolving into black plumes.

Everything was returning to a new dawn, to a daybreak consisting of millions of united determinations. Above all there was this host of men and women, thirsting for violence and conquest. They were assembled at the world's strategic points; they were drawing maps, naming countries, writing novels or compiling atlases: the names of the places they populated were lined up in columns:

Ecclefechan	Scotland	55.3. N.	3.14.W.
Eccles	England	53.28.N.	2.21.W.
Eccleshall	England	53.28.N.	2.21.W.
Echmiadzin	Armenia	40.20.N.	44.35.E.
Echternach	Luxembourg	49.48.N.	6.25.E.
Echuca	Victoria	36.7. S.	144.48.E.
Ecija	Spain	37.32.N.	5.9. W.
Ecuador, Rep.	South America	2.0. S.	78.0. W.
Edam	Netherlands	52.31.N.	5.3. E.
Eddrachillis	Scotland	59.12.N.	2.47.W.

and their own names filled the books that lay on the shelves in cafés:

Revd. William Pountney
Francis Parker
Robert Patrick
Robert Patton
John Payne
Revd. Percival
Robert de Charleville
Nathaniel Rayner
Abel Ram, Esq.

It was among them that he should have hunted. Then he'd have found everything, including Michèle seated at dawn in a deck-chair, cold and wet with dew, shivering amid these interwoven forces. They were all living the same life; their eternity was slowly fusing with the raw materials of which they were the masters. Fusion, the fusion brought about in blast furnaces, the fusion that boils amid smelting metal as though in a crater, was the weapon that raised them above themselves. In this town, as elsewhere, men and women were cooking in their infernal stew-pans. Protuberant against the hazy background of the earth, they were awaiting something, some supreme event, which would wrap them in eternity. They lived among their machines; naked, stubborn, invincible, they were making their earth resplendent. Their almost completed world would soon wrest them for ever away from all things temporal. It was as though an iron mask were already being laid over their faces; in another century or two they would be statues, sarcophagi: within their bronze and concrete moulds there would live on, concealed, frail but immortal, a kind of particle of electric fire. Then will come the reign of timeless matter; all will be within all. And it seems likely there will be only one man, only one woman, left in the world.

Adam was everywhere at once in the town streets. Outside a park drowned in the darkness, outside a dogs' cemetery, under a hewn-stone porch; sometimes along the tree-lined avenue, or seated on the cathedral steps.

Alone on this plain of stone and metal he kept an eye on everything; he was seen to smoke a cigarette beside the Fontaine Fusse and another under the railway bridge. He was quite incidentally under the arches of the Grand-Place, in the middle of the garden in the Square, or leaning on the railings of the promenade. Or on the beach, confronting a motionless sea. Being ubiquitous, he sometimes passed himself in the street, coming round the corner of a house. At this time, a quarter to four in the morning, there may have been 4,000 or 5,000 adams, the genuine article, going about the town. Some were on foot, others on bicycles or in cars; they were quartering the whole town, filling up even the smallest recesses in the concrete. An adam-woman, in a tight-fitting mauve dress, ran after the adam-man, her stiletto heels tapping loudly, and said:

'Coming with me, baby?'
and the adam-man followed her, as though reluctantly.

Further east in the town, other adam-men were going off to work, whistling. An aged adam-man lay asleep, curled up on a vegetable-barrow. Quite possibly another one of him was dying, with faint cries, in his old yellow, sweat-soaked bed. Or yet another was hanging himself with his belt, because he had no money left, or no woman.

In the Square, in the middle of the lawn, Adam halted at last; he leant back against the pedestal of a statue of himself; then, at about five o'clock, he stopped again, outside a laundry window. Drunk with fatigue and joy, he felt a kind of tears running down his cheeks; he suddenly began to weep, without looking at the hundreds and thousands of windows that were opening behind him. The adams ran past along the echoing pavement; with an effort, as though praying, he repeated two lines of a poem to himself. Exactly fifteen hours ahead of time, a strip of neon lighting reddened at the back of the window, performing a passage from a sunset.

With an effort, as though praying, no longer conscious of darkness or daylight, Adam repeated two lines from a poem:

"'Tis ye, 'tis your estrangèd faces,
That miss the many-splendoured thing.'

N. Sunshine, a man and woman lying on a double bed in a room with half-closed shutters, a terracotta ashtray between them on the sheet, which is grey in some places and scorched in others. The room is square, beige, squat, really set in the middle of the block of flats. All the rest of the town consists of concrete, hard corners, windows, doors and hinges.

On the night-table beside them a wireless set is turned on, pouring out a flood of words only interrupted every eight minutes by an islet of music.

'So we can safely say that the coming year will be, will prove more favourable to the tourist industry and we cannot fail to be gratified by this in view of the considerable importance the emphasis that has always been placed on the tourist industry and particularly on the influx of foreign tourists from which our beautiful country draws its chief source of income (. . .) for this purpose we have already made considerable improvements in our hotel system all along the coast, developing those hotels which were inadequate, improving those which offered no more than a modicum of comfort and thus establishing with more modern hotels the whole tourist organization which is becoming more and more necessary owing to competition from abroad and particularly from the Southern countries such as Italy, Spain and Yugoslavia (. . .) well Monsieur

Duter we are most grateful for the information you have so kindly given us and we shall soon be on the air again for another interview dealing with local tourist resources (. . .) it is exactly nine minutes thirty seconds past two o'clock, Radio-Montecarlo has chosen Lip to give you the correct time (. . .) Two o'clock in the afternoon is the time to relax, but not to relax just anyhow the only relaxation that does you good relax with a cup of coffee (. . .) appreciate the flavour of good coffee, hot or iced as you prefer and relax relax rela . . .'

There is no alarm-clock or clock of any kind on the night-table. The man is still wearing his wrist-watch, which makes a little leather coat right round his skin: apart from this he is naked. The woman is naked too; she has a wedding-ring on the fourth finger of her right hand. Between the first and middle fingers of that hand she is squeezing a cigarette; its crushed, sweat-damped paper shows the outlines of the strands of tobacco. And she is smoking.

Their clothes are rolled up carelessly on a chair, pushed right into the angle between the back and the seat. On the front of the wireless set there is a photo, slipped into the frame round the list of wavelengths; it shows the same man and woman, clothed this time, in a street in Rome; he is smiling, she is not. On the back of the photo they have written their names:

Mme and M. Louise and Jean Mallempart

They wrote their names like that two years ago, for a joke, because they were getting married next month; so they supposed. But that must be old stuff by now. Two hot summers, during which the heat from the valves of the wireless may have twisted the photograph right out of shape. There is nothing terribly tragic, or absurd, in the bedroom where, at this hour, at the third pip exactly ten minutes past two, with sun, closed shutters, sweat, cinema-organ music, nothing definite is moving, except the woman's hand as she smokes, and the round eye of the man, Jean Mallempart, shining below his forehead.

In the grocer's shop on the ground floor of this newish modern block of flats, in the grocer's shop called 'Alimentation Rogalle', the calendar says it is late August, getting near the end of August, something like the 26th or the 24th. This is marked on the square of white paper of the calendar which is sold as 'comic' because it has a joke every day, today's joke is 'What goes "ninety-nine *bump*"? A centipede with a wooden leg.' Above this is a square of cardboard with a picture of a blonde in a spotted dress. She is holding up a glass, and we are told, in red capital letters, that what she is drinking is 'B Y R R H' 'Apéritif'. The place is hot, almost boiling, with that sickly smell of geraniums and that sound of tyres gliding along the streets. We're in summer, and nearing the end of August. On the beaches the deck-chairs creak under the weight of broad, sunburnt, oily backs; dark glasses groan when folded up. In one or two dining-rooms, simultaneously, a red ant is eating straight off the greenish leaf of plastic that imitates a yellow rose or a pink carnation.

Men and women are entering the water; they bathe placidly, waiting a moment with their arms in the air for the slight ripple set up by a motorboat some way from the shore to reach them and wet another few inches of their stomachs; then they throw themselves forward, heads up, out of their depth, and advance through the water which gradually strips them of their names, making them absurd, breathless, jerky.

The water is quite round, and painted a gaudy blue; a mere eighteen inches from the shore a little boy in a bathing-suit is sitting in the sea, counting on his fingers the refuse washed up by the tide. He finds:

one banana-skin
one half-orange
one leek
one piece of wood
one strip of seaweed
one lizard, headless
one empty Artane tube, all twisted
two brown masses, of unknown origin
one piece of what looks like horse-dung
one scrap of cloth (Bedford cord)
one cigarette end (Philip Morris)

On the promenade, still in the sun, where it crosses the Boulevard de la Gare, an old lady is dying of sunstroke. She dies very easily, so easily she almost does it several times. Falling flat on her face on the pavement, without a word, she knocks her hand against the front mudguard of a parked car, and her old, dried-up hand begins to bleed imperceptibly, while she dies. While people go past, while they look for the police, the priest or the doctor, and a woman looking on stiffens and murmurs below her breath

'Hail Mary
Full of Grace
The Lord is with Thee
etc.'

An Italian, sitting on a bench, takes a packet of Italian cigarettes out of his pocket. The packet is three-quarters empty, so that the word 'Esportazione' loses its luxurious implications and meanders over the paper like a drooping pennon. He takes out a cigarette, and the expected happens: he begins to smoke. He looks at the breasts of a girl who walks by. One of those tight-fitting sailor-type jerseys they sell at the Prisunic. Two breasts.

143

What with all these buildings, these huge grey rectangles, concrete upon concrete, and all these angular places, one soon gets from one point to another. One's home is everywhere, one lives everywhere. The sun is exerting itself on the rough-cast walls. What with this series of old and new towns, one is landed full in the hurly-burly of life; it's like living in thousands of books piled one on top of another. Every word is an event, every sentence a series of events of the same kind, every short story an hour, or more, or less, a minute, ten or twelve seconds.

With flies buzzing round his head and that child yelling down in the yard like a scalded cat, Mathias is trying to write his detective story. He is writing it by hand, on exercise-book paper.

'Joséphime stopped the car:
"You want to get out here?"
"Okay, sonny," said Doug.
The moment he was out of the car he regretted it.
"You shouldn't have played the bloody fool."
The beautiful Joséphime had pulled out a little revolver inlaid with silver, a jewel of Belgian craftsmanship, and was now pointing it straight at Doug's stomach.
"It's really too bad," Doug reflected, "Now the women are beginning to want to put slugs into me too. Where's my well-known sex appeal?"
"So what's going to happen now?" sneered Doug. "You know, my life's insured."
"For your widow's sake I hope it's for a fat sum," said Joséphime.
And she pressed the trigger.'
and Douglas Dog died, or didn't die.
But there are still quite a lot of green, blue-sulphated vines to be seen from many windows. The children pick up

snails along the narrow paths, in the sunshine: the snails
have curled up in their shells, blindly trusting their lives
to the thin layers of rubbery secretion that hold them to the
branches of the oleanders. The café terraces are packed.
At the Café Lyonnais, people are sitting under the red
awnings, talking:

On the beach perhaps?

Waiter, a beer. A beer.

A beer.

Tickets for the National Lottery! Who'll have the prize?

Not me, thank you.

Waiter, a glass of vin rosé.

A vin rosé, yes Sir.

There you are, Sir.

How much?

One franc twenty, Sir.

Including service?

Yes, Sir.

Thank you.

Jean, where shall we sit?

I saw Monsieur Maurin yesterday, and d'you know what
he said to me?

Oh yes, he's a funny fellow.

Never. It's impossible, absolutely impossible.

After that I shall go, at any rate; I've got my shopping
to do you know, quite a lot of things to get butter meat
ribbon for the dressing-gown . . .

Shall we go? Waiter?

But what the hell does it matter, I ask you, what the hell
does it matter, so then he said to me all the same . . . But
what the hell does it matter to him, eh, what the?

It's a stylish café, where dark red predominates, on the
tables as well as on the walls; the tables, all round ones, are

arranged geometrically on the pavement, so precisely that on a sunny day when the awning is up, anyone looking out of a second-storey window might think they were seeing the pieces of a one-coloured set of draughts arranged for a game. The glasses on the tables are plain ones, and sometimes show on their edges a semicircle of whipped cream and lipstick, mixed together.

The waiters have white uniforms; with each order they put on the table, at the same time as the glasses, saucers whose colour varies according to the price of what was ordered; the men and women sit eating, drinking and talking quietly; and the waiters move silently, gliding past with empty or laden trays in their hands and napkins under their left arms, undulating along like skin-divers. Most of the noise comes from the street; it is manifold, though in its diversity it combines into a rich sound, more or less monophonic, such as is made by the sea, for instance, or the steady swish of rain; one audible note with millions of variants, tones, modes of expression accompanying it— women's heels, horns tooting, the engines of cars, scooters and buses. A tuning 'A' played simultaneously by all the instruments in an orchestra.

The movement of matter is all of one kind—the grey mass of cars, nose-to-tail in the background. There are no clouds in the sky, and the trees stand perfectly motionless, like dummies.

Whereas animal movement is at its height: strollers and pedestrians are walking along the pavement; arms are swinging and waving; legs are tensed to take the weight of a body, about twelve or thirteen stone; they bend slightly for a second and then become levers on which the rest of the body describes a tiny parabola. Mouths breathe, eyes turn rapidly in their moist orbits. Colours take on movement and their purely pictorial quality is attenuated; the white

146

man becomes more animal in movement. The black man, more Negro.

It is all this that gives him his gentleness, his slightly sinuous, slightly sour disdain, as though he had invented the moon or written the Bible.

He walks along the streets and sees nothing. He goes through whole squares, down entire boulevards—deserted, bordered with plane-trees or chestnuts—he goes past real police-stations, town-halls, cinemas, cafés, hotels, beaches and bus-stops. He waits for friends, for girls, or for nobody; often they don't come and he gets tired of waiting. He doesn't try to find reasons, that kind of thing doesn't interest him, and perhaps after all it's none of his business. So then he walks on again all alone, the sun scatters itself through the leaves, it's cool in the shade, hot in the sunshine. He wastes time, gets excited, walks, breathes, waits for darkness. We can bet he has seen *Libby* on the beach and talked to her, sprawling on the dusty shingle. She talked to him about clothes, boys' and girls' interests, classical music, etc. The bad film she saw.—It's in attending to such matters that one forgets the others; it does you good in the end, and you feel you're gradually recovering your invulnerability, a hero again, projecting all your concentrated brains on a heap of dirty shingle and the noise of retreating waves. Afterwards, an hour later, you go back to the street, quite proud of yourself and reeling like a punch-drunk boxer. Tragedy is a thing of the past? Who cares—we've still got petty details, general ideas, ice-cream cornets, pizza at five o'clock, Film Clubs and Organic Chemistry:

SUBSTITUTIONAL REACTIONS

H atoms may be successively replaced by certain atoms of identical value, such as Cl. Must be exposed to light.

(and bromide) (Br)

$$CH_4 + Cl_1 = CH_3Cl + ClH$$
$$CH_3Cl + Cl_2 = CHaCL_2 + ClH$$
$$CH_2Cl_2 + Cl_2 = CHCl_3 + Cl_4$$
$$CHCl_3 + Cl_2 = CCl_4 + Cl_4$$

(Carbon tetrachloride)

To begin with we've got no psychological reflexes any longer, we've lost them. A girl is a girl, a chap going down the street is a chap going down the street; he's sometimes a copper, a pal or a father, but he's first and foremost a chap going down the street. Ask, and what answer will you get? 'It's a chap going down the street.' Not that we're scatter-brained—not at all; in fact we're more like bureaucrats: under some kind of pressure: off-peak bureaucrats.

Like that woman, Andrea de Commynes. The only one with a face that was rather sallow, rather pale, among all the brown, shining ones; the only one who conceals green eyes behind dark glasses and who is reading, one hand hooked into the curve of her bronze necklace, the other holding her leather-bound book. The pages are worm-eaten and the title runs across the spine of the book, stamped in crooked letters from which the colour has faded:

INGOLDSBY LEGENDS

Not forgetting that plane that's silently crossing the naked sky; not forgetting that statue on which the sun shines in torrents from six a.m. onwards, and which also represents a naked man, in the centre of a basin. And the pigeons, and the smell of earth underneath the paving-stones, and the three old women sitting on the bench, nodding over their everlasting knitting.

Or the beggar—known as the Whistler. The kind of fellow you don't often come across. They call him that because when he isn't begging he walks along all the streets whistling an old tango tune :'Arabella'. Then he stops, settles down in some corner of an old wall, preferably all yellow from dogs and children peeing there; he pushes up his trouser-leg on the side that has the stump, and he calls to the tourists as they go by. When one of them stops, he explains:

'I live as best I can. I manage.

I sell waste paper. I suppose you wouldn't have anything for me?

A small coin for an old cripple?'

The other man says:

'Afraid not, I'm completely broke today,' and adds:

'Do you like—er—that kind of life?'

He replies:

'Well, I've no complaints,' and adds: 'So you really mean it? Not even one little cigarette for me? Sir? For a poor cripple?'

His stump develops scabs in the open air. It often looks like that sort of vegetable that's sold in the market in summer. Thousands of cars are making their way in Indian file to the 'Grand Prix Automobile'. One or two drivers may be killed, perhaps. They'll scatter sawdust on the ground and wait for Monday's paper. There it'll be: 'Tragedy Mars Big Car Race', handled no worse than anywhere else.

Hornatozi is having his wife followed. Hornatozi, the Son in Hornatozi & Son, Corn Merchants. He goes to work in his light-panelled office, and now and then he takes his wife's photograph out of his pocket. Hélène is tall, young and auburn-haired. Like Joséphime and Mme Richers, she often wears a black dress. Hornatozi knows that the day before yesterday, between 3 and 3.30 in the afternoon, she went to No. 99 Avenue des Fleurs. On the negative, which is smeared with finger-prints, Hélène Hornatozi is smiling into space, her head tilted a little to the left. She bears this drifting smile, and from her curved lips there flutters out the mysterious holy spirit that establishes relationships among men; it is as though she lay there dead, laid out on the marble surface of the film, offering beneath her glazed effigy the last vestiges of her woman's body, a parcel of white bones on a black background, a mask from which the flesh has been scooped out and where the colours are reversed; hovering between the air and this translucent screen, Hélène's memory contracts in her negative rigor mortis and her eyes, white pupils on black sclerotic, bore two holes through the rampart that surrounds the living, causing them to believe once and for all in ghosts. It is from this memory fixed by the developing fluid that the woman derives all her power; an insubstantial trace of maleficence draws all eyes to her voluptuous body, formed for love; in Hornatozi's fingers the white figure outlined in black burns with a thousand jealous fires. His thumbs, pressing on the edge, are sweating slightly and will yet again leave the greasy ridges of their prints behind them. He bends forward now, his hypnotized gaze plunging straight into the big hollow orbits where night seems to be falling; for he longs to make the journey, if only as a slave, and come at the end of his sufferings to the delicious intimacy of earlier days, the warmth of being hidden in being, the innocence, the assuaged yearnings, an almost alcoholic inhumation. But she, the woman of whom he is no longer sure whether she is dead or whether she has been unfaithful, shuts him out from her strange domain merely by indicating its celluloid walls; and it is vain for him to bend over the shiny card, vain for his breath to quicken, his mouth throwing rings of steam onto her picture, vain for his temples to swell and his shoulders to sag. Already, he perceives, the wickedness has faded to an abstraction, the powers of evil have destroyed themselves; nothing sharp remains in the photograph except a glint of light reflected from the window onto the rippled surface of the paper, running from side to side, captive, irrational and therefore human, like a bubble on a plate of broth.

Down below lies the long, flat, dusty expanse of the quays, still in the full glare of the sun; boats and derricks; the Customs House; the docks, with eleven dockers working there. Every three minutes the pulley lowers a bale of cotton or a cord of wood. In the globe of stale smells, the rattle of chains, the whiteness, the quivering air, the loads collapse onto the dock.

In a dark hotel room a Negro student is reading a Série Noire detective story. Old women are searching the depths of attic rooms through field-glasses.

Louise Mallempart, a pale dimness amid the silky folds of the sheets, is thinking of a table covered with a damask cloth and bearing enthroned in its centre one large glass of cold water.

All this comes of the heat that is branching out, crawling low down, just above the ground. A tiny, trembling breath of air makes wrinkles round the objects it meets. Earth, water and air consist of masses of black and white particles, mingling in a blur like a million ants. There is nothing really incoherent any more, nothing wild. One would think the world had been drawn by a child of twelve.

Little Adam will soon be twelve; one evening at the farm, one wet evening, while he can hear the cows being brought in along the lanes, while he listens to the Angelus and feels the earth withering, he picks up a big piece of blue cardboard and draws the world.

At the top of the blue cardboard, on the left, he draws a red and yellow ball with his coloured pencils; it's like the sun, except that there are no rays coming out of it. To balance it he draws another ball on the other side, high up on the right—a blue one, with rays. That must be the sun, since there are rays coming out of it. Then he draws a straight line right across the cardboard below the sun-moon and the moon-sun. With his green pencil he makes a lot of little vertical strokes going down into the horizon. These represent corn and grass. Some of them are barbed—those are fir-trees. Black in the white chalk sky, a horse with spider's legs is about to trample on a man put together from cylindrical tins and hairs. And wherever there is space left on the cardboard he draws big stars, brown or mauve stars ringed with yellow. In the middle of each star is a kind of black dot that transforms it into a live animal, watching us with its bacteria-nucleus, its strange, solitary maggot's eye.

A weird universe he is drawing, all the same, the little boy Adam. An arid, almost mathematical universe, where everything is easily understood in terms of a cryptographic code whose key is immanent; in the brown line round the cardboard a large population can be established without fatigue—shopkeepers, mothers, little girls, devils and horses. They are set there, line for line, in an indissoluble, independent, subdivided matter. Almost as though there were a kind of god in a box, giving orders for everything, with eye and finger, and saying to each thing, 'be.' It's also as though everything were contained in everything, to all infinity. That is to say, in this clumsy drawing by the little boy Adam as well as in the calendar from the wholesale grocer's or a square yard of checked cloth.

To give another example of a type of madness with which Adam had grown familiar, one might mention the well-known Simultaneity. Simultaneity is one of the necessary elements of that Unity of which Adam had one day had an inkling, either during the business at the Zoo, or because of the Drowned Man, or in connection with many other incidents we are deliberately omitting. Simultaneity is the total annihilation of time and not of movement; an annihilation to be conceived not necessarily as mystical experience, but by a constant exercise of the will to the absolute in abstract reasoning. The idea is, that when engaged in any particular action, smoking a cigarette for instance, one shall be indefinably aware, all along, of the millions of other cigarettes which are presumably being smoked by millions of other people all over the world. That one shall have the sensation of millions of flimsy paper cylinders, part one's lips and let a few grammes of air mingled with tobacco smoke filter through them; and then the gesture of smoking becomes single and unique. It is transformed into a Stereotype; the habitual mechanism of cosmogony and myth-making can come into play. In a way this procedure is the reverse of the ordinary philosophical method, which begins with an action or sensation and leads up to a concept that contributes to knowledge.

This process, which holds good for myths in general, such as birth, war, love, the seasons, death, can be applied to anything: any object whatsoever, a match-stick on a polished mahogany table, a strawberry, the striking of a clock, the shape of the letter Z, can be recaptured without limit in space and time. And by thus existing millions and milliards of times, as well as their *own* time, they become eternal. But their eternity is automatic: they need never have been deliberately created, and are to be met with in every century and every place. All the components of the telephone are present in the rhinoceros. Emery paper and magic lanterns have always existed; and moon is really sun and sun moon, the earth is Mars, Jupiter, a whisky and soda and that queer instrument that will soon be invented to create objects or destroy them, its structure being known by heart already.

To understand this properly one would have to follow Adam and try the path of certitudes, which is that of materialistic ecstasy. Then time shrinks and shrinks; its echoes become briefer and briefer; like a pendulum allowed to run down, what used to be years soon become months, the months dwindle to hours, to seconds, to quarter-seconds, to thousandths of seconds; and then all at once, abruptly, to nothing. One has reached the only fixed point in the universe and become virtually eternal. In other words, a god, since one needs neither to exist nor to have been created. It is not a question of psychological immobilization nor, strictly speaking, of mysticism or asceticism. For it is not prompted by the search for a means of communication with God, or by the desire for eternity. It would be only one more weakness in Adam were he to attempt to overcome matter, his own matter, by employing the same impulsions as matter itself.

It is not purely and simply a question of desire; just as, a while back, it was not purely and simply a question of the cigarettes people may be smoking *all over the world*. No, what drives Adam is reflection, lucid meditation. Starting from his own human flesh, from the sum of his present sensations, he annihilates himself by a dual system of multiplication and identification. Thanks to these two methods he can reason in the future as well as in the present and the past. Provided one takes these words at their proper value, that is to say as words. Whether close at hand or far off. He gradually obliterates himself by self-creation. He practises a kind of sympoetry and ends not in Beauty, Ugliness, Ideal, Happiness, but in oblivion and absence. Soon he no longer exists. He is himself no longer.

He is lost, a weak particle that still moves, still describes itself. He is no more than a vague ghost, solitary, eternal, measureless, the terror of lonely old women, who creates himself, dies, lives and lives again and sinks into darkness, hundreds, millions and milliards of an infinite time, neither one nor the other.

O. This is how, later on, Adam described what happened next; he told the story carefully, writing with a ball-point pen in a yellow exercise-book which he had headed 'My dear Michèle', as though beginning a letter. The whole thing was found later, half-burnt. Some pages were missing altogether, either because they'd been torn out to wrap something up in—basketball shoes, household refuse—or even as a substitute for toilet paper, or because they had been too badly burnt. So they will not be given here, and their absence will be indicated by blanks of about the same length.

'A few days before the owners would normally be coming back and throwing me out of the house, I got into trouble in the town. I'd gone down there as usual, about two or three o'clock in the afternoon, to try to see Michèle, or the dog, or somebody else, but more especially to buy cigarettes, beer and something to eat. I particularly wanted to see Michèle, because I needed to borrow another 1,000 or 5,000 francs from her; I had made a short list on the back of an empty cigarette-packet,

fags
beer

chocolate
stuff to eat
paper
newspapers if
possible take
a look round

and made up my mind to follow it in that order.

The cigarettes I found at a tobacconist's on the way into the town. A little bar, quiet and fairly cool, called "Chez Gontrand". There were picture postcards on the walls. The counter at the tobacconist's end was a wooden one, painted brown. The woman behind it was between sixty and sixty-five years old. She wore a striped dress. An Alsation dog lay asleep at the far end of the bar; the rolls of fur round his neck hid the aluminium plate rivetted to his collar and the name—Dick—that was engraved on it.

I bought the beer at a self service grocery which was spacious, clean and airy. As I went in they gave me a red plastic basket with perforated sides, to hold whatever I bought. Into it I dropped just one bottle of light ale, making a noise of glass hitting plastic. I paid and went out.

The chocolate, in the same shop. But I stole that. I pushed the tablet inside my shirt, one end wedged behind the belt of my trousers. It made a bulge, so as I went past the pay-desk I had to pull my stomach in hard, to hide the lump. I could scarcely breathe. The girl at the desk didn't notice, nor did the big lout who's supposed to watch what goes on along the shelves. It seems to me they don't give a damn, in that joint.

This left the stuff to eat, the newspapers and the paper.

The stuff to eat:

I bought a tin of stew at the Prisunic.

The newspapers:

I found these in my usual way, you know, by hunting in the refuse-bins that are hung on the lamp-posts. I found a magazine in good condition, the local dental magazine. Good-quality paper with lots of blank spaces; I said to myself this makes a change, I shall have fun mixing it all up, sockets and dentures, molars and killing the nerve by method B.

The paper:

At the Prilux, a school exercise-book. (This one is almost finished already; when I've filled three more like it I can begin to think about finding a publisher. I've already got a striking title—The Complete Bastards.)

The most important thing was: if possible take a look round.

~~That is to say, while I was walking round the town, keep a look out for things that might be useful later on, perhaps try to find an empty house, even a tumble down one, where I could live when the one up on the hill becomes impossible, and try to see the dog, lots of animals, play games of my own, have a bath at the Public Baths, and borrow 5,000 francs from Michèle. In the first place don't forget that I~~ If I could find some kind of work, something that didn't need much attention, some physical job, washer-up in a restaurant, layer-out at the Mortuary or crowd work at the film studios, I'd be satisfied with that. I should earn just enough to buy a packet of cigarettes when I want, once a day, for ex., & paper to write on, and a bottle of beer too, once a day. Anything more is luxury. I wish I could go to the ~~USA, they say one can live like that over there, and have sun in the South, and nothing to do except write, drink and sleep. Another idea would be to take holy orders, why not?~~ I once knew a fellow who was a potter. He married a woman called Blanche and he lives in a house up in the hills. I went to see him one day, at three in the afternoon; it was very hot, and there were beans climbing over a pergola. The sun was hardening everything into scabs. He was working under the pergola, half naked. He was scratching Aztec patterns on some kind of earthenware pots; and the sun was drying the clay, making little specks of powder all round the vase; afterwards he laid on the colours and they were fired in the oven, heat on heat. It was all in harmony. There was a salamander with a forked tail asleep on the sun-baked ground. I don't think I had ever in my life seen so much heat upon heat. The outside temperature was 39° Centigrade and the oven temperature was 500°. That evening his wife Blanche cooked the beans. He was a good chap; he was always nearly dead by the end of the day. Quite white, a patch of dancing air, an equilateral cube gradually baking.

I said to myself that I too might have a house in the country. On the side of a kind of flinty mountain; under the scorching stones there'd be snakes, scorpions and red ants.

This is how I should spend my day: I'd have a patch of ground, all covered with stones, exposed to the sun from morning till night. In the middle of it I would make bonfires. I'd burn planks, glass, cast-iron, rubber, anything I could find. I'd produce kinds of statues, like that, straight out of the fire. Black objects, scorched in the wind and dust. I should throw on tree-trunks and burn them; I should twist everything, blacken everything, coat everything with a crackling powder, send the flames soaring, thicken the smoke into heavy coils. The orange-coloured tongues would make the earth bristle, shake the sky right up to the clouds. The livid sun would fight against them for hours on end. Insects would come by thousands to fling themselves on my bonfire and burrow head-first into the colourless layer at the foot of the blaze. Then, blown upwards by the heat, they would climb the flames like an invisible column and fall back in a soft shower of ashes, delicate and fragile, transformed into charred specks on my head and my bare shoulders; and the blast of the flames would blow on them and make them shudder against my skin; it would give them new legs and new wing-sheaths, a new life that would carry them into the air and deposit them in swarms, soft as crumbs of smoke, in the holes between the stones, right down to the foot of the mountain.

About five o'clock in the afternoon—let's say—the sun would win. The sun would burn up the flames, leaving only a round black patch in the middle of the bonfire area, with all the rest as white as snow. The black patch would look like the sun's shadow, or a bottomless hole in the ground. And nothing would remain except charred tree-trunks, lumps of metal looking as though struck by lightning and melted, twisted glass, drops of steel like water among the ashes. Everything would have grown like dark plants, with grotesque stems, driblets of cellulose, crevices full of glowing coals. Then I'd collect all these convulsed shapes together and pile them up in a room in the house. I should enjoy living between a mountain of white stones and a burnt-up jungle. It's all connected with heat. It would decompose everything so as to reconstitute a world blighted by drought; heat, pure and simple. Thanks to that everything would be white and hard and set. Like a block of ice at the North Pole it would represent material harmony, so that time would cease to flow on. Yes, it would be really beautiful. By day it would be heat plus heat, and by night, blackness plus coal.

[

]

And one day I'd take an old car, run it into the middle of the bonfire site, and pour petrol over it. Then I'd pour petrol over myself, get into the car and set fire to it.

And I should keep on my dark glasses, so that when they found my charred body, my round skull, there would be a funny, black caricature of an insect there, its plastic body would have sunk boiling into the sockets of my eyes. Two wire rods, like spindly legs, would be sticking up on either side, making antennae for me.

I hope no one would recognize any trace of me in that blistered mummy. Because I would very much like to live all naked and all black, once and for all burning, once and for all created.

Michèle.

I made a very thorough search for you.

First of all there was that fellow Gérard, or François, I forget his name. I knew him in the days when I used to play pinball. Or when I was a student of some kind. He didn't recognize me, because since then I've grown a beard and I wear dark glasses. He told me he'd seen you going down towards the Vieux Port.

I went down there and sat on a bench in the shade. I waited a bit, with the idea of having a rest. I was just opposite the jetty and there were two Englishmen there, dressed up like yachtsmen, talking. They were pretending to be deathly bored with the Mediterranean, and one of them said:

"I am looking forward to the Shetlands."

Quite a lot of people were going past, pointing out the white boats to their children.

An hour later I went up again to the Grand-Place, the one with the fountain. In the Café I ran into a girl you must know, called Martine Préaux. I told her that Gérard, or François—anyhow, that dark chap in the pink shirt—had seen you going down towards the Vieux Port. She said something like this:

"He's crazy, I've just seen Michèle in the other Café, further down. She was with an American."

"An American? An American sailor?"

"No, not a sailor, just an American. A tourist."

I asked her if she thought you'd still be there. She said:

"I really don't know. Perhaps; it's not so very long ago," and added: "You'd better go and look."

You weren't in the other Café any longer, always supposing you ever had been. The waiter didn't know. He didn't want to know. It would have meant tipping him, and I couldn't afford it; so I sat down all the same and had a glass of grenadine-and-water.

As I wasn't sure what to do, and as I mostly can't think without doodling on a piece of paper, I tore out the first page from my exercise-book and drew a plan of the town, cross-hatching the places where you might be. It took me nearly an hour. In order of importance, the places were:

> at home
> the cafés in the Place
> the shops in the Avenue
> the seafront
> the church

the bus-station
the Rue Smolett
the Rue Neuve
the Descente Crotti

After that I got up, paid for the grenadine, and went straight off to look for you. I had about 50 francs left. Luckily I'd still got the [

]

what you said to me. He had a rather flabby face, a crew-cut, and long, fat legs. As it was dark, I went to the far end of the bar and asked for a glass of red wine.

At first I hadn't meant to drink so much. If I'd wanted to get tight I'd have started with something else; beer, for instance; I can't carry red wine. When I begin drinking that I always throw it up in the end, and I don't care for throwing up. It's the same with excrements, I don't like to think I'm leaving part of myself somewhere. I want to remain complete.

Why I drank too much this time was that I had the 5,000 francs in my pocket, I'd nothing else to do, and I didn't like the look of the American. I began by ordering:

"A glass of red wine"

when I might just as easily have said: "A Misty Isley" or "An espresso and two croissants".

The point is that after that I was too tired to call a different order to the waiter. I'd say:

"The same again."

"Red?" he'd ask.

And I'd nod.

A funny thing happened then. The Bar was crowded, the waiters were hurrying to and fro, and you were sitting near the door with that American fellow. I looked at all of you, one after another, and you were all doing the same thing, that's to say drinking, talking, crossing your legs, smiling, smoking and puffing out the smoke through your nostrils, etc. You all had faces, arms and legs, backs to your heads, sexual organs, hips and mouths. You all had the same lump of reddened skin on your elbows, the same tear-glands, their edges showing, the same double cleft in the small of the back, the same type of ears, curled like a shell, no doubt cast in the same mould, hideously identical. Not one of you had two mouths, for example. Or a foot in place of the left eye. You were all talking at the same time and telling one another the same things. You were all, all, all alike. You were living in twos, in threes, fours, fives, sixes, tens, twenty-nines, one hundred and eighty-threes, etc.

I amused myself by reconstructing your talk:
Suzanne's in a nursing-home.
    Of course not, never, why on earth? There's no
       reason!
    It's because of Georges, I saw him the other evening at
       the Mexico, he
      It's true in a way. But Ionesco isn't
      stinker if anyone asks you that say it's
      Hi! Jean-Claude, want a cigarette? You know

half a pint of draught you wouldn't have twenty
    francs
It's Henri, a pal of Jackie's. I've a job
Then what's the matter?
D'you want to know the truth? You know the truth?

necessarily modern, he's in the tradition of the
me, afterwards. I've had enough of this, shall we go?
on Thursday, when it rained, well, the thing worked
at the City Stores I unload packing-cases twice
to put a record on it's not worth mentioning
so then I had a good shower. He said to me it's
He tells you stories, okay, they're good ones, but you get
    tired of them, there isn't
realists, you know, of Monnier, Henri Monnier, for instance.
It's not ten o'clock yet, let's wait another
All the same I went to Monaco
it's all washed up now   here?
a week, it's quite well paid and it gives me a bit of exercise
no use counting on me for the next match
Hi, Claude!   No news
a word of truth in it all any more
five minutes anyhow. I'm sure he'll come, he kept saying
    he would.

But there was no sense in all these words, all these intermingled phrases. You were all men and women, and never
until then had I felt so strongly that you constituted a race.
I suddenly wished I could take refuge with the ants and
learn as much about them as I knew about you.

I drank four or five more glasses of wine; I'd had nothing
to eat, and drink on an empty stomach always makes me ill.
I drank more than a bottle of red wine, down there at the
far end of the bar.

I had a kind of sick taste on my tongue. It was very hot, and everything felt clammy. I remember tearing a page out of the exercise-book and writing in the middle of it:

> Interrogation concerning a disaster
> among the ants.

Then I wrote some stuff on the back of the sheet; but I've lost it since then and I can't remember what it said. I think it mentioned powder, mountains of white powder.

When I left the bar I was pretty well plastered. Going past you I saw you were showing some photographs to the American. I felt ill, so I went for a long walk in the Old Town. I staggered along, leaning against the wall. Twice I vomitted into the gutter. I had no idea what time it was, or what I was doing. I sat down on the rim of the Fontaine Saint-François; I put the parcels of food and the exercise-book down beside me. I smoked two cigarettes one after another. A cold breeze was flapping the awnings outside the shops.

My matchbox was empty; I made it into a boat, sticking a burnt match upright in the lid. I threaded a scrap of paper onto the match, to make a sail, and put the whole thing into the fountain. It began to drift across the black surface. Puffs of wind hit the sail and sent it zigzagging towards the middle of the basin. I watched it for over a minute, and then suddenly lost sight of it. The fountain swallowed it up in a shower of drops and hid it behind a curtain of mist. The water began to bubble round it, and a few seconds later it vanished downwards like a shadow and evaporated in the tumult of greyness and black whirlpools.

That was the moment when I'd have liked to hear somebody say, somebody say to me, Bastard!

[

In the end I went away after all, because a police car had seen me and slowed down. I went round through the Old Town and up again to the gardens behind the Bus Station. I thought I could lie down on a bench and get some sleep.

In the gardens I found you and the American fellow. When I recognized you I thought I'd have a ball, because it was dark and you looked as though you were enjoying yourselves. I sat down beside you and began telling you stories. I forget what they were, riddles, ghost stories or disjointed phrases. I have an idea I told you about my great-grandfather, who was Governor of Ceylon. But I forget. The American lit a cigarette and waited for me to go. But I didn't feel like going. I asked you for another 1,000 francs. Michèle said she'd given me enough for the time being; I replied that she had never returned the raincoat I'd lent her, and that it was certainly worth more than 5,000.

Michèle, you lost your temper and told me to clear out. I laughed, and said give me 1,000 francs. The American threw away his cigarette and said:

"Now, come on, get going."

I replied by swearing in American. Michèle got scared and gave me the 1,000 francs. The American stood up and said again: "Hey, get going". I repeated the same oath. Michèle threatened to call the police. But the American said not to worry, he'd manage by himself. I couldn't see straight. He made me get up off the seat and pushed me backwards. I came back at him, still talking, saying whatever came into my head, I can't remember what. I think I was telling him about the raincoat, that it had cost 10,000 francs, that it had a cloth lining; and also about everything we'd done that day up in the hills. Michèle began to walk away, saying she was going for the police. The police station was just across the gardens.

The American hadn't understood a word I was saying, because I'd spoken very fast, in a muffled voice.

He came back at me to push me backwards again, but I grabbed him by the collar. Then he hit me, first to the left of the chin and then again, under the eye. I tried to land a kick in his groin, but I missed. Then he began thumping me in the face and the stomach, with his fists and knees. Until I fell on the gravel path. He didn't stop at that. He put his two fat knees on my chest and bashed my face as hard as he could. He nearly knocked me out, and he broke one of my front teeth; in doing that he must have hurt his fist, because he left off at once. He got up, panting, and went out of the gardens, calling Michèle.

After a minute I managed to turn over, and I crawled on all fours to the bench. I sat down and wiped my face with my handkerchief; I didn't feel any pain except from my broken tooth, but I was bleeding a lot. He must have driven his fist into my nose. In any case both my eyes were swollen up like oranges. As I wiped away the blood I was muttering under my breath; I was still a bit tight, and I could find nothing to say except:

"Because of that stinker I shall have to go to the dentist, because of that bastard I shall have to spend 2,000 francs on going to the dentist."

Not more than five minutes later I saw the American and Michèle coming back with a copper. I just had time to get away through the bushes and over the hedge. I went back to the Old Town and washed my face and hands under a fountain. I had a cigarette to relax myself. My tooth was beginning to jag; it was half broken and felt as though the nerve had grown out through the enamel like a blade of grass. I thought to myself, I must be getting home, to the deserted house at the top of the hill.

I went back there as quickly as I could. Passing the church by the harbour I saw it was five-and-twenty to five. There were cars going by with their lamps alight, and animals all over the place, in pairs, uttering weird cries. I was thinking all the time, "I've been sick twice and to-morrow I shall have to go and see the dentist, the dentist—dentist." I was thinking all the time about the leather chair and the steel levers whirling and the sickly smell of fillings, in the square of stale, cool air, very hygienic.'

[

]

At this point three pages of the exercise-book have been torn out. The fourth has a drawing on it, an aerial view of some sort of town. The streets are drawn in with a ball-point pen. A red spot, like a Square, has been made by pressing on the paper a thumb covered with blood from a scratched pimple. A cigarette-end has been crushed out at the bottom left of the page. All this with considerable application, it would seem, and great self-satisfaction—as evidenced by an eyelash that must have fallen off during the exaggerated time for which Adam's head was bent over the paper. One may reckon that about three or four days elapsed between the page before the missing ones and the page that follows the gap. This is the last page in the famous yellow exercise-book. There are only a few lines on it, also written with a ball-point pen. The bottom of the page has been torn off, and there is a lot of scratching-out; in some places the words underneath are still legible, in other places they are completely obliterated. There are gaps in a few of the words, where the pen skidded on the greasy paper.

'Sunday morning, my dear Michèle,
Michèle and the American must have gone to the police and given away my hiding-place. Very early this morning I was woken by a noise; alarmed, I got up and looked out of the window. I saw two or three men climbing the hill, not talking. They were walking fast, and looking up at the house every now and then. ~~I thought at once they must be coppers,~~ anyhow I had just time to grab two or three things and jump out of the window. They didn't see me because there's a line of ~~rose bushes beans~~ rose-bushes in front of the window. I went uphill a bit, above the house, then I sloped off to the left and doubled back along the dry bed of a stream. ~~I passed not~~ very far from them, and at one moment I caught sight of them clambering up through the patches ▆▆▆▆▆▆▆▆ of briars. I took care not to make a noise by kicking any loose stones. The ▆▆▆▆▆ of them.

I came out on the road; at first I walked along the bank at the side, then I got down on the road. It wasn't long after sunrise; there was a glimpse of the sea to the left, between the pines. The scent of pines and grass was overpowering. After that I strolled along as though I were out for a walk. Five hundred yards further on I came to a narrow lane running down to the seashore, so I took that. I thought it was better not to keep on the main road, because the coppers would be bound to recognize me if they came past by car. I'd left my watch behind in the house, but by the sun it was eight o'clock, not more. I was hungry and thirsty.

Down below, near the beach, there was a café just opening. I had a cup of chocolate and an apple fritter. My broken tooth was hurting again. And I had about 1,200 fr.

left. I began to wonder whether I oughn't to go into exile. To Sweden, Germany or Poland. The Italian frontier wasn't far off. But it wouldn be   y with no passport or money. ~~Or I thought I might perhaps go and see my mother.~~ I no longer needed to write it on the back of an empty cigarette packet: what I was going to do was to take a look round. In a town there are two kinds of houses one can live in—ordinary houses, and homes. There are two kinds of homes—mental homes and homes for the night. Among homes for the night, some are for rich people and some for poor people. Among those for poor people there are some with separate rooms and some with dormitories. Among those with dormitories there are some that are cheap and some that are free. Among those that are free there's the Salvation Army. And the Salvation Army won't always take you in.

That's why, by and large, it was nice to live all alone in a deserted house at the top of a hill.

Of course it was short on what people call comfort. You have to sleep on the floor unless the owners have left a bed, which they hadn't in this case. The water is nearly always cut off (except the stand-pipe in the garden, you remember, Michèle?). You have no protection against burglars or animals: it means taking care of yourself; and when one's alone one rea   doesn't de   oneself efficiently against bugs, mosquitoes, spiders, or even scorpions and snakes. And then the owners are always liable to turn up suddenly. S   mes they get angry when they find there's somebody in their house. One hasn't much of an excuse, especially in hot weather and when one's a young chap, as tough as the next, in other words quite able to work—and particularly when one had a room of one's own in the town, with everything one needed. They may go so far as to call the police, and one's soon picked up, a tramp

declared to be "of no   wn   ress", a thief, a deserter—
breaking and entering, confidence trick, blackmail or
mendicancy.

I'm not blind or crippled. I shall go off to the cold
countries; I shall travel in a goods-train and bed in the
street in Rotterdam. I shall sit on a bollard beside a fishing-
net and go down to the beach to bathe. The dog will perhaps
come past here today, Sunday, 29th August, nearly nine
o'clock in the morning. It's hot and sultry; it seems there'll
be fires on the hill-sides round about. Here I'm hidden
away.

Unf [

]
On the back of the exercise-book Adam has signed his
name, in full: 'Adam Pollo, martyr.' Although one can't
say for certain, it is extremely probable that the above
passage was concluded in the place where it accidentally
turned up later on, in the 'Gents' at the Torpedo Snack-Bar.

P. Towards the end of the morning, about noon or nearing one o'clock, he had become just a man in the middle of the beach. His long, skinny body was stretched out on the scorching pebbles. To let the air through a little and reduce the roasting effect of the sun, he had propped himself backwards on his elbows, leaving a narrow gap between his spine and the ground. He had settled close to the water's edge, so that whenever a motorboat rushed past out at sea, towing somebody on water-skis, it wetted the soles of his feet with the ripples in its wake.

At a distance, and from behind, he looked much the same as ever. He was still wearing the dark blue shorts with oil-stains on them, and the sun-glasses with gilt wire frames. His clothes were folded in a heap beside him, topped by a two-month-old magazine; this had originally been open in the middle, at a page dealing with a railway accident; but the wind, blowing from one side, had closed it again; now it was the back cover that lay upwards, showing a little boy eating spaghetti and cheese. Further along the beach another little boy was playing all by himself, paddling barefooted in the water. Adam was not looking at him; Adam was about thirty years old now.

Adam Pollo had a longish head, with a slightly pointed top. His hair and beard, roughly hacked with scissors, were full of tangles and matted locks. His whole face had some lingering trace of good looks, rather large eyes, or perhaps a soft, immature nose, cheeks that were boyish, *beardless* under their covering of yellow beard. He had a narrow torso filled with dozens of ribs; it was stretched by his drawn-back arms and did not look very sturdy. His shoulders were bulgy in front, with muscles no doubt; his arms were bony. His hands were shortish, broad and plump, with an undeniable air of hands that couldn't undo the fastening on even the easiest bra. The rest was in proportion. But seen at close quarters, with the sun making patches on it, and the splashes of sea-water, Adam's body looked as though it were being gradually spotted with all kinds of colours, from bright yellow to blue.

Thus camouflaged, he was caught in a multitude of other spots—brown, green, black, black-and-grey, white, ochre, dirty red; from far off he looked like a small child, from nearer, like a young man, and from close to, like a kind of funny old man, centenarian and innocent. He was breathing rapidly. Each time he breathed in, the hairs round his navel straightened up to denote the fleeting presence of about 2 litres of air, which penetrated his bronchial tubes, dilated them down to the smallest, stretched his ribs and pushed away the top of the stomach and the smaller intestine with a thrust of the diaphragm. The air went right down inside, echoing with his heart-beats, the furthest recesses of his flesh turned blood-red and his veins were shaken at regular intervals by a great blue tide that swept up through his body. The air filtered in everywhere, warm, laden with smells and microscopic scraps. It invaded the mass of meat and skin and sent tiny electric shocks through and through it. Everything functioned along its course: the valves closed, the capillaries of the windpipe drove out the dust, and in the lowest depths of the great damp cavity, stained purple and white, the carbon dioxide accumulated, waiting to be driven upwards, ready to be exhaled and to mingle with the atmosphere; it would go to hover here and there on the beach, in the holes between the stones, on the sweating foreheads, adding to the density of the steel-grey skies. Deep down inside Adam was an agglomeration of cells, nuclei, plasma, atoms combined in any number of ways; nothing was airtight any longer. Adam's atoms could have mingled with the atoms in the stones, and he might have been drawn down quietly through the ground, the sand, water and slime; everything would have crumbled together, as though into an abyss, and have vanished into the blackness. In Adam's left femoral artery an amoeba had formed its cyst. And the atoms were revolving like infinitesimal planets in his immense, cosmic body.

Yet in confrontation with others, as he lay in the foreground of the beach with both feet trailing in the sea, he was an individual; the sun's yellow-white rays fell vertically on his sugar-loaf skull, and with his projecting jaw, his scrubby beard and his general air of being a specimen, he looked more and more like a character in the first part of a Greek play. Just now he was smoking a cigarette; sunblinks flew past his eyes like artificial flies and then burst like bubbles. Salt whitened on the hairs of his body. And the same little boy paddled about in the sea, singing in a drone:

> '. . .*Criaient la gloire*
> *de Dieu,*
> *Chantaient l'amour*
> *de Dieu . . .*'

He stopped for a glance at his mother, who was lying further up the shingle, abandoned to sleep; and then began again, on the wrong note,

> '. . . *Criaient la gloire*
> *de Dieu,* etc.'

Planes flew overhead without a sound, between two layers
of atmosphere. People were going off to lunch. A wasp
with one wing half torn off was running over the stones;
twice it nearly wheeled inland, but losing its sense of
direction in this chaotic desert it made a mistake and
crawled to meet its death—towards the sea, where a single
drop of salt water drowned it in the sunshine. Now the
little boy was singing:

> '*Oh Sarimarès*
> *belle amie d'autrefois,*
> *en moi tu demeures vi-ive.*'

in steadier voice. Then he climbed up the beach, knocking
Adam's magazine to the ground as he went past. After
which he went on more cautiously, staring at Adam's back
with his two small, heavy-lidded eyes; until he reached the
bath-towel where his mother lay asleep, pulled it towards
him, sat down and forgot.

Not long after this, Adam got up and went away. He
walked quickly to the Post Office nearest to the harbour
and went to the Poste Restante window. The clerk gave
him a bulging envelope, a fat letter. On the envelope was
written:

> Adam Pollo,
> Poste Restante No. 15

and the address.

Because it was cool there, and perhaps because he didn't
quite know where else to go, Adam opened the letter in the
Post Office. He sat down on a bench not far from the table
with the telephone directories. Beside him was a girl

making out a money-order. She had to have several shots at it, with pauses for mental arithmetic; she was sweating, and tightly clutching a ball-point pen with an advertisement printed on it and a rubber band twisted round it.

Adam unfolded the letter; there were three pages of large writing, much more like drawings or hieroglyphs than the Roman alphabet; it must have been traced by a heavy hand, a not very feminine hand, accustomed to bearing down weightily on flat surfaces, and more especially on sheets of paper. A touch of fantasy in the arrangement of the letters and the slope of the final 's's suggested affection, liveliness, or perhaps simply the faint irritation of having to write on the off-chance, with no guarantee that the letter would be read. The pages lay there, undeniably, offering a message which one must be able to read between the lines, kind of ingenuously cunning riddle. Changeless, at all events, as though engraved on some stone in a wall, a message from a mortal hand which could never be effaced by time, which offered itself, clear as a date, abstruse as the chart of a maze.

The letter had been waiting in its pigeon-hole at the Poste Restante for over a week.

19th August

My dear Adam,

When your father and I found your note in the letter-box we were very much surprised, as you can imagine. We were not expecting anything of the kind—neither what you have done, nor your way of telling us about it. We hope you aren't keeping anything from us—that there's nothing serious behind all this. Though neither your father nor I liked your showing so little confidence in us. We still feel hurt, I assure you.

Your father was terribly against the idea of writing to you Poste Restante, as you asked us to do in your note. We had a long argument about it and, as you see, I've gone against his wishes and taken it upon myself to indulge your whim.

But I feel somehow that I'm wrong, because I don't know what to say. I wish I could have a quiet talk with you, get you to explain why you acted as you did, and try to guess what it is you need. I don't feel that a letter will do much good in that way—particularly a surreptitious one like this. But since you wanted it, I'm writing it all the same. I'll try to make it a friendly one, to get you to understand the foolishness of your behaviour and the dreadful anxiety it is giving your father and me. As soon as you receive this letter, answer it by return, no matter what your plans are and what you may be doing. Tell me why you went off like that without a word, where you are now, and if there's anything you need. You must realize that's the first essential, so as to relieve our anxiety and soothe our feelings. Do that to please me, Adam, it's all I ask.

I'm enclosing the note you left us when you went away. If you read it you will understand that it was nothing like enough to set our minds at rest. We weren't expecting anything of the kind. You'd said nothing to us about a journey, or about holidays. We thought your national service had tired you and that you'd stay with us for a rest—we were thinking we might all go to stay in the country with your aunt for a time. We didn't say much about it, of course, but you had seemed tired lately, and I knew you didn't like making plans. Needless to say, this has put an end to our holidays.

Philippe had written to us the week before. He'd agreed to join us at Aunt Louise's as soon as he could get away from his work, and to have a family August. Your father had managed to get leave for the whole month, and I took it for granted you would like the idea. I was looking forward to being all together again, like old times; you and Philippe are grown up now, but you know we only have to get together, the four of us, and you're both my boys again and I forget your age and my own. Your father was very angry when he knew what you'd done. Why didn't you say anything about it beforehand, Adam? Why not have told us? Or at least told me, your mother? Yes, why didn't you try to explain things to me? If you had to go away for some reason or other, if it was absolutely necessary for you to be away for a time, you can be sure we should have understood. We'd have made no objection——

Remember the time before, fifteen or sixteen years ago, when you wanted to leave home—— You weren't twenty-nine then, only fourteen; but you remember I made no objection to the idea. I felt you needed to get away from us for a while. The quarrel with your father was a silly business, of course, but I could feel it went deeper than a row about breaking the blue bowl. Your father's a quick-tempered man, as you know—— He didn't really mind about the blue bowl either; but he thought you were being cheeky, defying his authority, and that was why he boxed your ears. He was wrong, and he apologized—but remember what I did. I caught you up on the stairs and asked you to think it over—I explained that you were too young to go away all by yourself, into the world—I said you'd do better to wait a bit and get over your anger. I said you might wait a week or two and then, if you still wanted to leave, you could look for a job somewhere, apprentice yourself, for instance. You could have made an honest living on your own, if that was what you wanted. You thought it over carefully, and you understood. You cried a little, because your pride was wounded and you felt you'd lost a battle. But I was glad for you, because I knew it was the only thing to do.

So, Adam dear, what I can't understand is, why didn't you do the same this time as over the blue bowl?

Why didn't you come and talk to me? I'd have advised you like I did then, and have tried to help you. You can't imagine how your note hurt me, it was so short and cold, and it put me in a position where I had no chance of helping you—— Your father was angry, but with me it's different. All these years of trust and affection can't just be washed out, my darling boy. I'm sorry you didn't think of all this before going away—for I'm certain you didn't. But I hope it's all nearly over now. As soon as you get this letter, do come home; we won't criticize you or ask you to explain —it will soon be forgotten. You're grown up, you came of age long ago, and you are free to go wherever you choose. We'll talk about that, if you like. If you don't want to come home right away, send us a long letter, addressed to both of us. But Adam, I do beg you not to leave us with the bad impression of a hasty note, scribbled at a café table. Don't leave us feeling worried and disappointed. Send us an affectionate letter, Adam, to show that we're still your parents, and not a couple of strangers you dislike. Tell us what you mean to do, where you want to work, how you're getting along, where you intend to go—— I see in the papers that teachers are wanted in central Africa and Algeria; it's not particularly well paid, but it might do as a beginning and lead to something else.

Then there are appointments as assistant professor of French in Scandinavia—and there must be lots of others like that. With your qualifications you could easily find a job in one of those countries, unless you'd rather stay here. In that case you could take a room in town, in whatever district you like. We would lend you the money, you could pay us back later on. You'd come to see us now and then during the week, or you'd write to us. In any case we should know what you were doing, if you were well, whether you were having difficulties about money or anything.

You see, Adam, you must realize things can't go on like this for ever. You can't spend the rest of your life with a wall between yourself and us; you can't arrange your life on a mere whim. You mustn't. Sooner or later you'll have to be on friendly terms with one or other of us—or else you'll have to get along with strangers. You must form a circle of friends, where you can find affection; otherwise you'll be unhappy and you will probably be the first to suffer for it. So as in any case you will have to give up this abrupt, suspicious attitude, why not do so right away, and with us? Everything your father and I have done for you we have done in the attempt to overcome your unsociability and shyness—we persist in our affection because we don't want other people to criticize you, because you're our own child. The Pollo clan, as you used to call it, must hold together. It mustn't split up, even over such a difficult member as you are. Please, Adam, do realize that we form a scrap of something indestructible. We brought Philippe up to look at it that way, and that's how we should have liked to bring you up.

So Adam dear, nothing is lost. With good will all round, everything can go back to what it was. In spite of the way things may seem to you, we are still the Pollo clan. You're called after one of our ancestors—your great-grandfather's name was Antoine-Adam Pollo. You have to be an important member of the clan, even if you behave differently from the others—even if you stand out in other ways. There are a thousand ways of sticking together, Adam, remember that. You can choose the one that suits you; and you can rely upon it that it will always suit me.

I shall look forward to a letter from you tomorrow, a long, friendly one. Be sure and tell me what you need. I'll put aside a little money for you and give it to you when you come to see us—enough to keep you going till you begin to earn your own living. And I'll get some clean clothes ready for you as well, if you like, some shirts and a suit and some underclothes.

There, that's all I wanted to tell you—forgive me for reminding you of the humiliating business about the blue bowl. But I feel so certain you haven't changed since the day I caught you up on the stairs and persuaded you, gently, that you ought not to go away like that. We'll keep all this a secret between the two of us, shall we? and we shall understand each other much better when you come to see us—— So I shall expect you very soon, Adam dear, I love you very much and I have great hopes of you.

Your affectionate mother,
Denise Pollo.

Adam folded up the letter; there was a scrap of paper in in the envelope as well. It was all crumpled and dirty. A few hurried lines were pencilled on it, in a different handwriting. They said:

> 'Don't worry about me. I'm going away
> for a time. Write to me at Poste Restante
> 15, down by the harbour. Don't be anxious
> about me, everything's all right.
> Adam.'

When he finished reading, Adam put the letter and the note back into the envelope, slipped it inside his magazine, picked up his belongings and left the Post Office. A kind of sweat was plastering his hair down on his forehead and his shirt to his back.

Everything was all right, indeed. The weather was still

lovely, for the end of summer, and the Promenade by the sea was swarming with people. Outside the cafés, boys in T-shirts were strumming guitars and handing round the hat. Everything was so white in the light that it might have been black. The whole scene had a sunburnt skin. A huge ink-pot, why not, had emptied its contents onto the earth; it was like looking at the world through a photographic negative.

Adam was no longer following anybody; in fact he was perhaps the one who was being followed now. He no longer strolled along casually. Each lingering step on the lozenges of gravel was calculated; he went straight ahead along the sea road, in the spirit in which one fills up an application-form.

    Surname.............................. First names...................
    Date and place of birth...
    Address ....
    Occupation..
Are you (*) a Civil Servant
           Employee of the Gas or Electricity Board
           Local Government employee
           Unemployed
           Student
           Old-age Pensioner
           Voluntary Welfare Worker
  (*) Strike out which does not apply.

On the other side of the street there was a wireless shop with an ice-cream stall next door to it. Adam bought an ice cornet and looked at the TV show: two kids, a boy and a girl, dressed in black tights and dancing to the tune of 'Paper Moon'; further back in the shop three other TV sets were tuned in to the same programme. They all looked terribly human, with their identical white rectangles traversed by thousands of greyish motes; superimposed on the picture, Adam's tall figure was reflected in the shop window, with his two eyes, one nose, one mouth, ears, a trunk, four limbs, shoulders and hips.

Adam smiled at all this, with a kind of smile that meant he was just getting over not understanding; he licked the ice-cream slowly, and for the first time for some days, he talked to himself aloud. He spoke in a melodious, rather deep voice, articulating each syllable distinctly. His voice rang out, fine and strong, against the plate-glass, drowning the bursts of music and the street noises. It was all that could be heard, as it emerged from Adam's lips in the form of a pyramid and spread over the surface of the window like a cloud of steam. From the very first second it appeared to be self-sufficient, to require no addition or response, rather like the words in balloons coming out of the mouths of the characters in children's comics.

'What I wanted to say. Here it is. We're all alike, all brothers, eh. We have the same bodies and the same minds. That's what makes us brothers. Of course it seems rather ridiculous, don't you agree, to make such a confession—here—in broad daylight. But I'm telling you because we are all brothers, all alike. Do you know something, do you want to know something? My brothers. We possess the earth, all of us, just as we are, it belongs to us. Don't you see how it resembles us? Don't you see how everything that grows on it and everything that lives on it has our faces and our style? And our bodies? And is indistinguishable from us? For instance, just look round you, to left and right. Is there one single thing, one single element—within sight, which isn't ours, which isn't yours and mine? Take that street-lamp I see reflected in the shop window. Eh? That street-lamp belongs to us, it's made of cast-iron and glass, it's upright as we are, and topped by a head like ours.

185

The stone jetty down there by the sea belongs to us as well. It is built to the scale of our feet and hands. If we'd wanted, it could have been a thousand times smaller, eh? Or a thousand times bigger. That's true. The houses are ours, houses like caves, with holes pierced in them for our faces, full of chairs for our buttocks, beds for our backs, floors that imitate the ground and consequently imitate us. We are all the same, comrades. We have invented monsters—yes, monsters. Such as these television sets or these machines for making Italian ices; but we have remained within the confines of our own nature. In that we show our genius— we have made nothing that merely cumbers the earth, like God himself, my brothers, like God himself. And I tell you, eh, I give you my word, there is no difference between the sea, the tree and television. We make use of everything, because we are the masters, the only intelligent beings in the world. There you are. The TV is us, men. It is our strength we have poured into a mass of metal and plastic, so that it may answer us back one day. And that day has arrived, the mass of metal and plastic answers us now, captivates us, enters our eyes and ears. An umbilical cord links this object with our own bellies. It is the useless, many-splendoured thing in which we are adrift, in which we lose ourselves, in a little pleasure, yes, in our general happiness. Brothers, I am the Telly and you are the Telly and the Telly is within us! It has our particular anatomy, and we are all square, all black, all electric, all sonorous with purrings and music when, drawn to the Telly by sight and hearing, we recognize in its voice a human voice and on its screen a figure identical with ourselves. Judge for yourselves, brothers. We share this image like love, and our vague, obscure unity begins to appear; behind that glazed surface it is as though thick, warm blood were flowing, it is like a set of chromosomes, with one extra

186

pair, which is at last going to make us into a race again. Who knows if we shall not draw the cruellest revenge from this, for having been so long separated. Having misunderstood one another. Having believed falsely. Who knows if we may not at last again discover some tyrannosaur, some ceratosaur, some deinotherium, some huge pterodactyl bathed in blood, against which we can fight side by side. Some opportunity for sacrifice and slaughter, which may prompt us to clasp our hands again at last and pray in a whisper to pitiless gods. And then there will be no more TV, brothers, no more trees or animals or earth or dancers in tights; there will be only *us*, brothers, for ever, us alone!'

Adam was now on the opposite pavement. He had laid his parcel of belongings and his magazine on the ground beside him. He stood with his back to the sea, and the wind flapped his yellow trousers. There was something slightly pedantic in the stance he had adopted: behind him the rail with its cross-pieces of painted iron; through the gaps one could see the stretch of quays and docks, with the dockers at work. All this bustle was supposed to form a contrast to Adam's impassive, vaguely oblong face. One felt that had there been a bench just there, Adam would have been standing on it. And yet his attitude was not that of a public speaker; he managed to convey a general impression of nonchalance by his whole bearing. His voice was now less vibrant in the lower register, at times it struck a shriller, rather flat note. In any case he was not trying to make a harmonious effect: nothing, in fact, was more discordant than the presence of this man, standing upright and motionless amid the shifting chiaroscuro of his surroundings; and nothing more disagreeable than the idea of this man talking aloud, all by himself, in front of a crowd of idlers, under the sun at approximately 1.30 p.m.

Adam was now speaking more distinctly; he had assumed a tone half-way between fanatical ranting and wedding-breakfast oratory. He was saying:

'Stop, ladies and gentlemen, and listen to me for a little. You don't pay enough attention to the speeches that are made to you. Although you hear them all day and every day, hour by hour. On the wireless, on the television, at church, at the theatre, at the cinema, at banquets and at fairs. Yet words come easily, and nothing is nicer than a tale told like that, at point-blank. Off the cuff. You're used to it. You are not human beings, because you are not conscious of living in a human world. Learn to speak. Try it for yourselves. Even if you have nothing to say. Because, I tell you, the floor is yours. Why not try, just as you are, to act as substitutes for your own machines: go ahead, talk, right and left. Spread the good word. You'll see, before long you won't need the radio or the telly any more. You'll just meet yourselves at the corner of a street, as I did today, and you'll tell yourselves stories. No matter what. And you'll see, your wives and children will come flocking up and listen to you with all their ears. You can go on telling them the loveliest things, indefinitely.'

By this time an audience had gathered, consisting more or less of:

(1) a dozen women, men and children, the hard core;

(2) about twenty others who moved on after a minute or two.

Altogether, an average of about thirty listeners, gathered in a knot on the pavement.

'I'll tell you something. Listen. I—a little time ago now, I was sitting on some steps, up in the hills, smoking a cigarette. There was a fine view from there, and I was enjoying it a lot. Across from where I sat there was a lower hill, and then the town, stretching away to the sea, and the long curve of the shore. Everything was very quiet. The sky took up three-quarters of the view. And below, the earth was so peaceful that one would have said—that it was a continuation of the sky. You see the kind of thing. Two hills, a town, a small river, a bay, a little sea, and a column of smoke curling up to the clouds. All over the place. I'm describing these features so you'll understand what comes next. You understand?'

Nobody answered, but a few people nodded, laughing.

Adam singled out one bystander, at random, looked at him and asked:

'You understand?'

'Yes, yes, I understand,' said the man.

'And—haven't you anything to tell us yourself?'

'Me?'

'Yes, you, why not? Do you live in the country?'

The man made as if to draw back, and the crowd seemed to do likewise.

'No, I——'

'Are you selling something?' asked a woman.

'Yes, the word,' said Adam.

The first bystander seemed to understand this:

'So you're a Jehovah's witness? Eh?'

'No,' said Adam.

'Yes, you—you're a prophet?'

But Adam did not hear him; he turned back to the mysterious enigmas of his embryonic language, to his desperate isolation, the blockade protecting him from being overrun by the populace, and he went on with what he had begun:

'Suddenly, on the earth, everything was different. Yes, at one stroke I understood everything. I understood that the earth belonged to me, and not to any other living species. Not to the dogs, not to the rats, not to the vermin, not to anything. Not to the snails or the cockroaches or the grasses or the fish. It belonged to the human beings. And so to me, since I was a human being. And do you know how I came to understand that! Something extraordinary had happened. An old woman had appeared. Yes, an old woman. An old woman. You'll see what I mean. The road I was sitting beside was one of those steep, mountain roads. From where I sat, on these steps, I could see it sloping down and vanishing round a bend. Ahead of me there was just a bit of road, not more than a hundred yards; it was tarred, and shining under the clouded sun. Suddenly I heard muffled sounds, coming in my direction, I looked down the road, and there, coming into sight slowly, terribly slowly, was an old woman, a fat, ugly old woman, in a flower-printed coat that billowed round her like a flag. First I saw her head, then her shoulders, then her hips, her legs, and finally the whole of her. She was toiling up the tarred road, on her fat, blotchy legs, puffing like a cow, her mind a blank. I watched her emerging from the hill, like getting out of a bath, and coming up towards me. She cut a paltry figure, a black silhouette against the cloudy sky. She was, that's it—she was the only moving thing in the whole region. Nature all round her was unvaried, motionless—except that—how should I put it?—it was making a halo round her head, as though she had the earth and sky for her hair. The town was still stretching away towards the sea, so was the river, the hills were still rounded and the trails of smoke still vertical. *But they extended from her head.* It was as though it had all tipped up. It had altered. It was she, you understand, she who'd made it all. The smoke, yes, that was a human thing all right. So were the town and the river. So was the bay. The hills—the hills had been cleared of trees and covered with telegraph poles, they were crisscrossed with lanes and gulleys. The road and the steps, the walls, the houses, the bridges, the dams, the airplanes—it wasn't the ants, all that! It was she. A quite commonplace old woman. Fat and ugly. Not even fit to live. Organically incapable. Bulging with fat. Unable to walk straight. With bandaged legs, varicose veins, and cancer somewhere about her, in her rectum or somewhere. It was she. The earth was round and tiny. And human beings had worked it all over. There isn't a single place on this earth, d'you hear me, not a single place on this earth that hasn't got a road, a house, an aeroplane, a telegraph pole. Isn't it enough to drive you mad, to think we belong to that race? It was she. It was she, this bundle of rags, full of entrails and stuff, of dirty, bleeding things, this dotty, muddy-eyed animal with a skin like a dried-up crocodile, its dewlap, its shrivelled uterus, its collection of drained-out glands, its lungs, its goitre, its yellow tongue all ready to stutter, . . . its gasps, like a stunned cow, its . . . its heavy cry . . . Huh-huh . . . huh-huh . . . swollen belly . . . broken veins . . . and its skull . . . bald, its hairy armpits scabbed with seventy-five years of sweat. It was she. She . . . You—you see?'

Adam was speaking faster and faster; he was getting to the point where one no longer forms sentences, tries to make oneself understood. He was pressing right back against the painted iron railing; all that could be seen of him now was his head, which rose above the crowd and faced them, with something prophetic, something friendly about it; he was the man people point at, the one that sends them hurrying for the police, the one for whom they go to fetch their cameras, the one who's either jeered at or insulted, according to choice.

'Want to tell you. Wait. Can tell you a story. You know. Like over the wireless. Dear listeners. I can argue. I can argue with you. Who wants to? Who'd like to talk to me?

Eh? Can we argue about something? We can talk about the war. There's going to be a war—— No . . . Or about the cost of living. What's the price of potatoes? Eh? It seems potatoes are enormous this year. And turnips quite tiny. Or about abstract painting. If no one has anything to say. Haven't you anything to say? I can tell a story. That's it. I can make up fables for you. On the spot. Here—I'll give you some titles. Listen. The legend of the dwarf palm that wanted to travel in Eastern Europe. Or the ibis turned into a girl by a commercial traveller. Or Asdrubal the two-mouthed. And the Love-story of a carnival king and a fly. Or How Zoe, the Queen of Peloponnesus, found the treasure of the rock-tomb without really trying. Or The courage of trypanosomes. Or How to kill rattlesnakes. That's easy. You need to know three things. Rattlesnakes. Are very vain. Don't like jazz. And as soon as they see an edelweiss they fall into a cataleptic trance. So. This is what you have to do. You take a clarinet. When you see the snake you pull an ugly face at him. Being vain, they get in a rage and rush at you. At that moment you play them Blue Moon or Just a Gigolo. On the clarinet. They don't like jazz. So they stop short. They hesitate. At that precise instant you take out. You take out of your pocket a real edelweiss, picked in the snow. And they fall into a cataleptic trance. So then. All you have to do is grab them and slip a p onto them somewhere. When they recover from the trance. They see they've become merely. That they've become merely prattlesnakes. And as they're so terribly vain, this kills them. They prefer to commit suicide. They hold their breath. For hours. In the end it kills them. They turn quite black. Do you hear? etc.'

Adam talked from 2.10 p.m. to 2.48 p.m. The crowd of listeners had grown appreciably. They were beginning to look really wary, and their interruptions drowned Adam's voice at times. He was talking faster and faster and more and more incoherently. He was hoarse with fatigue, and a kind of irritation had stolen over his face.

There were two deep furrows across his forehead now, and his ears were red. His shirt was clinging to his back and shoulders. He had talked so much, shouted so much, that he scarcely overtopped the crowd any more; he was fused with it, and his pointed head, with the thick hair and beard, seemed to hover among the listeners like somebody else's head; instead of degrading it, despair had carved it into an effigy. It was as though a dull hatred had severed it from the trunk, on the threshold of some peculiar revolution, and as in days of yore, the populace, aroused by the hero, was carrying in its sticky centre, like a sea, a noble countenance that was still alive. At once innocent and shameful, the eyes shone madly in their deep sockets, caught in the mass hysteria like marbles in a string bag. Among them all they had built up an agglomeration of human flesh and sweat, indivisible in aspect, where nothing that was comprehended in it could continue to exist. Sudden cries, laughter, jests, the roar of engines, motor-horns, the sea and the boats, were all stripped of logic. Everything was coming and going confusedly, in jerks, with the sound and colours of a riot.

The truth is hard to register; all of a sudden the pace quickened alarmingly. In a second, it was over. There was an eddy in the crowd, with cries, of anger perhaps. After that everything followed its natural course. Except for this strange, unexpected detail, nothing was left to chance. What I mean is that it was so simple and so automatic that when the crowd took action it was at least two hours ahead of its own schedule.

BEN BELLA SCORES TRIUMPH AT ORAN:
"One-party System Essential."

BETWEEN MANDELIEU AND LE TRAYAS FIRES CUT THE RAILWAY LINE IN SEVERAL PLACES

Many trains held up. Several houses threatened. A camping site hastily evacuated.

At Tizi-Ouzou, 100,000 Kabyles
cheer the G.P.R.A.

GENERAL STRIKE OF SAILORS AT MARSEILLES UNTIL TOMORROW AFTERNOON

Sailings for Corsica and Africa are cancelled until further notice.

VAR RESIDENT ON HOLIDAY MEETS DEATH BY DROWNING AT PALAVAS-LES-FLOTS

Montpellier. On holiday at Palavas-les-Flots (Hérault), M. Robert Mages, 47, of La Seyne-sur-Mer (Var) was accidentally drowned yesterday morning.

Overcome while in the water, M. Mages was brought to land by fellow-bathers and taken to hospital at Montpellier, where he died soon after admission, despite all attempts to revive him.

MYSTERY DEATHS IN CORSICA

The bodies of 2 German tourists were found in the sea, two miles away from each other, near Anghione beach.

The man's death appears to be due to a fractured skull. The woman showed no signs of violence.

(See page 7)

● **Missing from his home near Toulon since June 30, a farmer is found dead in a ravine. Accident, suicide, or foul play?**

● *Ariane district: A boy of twelve drowned in the Paillon.*

MANIAC ARRESTED AT CARROS

Young maniac barricaded in a school at Carros.

Police make arrest.

Short chase terminates escape of mental patient at Carros.

Strange behaviour

On Sunday afternoon the crowd strolling along the Promenade was alarmed by the strange behaviour of a young man, Adam P., who, clearly not in his right mind, was haranguing the crowd in an incoherent manner. Things would have gone no further, but that, for some unknown reason, the young man became so distracted that before the eyes of the spectators he began

(See page 7)

Verdict in the Locussol case:
STEFANI, 20 YEARS WITH HARD LABOUR ARTAUD, 5 YEARS

(Achard found guilty in absentia for the 2nd time)

MANIAC ARRESTED AT CARROS

(*Continued from page 1*)

what can only be described as a display of indecency.

Eventful chase

The police, sent for at once, set off in pursuit of the deranged youth, who had made his escape. They searched the upper part of the town; but it was not until the late evening, towards 10.30, that their quarry was reported to have been seen in a nursery school in the Carros district, which he had entered after climbing the wall of the playground. The young man then barricaded himself into one of the empty classrooms. When called upon to emerge, he threatened suicide. The police were obliged to drive him out with tear-gas bombs, whereupon he surrendered. He was armed with a kitchen knife.

Removed to mental hospital

Pending his appearance before the magistrate on several charges, the young man, the son of a good local family, is to be examined by a psychiatrist. It seems clear that he acted under the influence of sudden mental derangement. If Dr. Pauvert, who is a psychiatrist from the Institut Pasteur, finds him to be of unsound mind, he will remain at the mental home for treatment and the legal proceedings will be dropped. Otherwise he will be brought to trial on two charges—breaking and entering, and committing a nuisance. We understand that Maître Gonardi will appear on his behalf. The police ask all those who have or believe themselves to have suffered any loss or damage through the behaviour of the accused, to report the circumstances to the police station immediately.

As we go to press, we learn that the young man is alleged to have admitted, without apparent cause, to being responsible for fires in the district. He is said to have declared repeatedly 'I am an incendiary, an incendiary'. The information so far available seems to point to amnesia. Early this morning, however, two further complaints were lodged with the police—one by M. L., who declares that the accused broke into his house and caused damage, and one by Mlle. M., alleging indecent assault. The young man will be removed to the mental hospital at noon today, for examination by the psychiatrist.

MYSTERY IN CORSICA (*Continued from page 1*)

The bodies of a man and a woman were found yesterday morning on the beach at Anghione, a bathing resort on the east coast of Corsica, not far from Bastia.

The gruesome discovery is surrounded by considerable mystery.

It was about 7 a.m. and the camping-ground at Anghione, where many holiday-makers are enjoying a quiet seaside holiday, was beginning to wake up, when two amateur fishermen rushed to the manager's office to report that a woman's body was floating about 300 yards from the shore. A few minutes later the Moriani police arrived on the spot. Scarcely had the body been recovered from the sea, when the police sergeant was informed by telephone that another body had been found by a bather on the beach at Pinarello, two miles further north.*

FIRST OBSERVATIONS

It was at once discovered that the bodies were those of a German couple who had been camping at Anghione since June 28 and were intending to leave Corsica yesterday. The man was about 50 years old, the woman 42, and both were employed by a Hamburg firm. The bodies were clothed, and neither of them showed bullet-wounds. The man's forehead bore very extensive bruises, but the woman's body showed no traces of struggle or injury.*

Nevertheless, when brought out of the water, both of them bled freely from the ears. Dr. Marchesi, called to the spot, made a rapid examination and declared that the man, at least, had a fracture of the skull.

PUZZLING FEATURES

Questioned, the management declared that the couple were just like many others in the Camp and had attracted no special attention. It was said, however, that the man always carried a brief-case and never let it out of his hands.

A waitress had noticed that

Bastia removed the bodies to the mortuary, where Dr. Colonna will carry out an autopsy.

the couple were not on good terms and frequently quarrelled.

Asked whether they had quarrelled on Wednesday evening, a few hours before their death, she replied:

'No, they didn't come to the canteen that evening.'

Another curious point is that only two days after they arrived the woman asked to be moved to another hut, saying that her husband snored and kept her awake.

A strange couple indeed: did she discover for the first time, on this holiday, that the man in her life snored so loud as to keep her awake?

The obvious conclusion was that they were not married. Had they run away together? According to Dr. Marchesi, death had occurred at about 9 o'clock the previous evening.

THE INVENTORY

As required by law, the head of the municipality, M. Leonello, Mayor of Castellare di Casinca, was present when an inventory was made of the contents of the man's hut. Apart from the usual toilet articles and clothes, the police found the mysterious brief-case; but this proved to contain only some dirty handkerchiefs and other trifles. There was also a fairly considerable sum of money in French and German notes.

Theft could not, therefore, have been the motive of the crime. In the course of a thorough search of the hut, the police found some letters, which yielded no clues, a number of cuttings from literary newspapers dealing with philosophical or theological subjects, studies of man, the future, extinction, etc.

It was discovered later that neither of the couple was fond of bathing. They used to spend the day in the shade and never went on the beach.

Pliers in handbag

The first discovery which seemed to offer a promising clue was that the woman's handbag contained . . . a brand-new pair of pliers, bought in Germany. A curious possession for a woman! Did she intend to use it as a weapon of defence or attack? Several kinds of tranquillisers were also found, together with prescriptions showing that the dead man and woman had both been treated in Germany for nervous depression.

At 3 p.m. the representatives of the Public Prosecutor arrived —MM. Ricci, the Assistant Prosecutor, Leonello, examining magistrate, and Colonna, official pathologist. After they had inspected the scene of the discovery, the ambulance from

VIEWS ON THE CASE

It is difficult to draw any conclusions at this early stage. Certain hypotheses may be ventured upon, however. It is said that cries were heard about midnight; but this is not the hour indicated by the medical evidence. Moreover, the launching of a new yacht was being celebrated somewhat noisily that night in a neighbouring restaurant. The cries heard were no doubt those of the festive guests.

As for the boats which are reported to have passed soon after nightfall, they were probably fishing-boats, of which several put out every evening.

Was this a double crime, perpetrated by a killer who had come to pay off some score?

The police considered this possibility. But the following theory seems more convincing.

Did the woman discover that the man she loved was about to leave her? That the end of the holiday would mean the end of her love? The man was not physically strong (he also had a slight limp); did she knock him on the head, throw him into the water, and then drown herself?

All this, of course, is pure hypothesis; and unless the postmortem yields some fresh clues the police will have a difficult task.

R. At last he was in the shade, sitting in a cool, clean little room which faced north and was thus hermetically sealed against the sun. Not a sound to be heard except the faint plash of water flowing into a tank somewhere in the distance, and the cries of children playing a long way away, at 5 o'clock in the afternoon, in some park with sand-pits and benches. The walls seemed to match these faint sounds, for they did not look strong; they were of hollow bricks, plastered over and then painted; the paint was cream-coloured and grainy-surfaced. These walls must be pleasantly damp with condensation, summer and winter alike. There was an open window in the exact centre of the outer wall. It was barred, and the sun, thus intercepted, threw vertical and horizontal shadows across the blankets on the bed and Adam's striped pyjamas. The bars—three vertical and two horizontal—divided up a sky that was just like the walls. It was an arbitrary yet harmonious division into squares, and their number, twelve, brought a quaint reminder of the Celestial Houses as described by Manilius.

Adam was thinking of it at this very moment, as he sat in his striped pyjamas on the edge of the iron bed. They had given him permission to smoke, and he was making use of it and of a plastic ashtray. His cigarette, smouldering tip downwards at the bottom of the ashtray, was helping him to pursue an unlimited train of thought which could not be interrupted as long as the tobacco lasted. They had cut his hair and shaved him, and his face looked very young again. It was turned towards the monochrome rectangle of the window; Adam had already got as far as choosing one of the compartments formed by the intersection of the bars; owing to his bad taste, or perhaps accidentally, he had chosen the eighth, starting from the left. In any case, whether his choice had been deliberate or no, Adam was well aware that, according to Manilius, the Eighth Celestial House is that of Death. Knowing this made it virtually impossible for him to be sincere; there was no importance in anything he might imagine or believe on the basis of this single fact (irrespective of the data relating to angles, quadrille, sextile, etc., whether or no they could be confirmed by the ecliptic, the North–South line, the meridian or the First Vertical, or assimilated to the famous points on the equator, 30° and 60°—Whether or no one agreed with Manilius that the Eighth Celestial House was potentially the Third); he had chosen to play that game as he might have played Battleships, Consequences, hopscotch or Animal, Vegetable or Mineral—prepared from the start to keep to the basic rules.

That having been said, it was not too exactly himself, any longer. And what is more, it was not too exactly the window-bars either; it was six crosses intermingled, in the style of:

Elohim ADONAI ZEBAOTH Eloher

199

which made frames for other symbols, such as Aglaon and Tetragrammaton, with 2 Maltese crosses, one inverted swastika, and one Star of David, or else Ego Alpha et Omega, or perhaps an alternation of Stars of David and suns.

If one had suddenly been transformed into that window, or if one had been facing Adam, one would have seen that he was sitting bolt upright on the raised edge of the mattress, with his head bent slightly forward and his hands resting on his knees, like someone just looking at the time. Seen thus, he looked as though he were thinking or as though he felt cold. He kept on staring at the same point, to the left.

The floor beneath his parallel feet was covered with dark red tiles, which had once been glazed; they were hexagonal in shape, and so strictly geometrical as to resemble a scale model of the room itself. The light coming through the window must undergo prolonged reverberation, as though the walls were covered with bevelled mirrors. It was the shiny paint and the innumerable facets of its grainy surface that reflected the light and threw it back continuously from point to point. He, Adam, knew the room well, having inspected it carefully at the very beginning: he granted it, despite its small size, a familiar, even family appearance, in fact soothing. It was deep and hard and austere. Everything, particularly the walls, stood out in cold, unmistakable relief. Yet it was this very coldness that he appreciated, without seeing it; he did not dislike the matter of the place, because of the implication that a game was in progress, a game that required him, Adam, to adjust himself, to give way, and not the things around him. He knew he was succeeding, by stages; he remained hard, insensitized, motionless, and his temperature was going down. From 36.7°C. to 36.4°. Sitting to the right of his cigarette, he was bathed in the cream-coloured half-light, grainy, moist, with no thought of passing time. There were lots of such moments in the day. He had been collecting them since early childhood: for instance when you're lying in the bath and you feel the water changing gradually from hot to warm, warm to cool and cool to cold; and you lie stretched out, up to your chin in an alien element, looking up at the ceiling between two layers of steam and wondering how long the water will take to get icy cold again; you pretend you're in a boiling pot and that by sheer force of will (or of Zen) you're enduring the heat, getting the better of something like 100°C. You are destined to emerge shamefaced, deserted, naked or shivering.

And the bed: he often thought that later on, when he had money, he would get his bed put on wheels, and have himself pushed out of doors. He'd be warm, knowing it was cold outside, and he would keep himself to himself under the blankets, while remaining completely in touch with the outer world. The room was so cramped, so stifling, that he felt sure of this. That was perhaps what he wanted more than anything else. In any case it seldom happened to him, in fact hardly ever. He felt certain that if he fell asleep there he would have no need to turn over noiselessly in bed in the middle of the night and look all round, trying to understand what he was seeing, translating mentally, here an empty coat-stand, there a chair and a towel, further on the shadow of a bar enlarged by the moonlight, etc. No more need, before getting into bed, to learn by heart where things stood; no more need to lie with his head towards the door, so as to keep watch. Here there was a bolt on the door and bars across the window. He was enclosed, alone, the sole one of his kind, right at the centre.

Adam was listening slowly, without moving his eyes half an inch; there was nothing he needed. All sounds (the gurgle of water in the pipes, the dull thuds, the bursting of seed-pods, the cries from far away that came into the room, cut off one by one, the whispering of a fall of dust nearby, somewhere beneath a piece of furniture, the slight vibrations of the phagocytes, the tremulous awakening of a pair of moths because of a heavier knock on the other side of the wall) seemed to come from inside him. Beyond the walls there were more rooms, all of them rectangular, architecturally designed.

The same design was repeated in every section of the building, room, corridor, room, room, room, room, room, room, room, room, room, W.C., room, corridor, etc. Adam was glad to detach himself like that, with 4 walls, 1 bolt and 1 bed. In the cold and in a clear light. It was comfortable, if not durable. One ended sooner or later by suspecting as much and calling for it.

Outside, outside the sun was perhaps still shining; there were clouds, perhaps, in little wisps or perhaps only half the sky was covered. That was all the rest of the town; one felt that people were living all around, in concentric circles, thanks to the walls; one had, wasn't that so, a great many streets, going in all directions; they divided the blocks of houses into triangles or quadrilaterals; these streets were full or cars and bicycles. By and large, everything was repetition. One was practically sure to find the same planes a hundred yards further on, with exactly the same basis angle of 35° and the stores, the garages, the tobacconists, the leather goods shops. Adam was working out the plan in his head and adding a lot of things to it. If you took an angle of 48.3°, for instance, well, you could be sure of finding it somewhere in the Plan. It would be a funny thing if there were no place for that angle at Chicago; and then, after finding it again, one need only look at the drawing to realize at once what had to be done. At that rate Adam could never get lost. It was the curves that were the hardest; he didn't understand how to react there. The best thing was to draw a graph; the circle was less complicated: one only had to square it (so far as possible, of course) and decompose it into a polygon: then there were angles, and one was saved. For instance he would extend the side GH of the polygon and get a straight line. Or he could even extend two sides, GH and KL, which would give him the equilateral triangle GLz, and then he would know what to do.

The world, like Adam's pyjamas, was striped with straight lines, tangents, vectors, polygons, rectangles, trapezoids of all kinds, and the network was perfect; no parcel of land or sea but was divided with great precision and could be reduced to a projection or a diagram.

In fact one need only start out with a polygon of about 100 sides, drawn on a piece of paper, and one would be sure of finding one's way about, anywhere in the world. By walking on along the streets, following one's own vectorial inspiration, one might perhaps even—who can say?—get as far as America or Australia. At Chu-Cheng, on the Chang, a little hollow house with walls of papyrus is waiting patiently in sunshine and shade, amid the soft rustle of leaves, for the messiah-surveyor who, compass in hand, will one day come to reveal the obtuse angle that is splitting it asunder. And many others as well, in Nyasaland, in Uruguay or in the heart of Vercors, all over the world, on stretches of arid, eroding land, among the bushes of broom, covered with millions of angles swarming like vermin, with millions of squares as fatal as signs of death, of straight lines splitting the sky on the far horizon with lightning gestures. One ought to have gone everywhere. One ought to have had a good plan, plus faith; a complete confidence in Plane Geometry and a Hatred of all that is curved, all that undulates, sins on the side of pride, the circle or the terminal.

In the room at that moment, with the daylight coming in

through the window, leaping forward and back in all directions and enfolding him as though in a sheet of sparks; with the cool, monotonous sound of waters; Adam was growing more tense; he was watching and listening intently, he felt himself growing, becoming a giant; he saw the walls extending to infinity, squares being added to squares, larger and larger, always a little larger; and little by little the whole earth was covered with this scribble, lines and planes intersecting with sharp cracks like rifle-shots, marked at their intersections by big sparks that fell away like round balls and he, Adam Pollo, Adam P . . . , Adam, not severed from the Pollo clan, was in the centre, right at the heart, with the drawing all made out, all ready for him to take to the road, and walk, go from angle to angle, from segment to vector, and name the lines by scratching their letters in the ground with his forefinger: xx', yy', zz', aa', etc., etc.

Quite naturally Adam took his eyes off the eighth intersection of the bars and let himself fall backwards on the bed. He reflected that he still had two or three hours before supper-time. After that he would smoke his last cigarette of the day, and go to sleep. He had asked for paper and a black ball-point pen as well; but those were evidently not allowed, for the nurse had not mentioned the subject that morning, nor at lunch time. In any case he realized he had nothing much left to write. He had lost the wish to do anything tiring. He wanted to eat, drink, urinate, sleep, etc., taking his own time, in the cool, in the silence, in a kind of comfort. He had a vague impression that there were trees over there, all round. Perhaps one day they'd let him go out in the garden, in his pyjamas. Then he could carve his name surreptitiously on the tree-trunks, like that girl Cécile J. had done on the cactus leaf. He would steal a fork to do it with, and dig it in hard, in capital letters. Then the name would harden slowly into a scar, under the action of sun and rain, for a long time—for twelve years or twenty, for as long as a tree lives:

ADAM POLLO   ADAM POLLO

He threw the bolster off the bed and laid his head flat on the mattress; then he stretched his legs as far as possible, so that his feet stuck out beyond the end of the bed. The night-table was on his right, close beside his head; it had two movable aluminium shelves without doors. On the bottom shelf there was an empty chamber pot. On the top shelf were: a pair of sun-glasses with gilt wire frames; one bottle of tranquillizer pills with passiflora and quinine as their chief ingredients; one cigarette, but no matches— when he wanted a light he had to ring for the nurse; one handkerchief; *La Sarre et son Destin*, by Jacques Dircks-Dilly, out of the hospital library; one glass of water, half full; one white comb; one photo of Zsa-Zsa Gabor, cut out of a magazine. All the furniture and cubic space in the room was supposed to form a setting for Adam alone, as he lay flat on the bed with his arms at an oblique angle and his feet together, as though crucified in sloth and repose.

And, a little before 6 in the afternoon, long after he had finished his cigarette and his thoughts—if they could be so called—the nurse pushed back the outside bolt and came into the room. She found Adam asleep. She had to put a hand on his shoulder in order to wake him. She was a young woman, and attractive, but so completely annihilated by her nurse's uniform that it was impossible to make out her age or whether she was really pretty or really commonplace. Her hair was tinted a red-gold shade and her palish complexion stood out against the beige walls of the room.

Without saying a word, she picked up the plastic ashtray

205

from the floor where Adam had deposited it, and emptied it into the slop-pail. Time did not in any case pass quickly in this place; and the position she thus suddenly took up, for some obscure reason deriving, perhaps, from the thousands of hours she had given to waiting on the mentally sick, seemed to place her in contradiction to herself, render her more ridiculous, reduce her by repercussion to four colour-slides projected on walls which had become a screen; her body bent sharply at hip-level and stayed like that, stuck, for an indefinite period of time. Awakening echoes of toil and distress in the world, memories of days without food, of degradation and old age. Abolishing all colour-contrasts by a succession of possible movements on different planes where a watery grey was dominant. Driving to madness whoever had the misfortune to catch sight of her and to shut his eyes immediately afterwards. For now the colours were reversed—her white face and apron were ink-black, the once-yellow walls powdered with a sort of cloak of bitter slate-grey and every cool, soothing colour suddenly transformed to a hellish atrocity. Nightmare drew close, pressing against the temples, making every object shrink or expand at its will. The woman seen just now was a medium putting the final touch to delirium in its most horrible form—the fear of going really mad. She clung to the eyeballs like a twining root, multiplying her faces to infinity. Her eyes were immense, wide open like caverns. She emerged from a dark pyrosphere, shattered the ramparts of the background like glass, and stood there, half-revealed, bending over a world simulated in her own image, awaiting some infinitesimal changes. Slowly she shrivelled, until her bones could be seen; until she resembled a drawing traced heavily with the pen, a pattern stamped on some object made of snake-skin; some figure, or rather some strange letter, a capital Gamma, piercing the brain through and through. Within a few seconds she had been devoured by incandescent fire, she had overthrown boundaries; in the ebb and flow that was now slowing down she stood motionless, became mechanical, was transformed into a dead bough that the flames have left behind. She offered every possibility of lingering in her torment, a thousand ways of perpetuating her gesture; Adam's choice was to sit up up the edge of the bed. Then, drained of all volition, he waited for the nurse to begin moving again; her movement led up to words, pleasant ones, for she asked:

'Well? Had a nice nap?'

And he replied:

'Yes, thank you, very nice,' adding, 'Have you come to do the room?'

She moved the slop-pail a few inches before saying:

'That I have not. You should do a little work yourself today, don't you think? We can't afford to pay for chambermaids for you here, you know. So make your bed, nice and tidily, and then sweep the floor a bit. I've brought you a broom and a dust-pan. All right?'

'All right . . .' said Adam. 'But . . .' he added, looking with curiosity at the young woman, 'But—shall I have to do this every day?'

'I should think so,' she retorted, 'Every morning. Today it was rather different, because you're new here. But from now on you'll have to get down to work every morning at ten o'clock. And if you're a good boy you'll soon be allowed out, like the others. You'll be able to go out in the garden and read, or dig flowerbeds, or talk to the rest of them. You'd like to go out in the garden, wouldn't you? You'll see. You'll enjoy being here. They'll give you little jobs to do, making little wicker baskets, or decorations. There's even a carpenter's shop with all the gadgets, planes, electric saws and so forth. You'll see, you'll enjoy it. Provided you do just as you're told, you understand? To be going on with, make your bed now, and sweep the floor. Like that, everything will be tidy for visiting time.'

Adam nodded, got up, and set to work at once. He did it well, while the young woman in her white uniform watched him. When he had finished, he turned to her and asked:

'Will that do?'

'Is the pot empty?'

'Yes,' said Adam.

'Good. Then that'll do. We shall get along splendidly.' She picked up the slop-pail and added:

'Right. Visiting time is an hour from now.'

'Is someone coming to see me?' queried Adam.

'I'll come and call you then.'

'Is someone coming to see me?' he asked again.

'I should just think so.'

'Who? My mother? Tell me.'

'Half a dozen gentlemen will be round to see you an hour from now, with the head doctor.'

'From the police?' Adam asked.

'Oh no,' she laughed, 'Not from the police.'

'Then who?'

'Some gentlemen who're interested in you, you inquisitive boy! Some very solid citizens, who can't wait to meet you! You'll behave nicely, won't you?'

'Who are they?'

'They're what I've told you. Half a dozen of them. Very much interested in you.'

'Journalists?'

'Yes, that's it. Journalists, in a way.'

'They're going to write some stuff about me?'

'Well, that's to say—they're not exactly journalists. They won't talk about you in the papers, certainly . . .'

'Then they're the people I saw when I came in here?'

The nurse picked up everything she had to carry away, and took hold of the door-handle with her left hand.

'Oh no, not them. Young men like yourself. They'll come to the infirmary with the head doctor and ask you questions. You must get on the right side of them. They may be able to help you.'

'You mean coppers, don't you?' Adam persisted.

'Students,' said the nurse as she left the room, carrying the slop-pail. 'Students, if you must know.'

Adam went to sleep again till they arrived, at about ten past seven.

The nurse woke him as she had done the first time, shaking him by the shoulder, told him to make water, to straighten his pyjamas and comb his hair, and then led him to the door of a room just across the corridor. She left him to go in alone.

The room was even smaller than his own cell, and full of people sitting on chairs. There was a medicine cupboard in one corner and a weighing-machine in another, to show that this was the infirmary. Adam made his way between the seated people, found an empty chair at the far end of the room, and sat down on it. He sat there for a little time in silence. The other people seemed to take no notice of him. Except when Adam asked a girl who was sitting next to him whether she happened to have a cigarette; she said yes, opened her black leather handbag and held out the packet to him. They were rather expensive Virginia cigarettes, Blacks or Du Mauriers. Adam asked if he might take three or four. The girl told him to keep the whole packet. Adam took it, thanked her, and began to smoke. After a few minutes he raised his head and looked at them; there were seven in all, young ones, some male, some female, aged between nineteen and twenty-four, and a doctor, a man of about forty-eight. None of them was looking at him. They were talking in undertones. Three of the young ones were making notes. A fourth was reading something in an exercise-book; this was the girl who'd given him her packet of cigarettes. She was twenty-one and a bit, her name was Julienne R., and as it happened she was slim and astonishingly pretty; she had fair hair twisted into a chignon and a beauty-spot above her right ankle; she was wearing a dark blue cotton dress that had a leather belt lined with gold plastic. Her mother was Swiss. Her father had died of an ulcer ten years ago.

She was the first who really looked at Adam. She gazed at him with grave eyes, faintly dark-circled, full of gracious understanding. Then she folded her arms, locking her little finger into the bend at each elbow, scarcely moving the tips of the first fingers, and craned her neck slightly forward, more than usual. Her forehead had a faint suggestion of something childish, yet material; it was broad but not vulgarly so, it made way naturally for the roots of her hair, which began by parting to right and left and was then brought up at the back of the head and coiled down again at the end of a twisted parting.

She was unquestionably the one who had listened most to the others, whether to the doctor or to her fellow students. One could sense this in her remarkably well-proportioned features; they had a symmetry which, instead of hardening the lower part of the face, particularly the lips, gave an added tenderness, an extra touch of enquiry. She opened her mouth slightly in breathing, and gazed unblinkingly. Her gaze, by infinitesimal degrees, bore down Adam's, took on a thousand presumed emotions, a thousand delicate touches, an intimacy as powerful as sin, as perfect as incestuous love. She was a citadel of consciousness and knowledge, not vindictive, not violent, but almost senile in its sweet confidence.

She was the first to speak; at the nodded permission of

the doctor, she leant slightly forward towards Adam, as though to take him by the hands. But her arms were still folded. She said, in her deep voice:

'Have you been here long?'

'No . . .' said Adam.

'How long?'

Adam hesitated.

'A day? Two days? Three days? Or more?'

Adam smiled.

'Yes, that's it—three or four days, I think . . .'

'You think?——'

'Three or four days?' asked a boy in dark glasses.

Adam hesitated again.

'Do you like being here?' asked Julienne.

'Yes,' said Adam.

'Where are you?' asked another girl, whose surname was Martin.

'Do you know where you are, here? What the place is called?'

'Er——the lunatic asylum,' said Adam.

'And why you're there?' asked the Martin girl.

'Why you're here?' Julienne repeated after her.

Adam pondered this.

'The coppers brought me here,' he said. The girl made a note—of his reply, no doubt—in her exercise-book. A lorry was grinding up a steep bit of road, somewhere outside the window. The dull roar of its engine came into the infirmary like the drone of a bluebottle, weaving a web of sound-waves between the white-tiled walls; it was a garbage-lorry, no doubt, climbing the mimosa-bordered hill that leads to the incinerating plant. Lead pipes, rolls of cardboard and heaps of springs would fall pellmell over the sides of the artificial mountain, waiting to be thrust into the annihilating flames.

'How long will they keep you here?' asked Julienne R.

'I don't know—they haven't told me.'

Another young man, a tallish boy on the other side of the room, raised his voice now:

'And how long have you been here?'

Adam looked pensively at him.

'I've told you already. Three or four days.'

The girl glanced round and made a sign of disapproval at the young man. Then she went on again, in a slightly softer voice:

'What's your name?'

'Adam Pollo,' said Adam.

'And your parents?'

'The same.'

'No—I mean, your parents? They're still alive?'

'Yes.'

'Do you live with them?'

'Yes.'

'You always have done?'

'Yes, I think so.'

'You have lived somewhere else?'

'Yes—once . . .'

'When was that?'

'Not long ago.'

'And where was it?'

'It was on a hill. There was an empty house.'

'And you lived in that?'

'Yes.'

'Were you comfortable?'

'Yes.'

'You were alone there?'

'Yes.'

'Didn't you see anybody? Didn't anyone come to see you?'

'No.'

'Why not?'

'Because they didn't know where I was.'

'Did you like that?'

'Yes.'

'But you don't sug . . .'

'It was nice. A fine house. And the hill was nice, too. One could see the road at the bottom. I used to sunbathe with nothing on.'

'You like that?'

'Yes.'

'You don't like wearing clothes?'

'Not when it's hot.'

'Why not?'

'Because one has to button them. I don't like buttons.'

'What about your parents?'

'I'd left them.'

'And gone away?'

Adam took a flake of tobacco out of his mouth.

'Yes.'

'Why did you go away?'

'Where from?'

The girl jotted down something in her exercise-book; now it was she who hesitated, hanging her head. Adam saw that the parting turned round the top of her head in an S shape. Then she looked up and her big, heavy, sleepy eyes rested on Adam again. They were huge eyes, blue, intelligent, inflexibly and resolutely hypnotic. Her voice seemed to flow along her gaze and slide to the depths of Adam's guts. Before it reached maturity, three other questions, fired at him by two girls and a boy, were left unanswered:

'Are you ill?'

'How old are you?'

'You say you don't like clothes. But—do you specially like being naked?'

At last Julienne R's words burst out from the midst of a kind of fog, like a spark running through damp gunpowder. Like a match used for picking one's ear, on which the wax-coated phosphorus is consumed without a flame and gives off an acid smell of singed flesh. Like a burning torch thrusting through the opposing layers of water.

'Why did you leave your parents' house?'

Adam had not heard this; she repeated, without annoyance, as though speaking into a microphone:

'Why did you leave your parents' house?'

'I had to go,' said Adam.

'But why?'

'I don't quite remember,' he began. They all made notes of this. Only Julienne R. did not lower her head.

'I mean to say——'

'Were you in trouble?'

'Had you quarrelled with your parents?'

Adam waved his hand. The ash from his cigarette fell on Julienne's shoe; 'Excuse me,' he murmured, and then went on:

'No, not in trouble, exactly. Put it this way, I ought to have gone a long time before. I thought——'

'Yes? You thought?' asked the girl. She seemed to be really listening.

'I thought it would be better,' said Adam. 'I wasn't having trouble with my parents, no but—— Perhaps I was just giving way to a childish need to be alone . . .'

'Children are usually pretty sociable,' said the boy with dark glasses.

'Yes, if you like—— Yes, that's true, they are pretty sociable. But at the same time they try to establish a kind of—how can I put it?—a kind of faculty of communication with nature. I think they want—they easily give way to purely egocentric—anthropomorphic—needs. They try to find a way of getting inside things, because they're afraid of their own personality. It's as though their parents had made them want to minimize themselves. Parents make their children into *things*—they treat them like objects of poss—like objects that can be possessed. They give this object psychosis to their children. So some children are afraid of company, of the company of grown-ups, because of a vague inkling that they're on an equal footing there. It's equality they're afraid of. They have to play their part. Something's expected of them. So they choose to withdraw. They try to find some way of having their own universe, a rather—well—mythical universe, a make-believe universe where they're on a level with dead matter. Or rather, where they feel they've got the upper hand. Yes, they'd rather feel superior to plants and animals and what have you, and inferior to grown-ups, than on an equality with anything at all. If necessary they'll even reverse the situation, making the plants play their role, the children's role, while they play at being grown-ups. You see, for a kid, a Colorado beetle is always more like a man than another kid. I—yes . . .'

By this time the girl was bolt upright on her chair. Her eyes were shining like spectacles; she was frowning, as though in thought. The weighty appearance of her brow and nose had altered a little, deviating into a kind of snobbish pleasure at the incongruous encounter between elements reputed to be incompatible; it was like writing whimsical associations of words right in the middle of a blank page. This kind of thing:
'proton—already'
  'Jesus—bather'
    'grandmother—cracker'
      'island—belly'

One would have said she was now showing the reverse side of her mask; she seemed like, heaven knows what, a young Methodist girl who'd discovered a spelling mistake in a paragraph of the Bible—she looked half amused and half disgusted.

The boy in dark glasses leant forward and said:

'But you—you're not a child any longer!' The others giggled; the doctor cut them short by saying:

'Please, please. We are not here to amuse ourselves. I suggest you go on with your interview. Though I warn you that so far it's not very satisfactory. How can you expect to form any interesting ideas unless you manage the questions and answers better? You put your questions anyhow, at random, you pay no attention to the patient's behaviour, and then you're surprised that you can't diagnose the trouble. You let the clues escape you.'

He got up, took the spectacled student's notebook from him, glanced at it briefly and handed it back.

'You don't know how to set about the thing,' he said, and sat down again. 'You jot down a whole lot of useless details in your notebooks. You put "doesn't remember how long he's been in hospital—three or four days", and further on, "doesn't remember why he left home," and then, "doesn't like wearing clothes. Reason: dislikes buttons." That's all quite pointless. Whereas what might have been interesting, you don't mention—instead of writing all that, you need only have put: lapses of memory—sexual obsession accompanied by rejection of responsibility through fabulization —and there you would have had the beginnings of a diagnosis. But never mind, go ahead.'

Turning to Julienne R., he added:

'Come along, Mademoiselle. You'd made a good beginning.'

Julienne R. thought for a moment. During this time,

there was silence except for the creaking of chairs, the rustle of one or two exercise-book pages, the swallowing of saliva, and a curious smell of sweat and urine given off by the walls of the infirmary, or perhaps by Adam himself. He had managed to prop his elbows on his knees without hunching his shoulders too much, and in this position, with his right arm quite vertical, his hand was level with his chin and the butt-end of his cigarette just opposite his mouth. It was a pose carefully calculated to involve the minimum of effort. Allowing for the uncomfortable effect, in this company, of striped pyjamas and hair cut too short, almost shaved, and for the general chilly atmosphere of the infirmary, Adam was getting along fairly well. With his long, lanky body, thin arms and closed mouth, he gave an impression of exceptional, eccentric intelligence together with a slight tendency to pose. Moreover, his bare feet in their felt slippers were exactly parallel. One could see he had ceased to expect anything much—a breath of air, perhaps, a little fresh-turned soil, the sound of a wash-basin emptying; he had been a long time in the world, there was nothing about him that could be restored to life or firmly resist the heavy gaze of the fair-haired girl with the pair of blue eyes, deep as bottles, strained, avid to encircle the whole world, himself included, in the power of knowledge. He could read her, and the rest of the group, like a postcard. But he stopped at that. And he was outstripped, carried away on a black stream, amid whirlpools of pulverized granite, between the shifting layers of immense zinc plates where he was reflected an infinite number of times, a solitary, weedy man.

Julienne R. did not look at the others again. It was difficult to tell whether she was ashamed, afraid, or what. She said:

'Why are you here? Why are you here?'

It might pass for just another question; but it was almost a compassionate appeal, almost a diffuse love-formula. She repeated:

'Can you tell us—— Will you tell me why? Why you're here? Do try to tell me . . .'

Adam refused. He took another cigarette out of the packet and lit it from the stub of the first; then he dropped the stub on the floor and crushed it out, lingeringly, with the toe of his slipper. The girl watched him, her fingers clenched on her exercise-book.

'You won't—tell me why you're here?'

The other girl, Martin, put in:

'You don't remember.'

One of the young men nibbled the end of his pencil.

'Just now you were saying something interesting. You were talking about children, about minimization, etc. Don't you think—don't you think that may be an obsession with you? I mean, mightn't it be that you assimilate yourself to these children? That is—I mean——'

'How old are you?' asked the boy with the dark glasses.

'Twenty-nine,' said Adam; then, turning to the first speaker:

'I see what you mean. But I don't feel one can answer that kind of question. I think—— Unless that belongs to the general attitude of a lunatic, a nut. In which case it wouldn't matter much if I answered yes or no.'

'Well then, why did you mention it to us?' asked the young man.

'To explain,' said Adam. 'I'd mentioned the solitary spirit of children. I wanted to explain it. Perhaps it wasn't worth while.'

'But it was you we were talking about.'

'Yes, of course—anyhow, it answered your question.'

'Because you're a case of micromania.'

'Or perhaps because one may still have something childish about one even at twenty-nine.'

The girl opened her mouth to say something, but she was forestalled:

'Have you done your national service?'

'Yes.'

'And your job?'

'What work were you doing?'

'Before?'

'Yes, before——?'

'I did all kinds of things,' said Adam.

'You had no settled job?'

'No——'

'What things have you done?'

'I don't know, really . . .'

'What work did you have that you enjoyed doing?'

'Odd jobs, I enjoyed them.'

'What odd jobs?'

'Well, washing cars, for instance.'

'But you——'

'I enjoyed being a bathing attendant, too. But I've never been able to do what I'd have liked. I'd have liked to be a chimney-sweep or a grave-digger or a lorry driver. But one needs references.'

'You wanted to do that all your life?'

'Why not? You do find old grave-diggers, you know . . .'

'But you've had a good education, haven't you?'

'Yes.'

'Have you any qualifications?'

'Yes, a few.'

'Wh——'

'I have a diploma in Regional Geography, for one thing . . .'

'Why didn't you make use of it?'

'I wanted to be an archaeologist—or an excavation over-seer, I don't quite remember which . . .'

'And——?'

'It didn't last . . .'

The fair-haired girl looked up and said:

'Honestly, I can't think what you're doing here——'

Adam smiled. 'You mean you don't think I'm a nut? is that it?'

She nodded. Her eyes were unfocused, inscrutable. She turned towards the head doctor and asked:

'Who said he was insane?'

The doctor stared hard at her and then slowly drew his legs in under his chair.

'Listen, Mademoiselle. This should be a lesson to you. You always jump to conclusions before you have collected all the facts. At least wait till you have finished this conversation. You know what he did?'

She nodded, her brow slightly furrowed. The doctor's expression was amused.

'You know. Not all cases are equally simple. Not all cases are as simple as the last one. You remember, the sailor? This may surprise you, but the fact is that there are no extremes in madness. There is no real boundary between a madman who commits murder and one who seems perfectly harmless. You came here expecting to see extraordinary people, taking themselves for Napoleon or unable to utter two coherent words, and you're disappointed to find nothing of the kind. Sometimes, like today, you even come across a patient who is extremely intelligent.'

He paused, cautiously.

'Well, as this is an exceptionally difficult case, I will help you. According to you, the patient is quite sane. But let me tell you that the first psycho-pathological tests for which I gave instructions when he was admitted showed him to be not merely abnormal, but definitely insane. I'll read you the results . . .'

He picked up a sheet of paper and read:

'Systematized paranoid delirium.

Tendency to hypochondria.

Megalomania (sometimes reversing to micromania).

Persecution mania.

Theory of justified irresponsibility.

Sexual deviations.

Mental confusion.

In short, the patient is in a permanent manic-depressive state which may evolve towards confusion or even to acute psychotic delirium. In such cases as his the delirium takes on what I might call an orderly appearance, owing to memories of culture and to the patient's potential intelligence. But his condition is dominated by frequent changes of mood, relapses and depressive states, and most of all by mythomania, confusion, and the different phases of sexual obsession.'

The doctor passed his hand over the back of his neck, which was rather greasy although he rubbed it with lavender-water several times a day. He seemed to relish more and more the embarrassment he had brought upon his audience. In the case of Julienne R. he was particularly pleased. He leant slightly forward in her direction.

'So you see, Mademoiselle, we have come to very different conclusions. Try to check mine by continuing your conversation with M. Pollo. I am sure you will persuade him to say some very interesting things—— No, seriously, depressive patients respond tremendously to a sympathetic attitude. What do you say to that, M. Pollo?'

Adam had only heard the last words, all the rest having been uttered in a confidential tone intended only for the students. Adam glanced for a moment at the doctor and then at the tip of his cigarette, projecting, white and slender, from his fingers; and said:

'I'm sorry, I didn't hear the beginning of your question.' Then he lapsed into a kind of torpor. He could already feel himself slipping away from his real surroundings. Julienne R. cleared her throat and said:

'Very well—let's go on . . . What do you think? I mean, what do you think is going to happen to you?'

Adam looked up:

'What did you say?'

Julienne repeated: 'What do you think is going to happen to you now?'

Adam looked into the girl's eyes, two cavities that were almost familiar by this time; she had prominent brow ridges, so that the light falling from above cast two grey-blue shadows on her white cheeks, like the eye-holes of a plaster skull. Adam sighed faintly.

'I've just remembered a queer thing,' he said. 'I don't know what reminded me of it—it's funny . . .'

Looking at the edges of Julienne's eyelids, he went on:

'It was—let's say when I was twelve. I knew a funny chap, his name was Tweedsmuir, but they called him Sim, because his first name was Simon. Simon Tweedsmuir. He'd been brought up by the Jesuits, so there was a kind of style about him. He was friendly enough, in his own way, but he didn't talk much to the rest of us. He liked to keep himself to himself. I think it was because he knew that all we other fellows knew his father used to beat him with a stick. He would never talk about it to anyone. He was certainly the cleverest chap I've ever known, and yet he was always at the bottom of the form. But you could feel he could have been top if he'd wanted to. Once he had a bet with another boy that he would come out top in Latin composition and algebra. And he did. And the funny thing is that nobody was surprised. Not even the boy who'd had the bet. I think Sim regretted it afterwards, because the masters began trying to take an interest in him. He got himself expelled from school on purpose and no one ever heard of him again. The only time he ever really spoke to me was at the end of the Christmas term, just before he left the school. He'd turned up that morning black and blue with bruises, and in the cloakroom at break he told me about his way of praying. He said he thought the only way to get nearer to God was to do over again, in spirit, what God had done in the material sense. One must gradually rise up through all the stages of creation. He had already spent two years as an animal; when I knew him he'd just got up to the next level, the Fallen Angels. He was going to have to worship Satan out and out, until he managed to establish perfect communication with him. You understand. Not merely what one might call a physical relationship with the Devil, like most saints or mystics. Like St. Anthony or the Curé d'Ars. Complete communication, that's to say a state where he would understand the Works of the Evil One, their aim, their relation to God, to the beasts and to mankind. Put it this way, God can be understood as well through his opposite, his Devil, as through Himself, in his own essence. Every evening for two and a half hours, Sim was giving himself up entirely to Satan. He had written prayers and hymns of praise to him; he made him offerings —sacrificing small animals, and sins. He'd tried magic too, rejecting what he felt to be too childish or too daring, in view of his age and of the twentieth century. It was a stage in the manner of the Khlystys, you know, or Baron Samedi. But the difference was that for Sim this was only one step in the religious life. Taken entirely for love of God. From a wish to re-enact the Creation in the spiritual sense. He'd determined——'

223

Adam paused, then decided to go on. The fair-haired girl was sitting very stiffly on the edge of her chair, and trembling. Her fingers had made damp sweat-marks on the cover of the exercise-book. Every now and then a shadow travelled along the line of her eyebrows, thrown by a flight of birds passing the window; after so many long-drawn-out words and memories there was no difference any more between her and the fabulous characters in dreams. The words were alive, or she was, or the unicorn and the Yink, or anything.

'Yes—he'd determined to get through his worship of Satan by the time he was about sixteen—sixteen or seventeen. So he would have four years left before coming of age, four years to devote to the stage of human beings. Then nine years for the Angels. And then, by the time he was thirty, if he worked without ever letting up, if he didn't indulge his personal ambitions or pleasures, he could have ceased to exist except in God, in Him, through Him and for Him. In the ineffable—bang in the ineffable. No longer Sim Tweedsmuir, but God in person. You see. You see.'

One would have said his words had rung strangely in the infirmary, that cramped little room with its white-tiled walls like the walls of a bathroom or a public lavatory; one would have said there was an immense rectangular emptiness somewhere on earth and that this altered the depths of the sentences and dimmed the meaning of the words.

'Tweedsmuir. Tweedsmuir' Sim Tweedsmuir. He never talked to me again after that, after that day. I believe I heard that he'd died some time ago. He must have caught syphilis somewhere, during his satanic period. While honouring the Devil with a tart. You see the kind of thing. In a way, yes, he was an intelligent fellow, and all that. If he'd managed to see it through, he'd have ended by getting into the newspapers.'

224

Adam gave a short laugh. 'You know the funny thing about it? It's that if he'd been only the slightest bit more sociable lots of the chaps at school would have followed him, and his religion. I would have, for instance. But he didn't want any of that. He distrusted people. He wouldn't even listen if one mentioned Ruysbroek or Occam. In fact he had a petty side to him, and that was his downfall . . .'

'You're sure you didn't follow him a little way all the same—I mean his religion, his doctrine?' Julienne asked.

'How old did you say he was?' added the boy with the dark glasses.

'Who, Sim?'

'Yes.'

'He must have been a little older than me, about fourteen or fifteen . . .'

'Yes, that makes it easier to understand. It must have been the kind of mysticism kids do invent for themselves at that age—no?'

'You mean it was unsophisticated?'

'Yes, and I——'

'That's true. But it was rather fine, all the same. I think—I think if one remembers he was at the age for being confirmed, and all that, it seems rather fine, don't you think?'

'And you yourself thought it so fine——'

Julienne R. frowned, as though her head had suddenly begun to ache.

'——so fine that you followed him, didn't you?'

The head doctor agreed with this. 'Yes, that was it,' he said. 'And I would even go further and ask whether you are sure the whole story isn't about you. This Sim what-d'you-call-him—did he really exist?'

'Sim *Tweedsmuir*,' said Adam.

He shrugged his shoulders; the cigarette was burning the

nail of his first finger and once again he had to crush it out on the floor with the toe of his slipper.

'After all, I . . . I couldn't tell you. I mean it doesn't really matter whether it was I or he, you understand? In fact it doesn't really matter whether it was you or me or him.'

He thought for a moment, then swung round to face the fair girl and asked abruptly:

'What have you put me down as? A schizophrenic?'

'No, a paranoiac,' replied Julienne.

'Really?' said Adam, 'I thought—I thought you'd have put me down as a schizophrenic.'

'Why?'

'I don't know. I don't know. I thought so. I don't know.'

Adam asked if he couldn't have a cup of coffee. He pretended he was thirsty, or cold, but what he really wanted was to make a slight change in the appearance of the room. He was tired of being in an infirmary, with infirmary chairs, an infirmary discussion, an infirmary smell and a great infirmary emptiness. Anyhow the doctor rang for the nurse and asked her to bring a cup of coffee.

His cup of coffee came very quickly; he put it down on his left knee and began stirring it slowly, to melt the sugar. He drank in sips, seldom raising his head. There was something in his mind, a kind of swelling; he couldn't make out what it was. It might be like the memory of a dead person, the absurd idea of someone being dead and gone. Or, at a pinch, like being on a boat at night and remembering thousands of things, the waves for instance, and the gleams that are hidden by the darkness.

'So you don't know—do you know what you're going to do now?' Julienne began again; then she broke off and asked 'Can you let me have a cigarette?'

226

Adam held out the packet. She lit her cigarette with a little mother-of-pearl lighter she took out of her handbag. She had clearly forgotten the others, and that might mean, at a pinch, that she would soon forget Adam too.

'You don't know what will happen to you . . .'

Adam made a gesture that brought his hand down on his trouser-leg, a fraction of an inch away from the kneecap.

'No—but I have a pretty good idea, and that's enough for me.'

She made a last effort to talk to him.

'So there's nothing you want?'

'Yes there is—why?'

'Well, what do you want? To die?'

'Oh, not at all!' smiled Adam. 'I don't in the least want to die.'

'You want——'

'You know what I want? I want to be left in peace. No, not exactly that, perhaps . . . But I want lots of things. To do what isn't me. To do what I'm told. The nurse told me when I first came that I must be good. There! That's what I'm going to do. I'm going to be good. No, I don't really want to die. Because—because it can't be so very restful to be dead. It's like before birth. One must be bursting with eagerness to be born again. I think I should find that tiring.'

'You've had enough of being by yourself . . .'

'Yes, that's it. I want to be with people now.'

He breathed in the smoke as it came out of Julienne's nostrils.

'I'm like that bloke in the Bible, you know, Gehazi, the servant of Elisha. Naaman had been told to bathe seven times in the Jordan, or something like that. To cure his leprosy. When he was cured he sent Elisha a present, but Gehazi kept it all for himself. So then, to punish him, God

227

gave him Naaman's leprosy. You understand? I'm Gehazi. I've caught Naaman's leprosy.'

'You know what?' said Julienne—'Do you know what are the most beautiful lines of poetry ever written? It seems pretentious, of course, but I'd like to say them to you. May I?'

Adam nodded. She began:

'It goes: "*Voire, ou que je*——" '

But her voice faltered. She cleared her throat and began again:

'*Voire, ou que je vive sans vie
Comme les images, par coeur.
Mort!*'

She looked to the left of Adam, a couple of inches to the left. 'That's by Villon. Did you know it?'

Adam drank some coffee and made a negative gesture with his hand. He looked at the others, who had been listening, a little embarrassed, a little ironical. And he wondered why he was left in pyjamas the whole blessed day. So he shouldn't escape, perhaps? And perhaps, in spite of the vertical stripes, the things were not pyjamas. This might be the uniform worn in an asylum, or by sick people. Adam picked up the coffee cup from his knee and drank the rest. A little damp sugar was left at the bottom. He scraped it out with the spoon and licked it. He would have liked another cup of coffee, dozens of cups of coffee. He would have liked to talk about it, too. To the fair-haired girl, perhaps. He'd have liked to say to her, stay with me, in this house, stay with me and we'll make coffee at any time of the day or night, and then drink it together; there would be a big garden all round, and we could walk about in it until morning, in the dark, with the planes flying overhead. The young man with dark glasses took off his glasses and looked at Adam.

'If I've got it right,' he said, 'the idea of your friend's religion was a kind of pantheism—or mysticism. A sort of link with God by means of knowledge? The path of certitude, what?'

Julienne R. added:

'But what does it all matter to you? This stuff about mysticism? What does it all mean? Does it really interest you so much?'

Adam flung himself back in his chair, almost violently.

'You haven't understood. Not in the very least. It's not God that interests me, you see. It wasn't God for Sim either. Not God as such, as the creator, or what have you. Responding to a sort of craving for the final or the absolute, there, like a key unlocking a door. Good heavens, you'll never understand in that way! That doesn't interest me. I don't need to have been created. It's like this discussion. It doesn't interest me for what it is, for what it appears to be. Only because it fills a vacuum. A terrible, unbearable vacuum. Between two levels of life . . . Between two stages, two periods, you see what I mean?'

'But then what good does it do, all this mystical stuff?' asked the spectacled student.

'None at all. Absolutely none. It's as though you were talking to me in a language I don't understand. What good do you expect it to do? I can't tell you. It would be like trying to explain why I'm not you—— Take Ruysbroek, for instance; what good did it do him to draw distinctions between the material elements, earth, air, fire and water? It might have been poetry, of course. But it wasn't. Mysticism served to raise him to the level—not the psychological level, eh? not that—the level of the ineffable. It doesn't matter where that level lay. No matter what level. The important thing is that at a certain moment in his life he believed he had understood everything. Since he had made the connection with what he had always called God, and that God being by definition eternal, omniscient, omnipotent and omnipresent, Ruysbroek too was all those things. At least during his attacks of mysticism. And towards the end he may even have been permanently at his level, his state of full effusion. That's it. It isn't knowing that matters, it's knowing one knows. It's a state in which culture, knowledge, speech and writing become worthless. By and large, if you like, it might be a sort of comfort. But never an end in itself, you see, never an end in itself. And at that level, of course, there haven't been so very many real mystics. You understand—speaking in the dialectical manner—but the relationship is different, of course—or perhaps one is oneself. It's simply a state. But when you get down to it, it's the only possible outcome of knowledge. In any other way, knowledge leads to a dead end. And then it ceases to be knowledge. It takes a form in the past tense. Whereas there it's suddenly exaggerated, it becomes so enormous, so overwhelming, that nothing else matters. One is that one is—— Yes, that's it. To be is being . . .'

Mlle R. gave a faint shake of the head; her lower lip quivered, as though she were torn between contradictory ideas.

'Very clever, all that,' said the spectacled fellow, 'But that's all one can say for it . . .'

'It's meaningless, a lot of metaphysical bombast,' another student interrupted. The spectacled fellow went on:

'I don't know—I don't know if it has occurred to you that it's a kind of argument that has no end to it. Like the reflections in a triple mirror. Because, for instance, I can reply that one is that one is that one is that one is. And so forth. It seems to me to be more like rhetoric. The type of rhetoric that amuses a boy of twelve. Syllogisms. This kind of thing: a boat takes six days to cross the Atlantic, therefore six boats will take one day.'

'I don't——'

'Because, because the concept of existence implies a unity. A unity which is the consciousness of being. And because this consciousness of being is not the same as its definition in words, which can be multiplied *ad infinitum*. Like anything imaginary. There's no reason why it should ever stop. Eh?'

'That's not true,' said Adam. 'That's not true. Because you're making a confusion. You're confusing existence as real experience with existence as *cogito*, as the point from which thought starts and to which it returns. You think I'm talking about psychological concepts. That's what I dislike about you. You're always trying to drag in your blasted analytical systems, your psychological stunts. You've adopted a particular system of psychological values, once and for all. Useful for analysis. But you don't see, you don't see that I'm trying to make you think—of a much wider system. Something that goes further than psychology. I'm trying to get you to think of a huge system. Of a kind of universal thought. Of a purely spiritual state. Something representing the culmination of reasoning, the culmination of metaphysics, of psychology, philosophy, mathematics, the lot. Yes, it's exactly that: what's the culmination of everything? It's to be to be.'

He switched to Julienne R.

'It's because just now I said something about a state of ecstasy. So you assumed it was a psychological condition. Something that will yield to treatment. Something like paranoid pathological delirium and so forth. I don't give a damn for that. I'll try to tell you what it is, and have done with it. After that, don't ask me what I think about Parmenides, because I shan't be able to tell you any longer . . .'

Adam pushed his chair back and wedged his shoulders against the wall. It was a cold, solid, white-tiled wall that one could easily take into partnership, either for a struggle or for a doze. Besides, it would certainly re-echo the vibrations of Adam's vocal chords, transmitted through his back, and carry them all over the room, thus sparing him the fatigue of speaking loudly. Adam explained, his words hardly articulated:

'I could tell you about something that happened a year or two ago, and which has nothing to do with stuff about God or self-analysis or anything of that kind—— Of course you're at liberty to analyze it by the usual psychological criteria if you want. But I don't think that would be any use. In fact that's the very reason why I'm choosing something that seems to have no connection with God, metaphysics and all that stuff.'

He stopped and looked at Julienne. He saw her face move almost imperceptibly, at the base of the nostrils and round the eyes, as though stirred by some complicated rage. And suddenly, without anyone else having noticed the change, he felt terribly ridiculous. He bent forward, away from the supporting wall, exposing himself to the biting gaze of his enemies. And he said calmly, aware throughout his being that only this fair-haired girl could understand him:

'Yes . . .'

At intervals of 7 seconds he said again:

'Yes—— Yes.'

She said: 'Go on.'

Adam reddened. He drew his legs in under his chair, as though about to get up. It was as though thanks to those few seconds, to a dark-ringed glance from an unknown girl and to the words 'Go on', brought out in a muffled tone after an infinitesimal mental hesitation, a pact of friendship had been signed between them. In her turn she crushed out her cigarette end with the toe of her black court shoe. In form and substance, the situation curiously resembled that of a man and woman, strangers to each other, suddenly aware of having been photographed side by side by some street photographer.

'It's not worth it,' Adam grunted, 'you don't like the anecdotal style.'

She said nothing, simply bent her head; not quite as low as the first time, however, so that only the front half of the S came into view. On the other hand the movement was sufficient to loosen the front of her dress, and Adam saw two silver threads, the two sides of a chain, that met in the cleft of her breasts. The chain certainly ended lower down, between the cups of her brassière, with a little mother-of-pearl cross, or a medal of the Virgin set in aquamarines. The idea of concealing something rather sacred, the picture of a divinity, against the most eminently biological part of a woman's body was slightly fantastic. It was childish, touching, or else pretentious. Adam looked round at the others. Except for the spectacled student, who was writing in his notebook, and the Martin girl, who was talking to the head doctor, they all showed signs of weariness. Embarrassment had given way to boredom and was taking strange, nightmarish forms, prompting, it seemed, a perpetual repetition of the same gestures, sounds and smells.

Adam sensed that this might last for another fifteen minutes, certainly not more, and decided to make the most of what time remained to him.

'No, I'll tell you, it's not worth while. For one thing you don't like the anecdotal style, and for another thing, in a way, from the point of view of truth, from a realistic standpoint, that's not it, either . . .'

'Why not?' said Julienne.

233

'Because it's literature. Just that. I know we're all more or less literary, but it won't do any longer. I'm really tired of—— It's bound to happen, because one reads too much. One feels obliged to put everything forward in a perfect form. One always feels called upon to illustrate the abstract idea by an example of the latest craze, rather fashionable, indecent if possible, and above all—and above all, quite unconnected with the question. Good Lord, how phoney it all is! It stinks of fake lyricism, memories, childhood, psychoanalysis, the springtime of life and the history of the Christian religion. One writes cheap novelettes full of masturbation, sodomy, Waldensians and sexual behaviour in Melanesia, when it isn't the poems of Ossian, Saint-Amant or the canzonettas placed in the tabulary by Francesco da Milano. Or 'Portrait of a Young Lady' by Domenico Veneziano. Shakespeare. Wilfred Owen. Joâo de Deus. Léoville Lhomme. Integralism. Fazil Ali Clinassi, etc. etc. And the mysticism of Novalis. And the song of Yupanqui Pachacutec:

> *Like a lily of the fields I was born*
> *Like a lily I grew tall*
> *Then time went by*
> *Old age came*
> *I withered*
> *And so died.*

And Quipucamayoc. Viracocha. Capacocha-Guagua. Hatunrincriyoc. Intip-Aclla. The promises of Menephtah. Jethro. David's kinah. Seneca the Tragedian. Anime, parandum est. Liberi quondam mei, vos pro paternis sceleribus poenas date. And all that: Markovitch cigarettes, the Coupe Vétiver, Wajda, Cinzano ashtrays, ball-point pens, *my* ball-point pen, BIC No. 576—reproduction

234

"APPROVED 26/8/58, Pat. Off." All that. Eh? Is it correct?
Does it mean anything? Is it correct?'

Adam ran his hand through his close-cropped hair. He
felt that the gesture gave him an American air.

'You know what?' he said, 'You know what? We spend
our time turning out rubbishy cinema. Yes, cinema. Theatre
as well, and psychological novels. There's hardly any
simplicity left in us, we're croakers, half-portions. Weary
Willies. You'd think we'd been invented by some writer
of the 'thirties, who'd wanted us to be affected, handsome,
refined, full of culture, full of filthy culture. It sticks to
my back like a wet coat. It sticks to me all over.'

'Eh—what *is* simple, at that rate?' The rather ill-timed
interruption came from the spectacled student.

'How d'you mean, what's simple? Don't you know?
Haven't you even the faintest idea, then?' Adam's hand
went to his pocket in search of the packet of cigarettes, but
stopped, tense, before getting there.

'Do you really not see it, life, life the whore, all round
you? You don't see that people are alive, alive, that they're
eating, etc.? That they're happy? You don't see that the
man who wrote "the earth is blue like an orange" is a
lunatic or a fool?—— Of course not, you say to yourself
there's a genius, he's dislocated reality in a couple of words.
You run them off, "blue, earth, orange". It's beautiful.
Whatever you like. But I personally need a system, or I
go mad. Either the earth is orange or the orange is blue.
But in the system that consists of employing words, the
earth is blue and oranges are orange. I've reached a point
where I can't stand freak talk any longer. You understand,
it's too difficult for me to find my way to reality. Maybe I've
no sense of humour? Because according to you it takes a
sense of humour to understand that stuff? You know what I
say? I'm so far from lacking a sense of humour that I've

235

gone much further than you. And there it is. I've come back ruined. My kind of humour lay beyond words. It was hidden and I couldn't give it expression. And as I couldn't put it into words, it was much vaster than yours. Eh? In fact it was boundless. You know. Myself, I do everything that way. The earth is as blue as an orange, but the sky is as bare as a clock, the water as red as a hailstone. Or better still— the coleopterous sky floods the bracts. To want to sleep. Cigarette cigar besmirches the souls. 11th. 887. A, B, C, D, E, F, G, H, I, J, K, L, M, N, O, P, Q, R, S, T, U, V, W, X, Y, Z & Co.'

'Wait, wait a minute, I——' the girl broke in. Adam continued:

'I'd like to stop this silly game. If you knew how I'd like to. I'm crushed, soon nearly crushed . . .' he said, his voice not weaker but more impersonal.

'You know what's happening?' he asked. 'I'll tell you, just you. What's happening is that people are living, here, there and everywhere; what's happening is that some of them are dying of heart-failure, quietly, at home, in the evening. What's happening is that there are still people who are unhappy, because their wife's left them, because their dog is dead, because their little boy chokes when he swallows. You know—— And we, we, why do we have to put our oar in?'

'Is that why you did all THAT?' the girl demanded.

'All WHAT?' shouted Adam.

'Well, those things—all those things that they——'

'Wait!' said Adam. He was hurrying, as though ashamed of explaining himself:

'I've had enough of it! That's enough psychopathology for today—I mean—there's nothing left to understand. It's all over. You're you and I'm me. Stop trying to put yourself in my place all the time. The rest is balls. I've had enough of it, I—do please stop trying to understand. You know, I—I'm ashamed—I don't know how to put it. Don't talk about it all any more . . .'

He suddenly lowered his voice and bent towards Julienne R., so that only she could hear him.

'This is what we'll do: I'll talk to you very softly, just to you. And you must answer in the same way. I'll say to you hello, how are you? and you'll say to me, I'm very well, thank you. You see how I want it to be: and then, what's your name, you're pretty, I like the colour of your dress, or of your eyes. What's your sign? Scorpio, Libra? You'll answer yes, or no. You'll talk to me about your mother, what you had for your meal, or the film you've seen at the cinema. The countries you've been to—Ireland, the Scilly Isles. You'll tell me something that happened during your holidays, or your childhood. The first time you ever used lipstick. The time you got lost on a mountain. You'll tell me whether you like going for walks in the evening, when it's getting dark and one can hear hidden things moving. Or about when you went to look at the exam results, standing out in the rain, and what you were thinking as your eye ran down the list of names. You'll talk to me very softly, telling me such tiny things that I shan't even need to listen. Stories of storms or equinoctial gales, autumn in Brittany with heather growing above your head. When you were scared, when you couldn't get to sleep and you used to go and look out into the darkness through the slats of the shutters. And for the others, for the others, I'll go on with my own story. You know, that complicated story that explains everything. The mystical business. Shall we?'

The others were leaning foward, watching; some of them —the fair-haired boy, for instance—were grinning sarcastically. They didn't take the thing seriously; they were all eager for this other-world rigmarole to come to an end, so that they could get home, have dinner and go out for the evening. There was something on at the cinema and at the Opera it might be Gluck.

Adam could read consent all over the girl—on her neck, all round her neck, in the corners of her mouth, on her shoulders and breasts, down her spine and right down to her feet, which were rigid in their gold-buckled court shoes set at an infinitesimal angle. He pushed back his shoulders until they touched the wall; he stretched out his legs till they brushed against her bare knees. He could feel the red and black pyjama-stripes on his skin; they extended from him to a kind of solid, impenetrable surface that was now forming between himself and the group of students. He groped in the jacket pocket and found the packet of cigarettes. The student with the sun-glasses held out a box of matches to him at arm's length. There were five matches in the little cardboard drawer, three of them used and two fresh. Adam lit the cigarette flawlessly; as the only temporal detail in his successful bearing, a drop of sweat ran down from his armpit and fell like a cold pin-prick, level with his second rib. But it happened so rapidly, and was after all so well tolerated, that nobody could have guessed. Julienne R., hunched up on her chair, showed the greater fatigue; she was obviously waiting for something. Not anything novel or strange, something socially inevitable; something calm and icy, like crossing out a word in a sentence, for example.

'A year or two ago,' Adam began, '—to go on with the story I was telling just now——'

Julienne R. picked up her exercise-book and prepared to jot down essentials.

'I was on the beach with a girl. I'd been bathing, but she'd not gone in; she was lying on the shingle, reading a science-fiction magazine. There was a story in it called "Bételgeuse", I think. When I came out of the water she

238

was still there. I could see she was hot, and I don't know why—probably to annoy her—I put my wet foot on her back. She was wearing a bikini. At that she jumped up and said something to me. I don't remember what it was. But that's the important thing. Two minutes later she came back to me and said, "Because you made me all wet just now, I'm going to take one of your cigarettes." And she felt in the pocket of my trousers, which were lying beside me on the beach, to find the cigarette. I said nothing, but I began to think. Two hours later, I remember, I was still thinking about it. I went home and looked in the dictionary. I swear this is true. I looked up every word, so as to understand. And even then I couldn't understand. I spent the whole night thinking about it. By about 4 in the morning I was crazy. I'd got what the girl had said on my brain. The words were flying in all directions. I could see them written up everywhere. On the walls of my room, on the ceiling, in the squares of the windows, along the edge of the sheet. It was bothering me to death. Then I began to get things straight again. But it wasn't the same now. It was as though everything had become either false or correct, from one day to the next. I said to myself, no matter how I twist The Sentence, or the facts that are parallel to it, it MUST be pure logic. I mean I began to understand everything, clearly. And I thought I must go, push my motor-bike into the sea, and all that. I said to myself that the——'

But Adam had already become invisible to them all, as he had been obliged to do with his mother, with Michèle and with many other people; sitting alone at the lightest end of the infirmary, he seemed to be hovering slightly, with his thin limbs, his egg-shaped head and his left hand, from which the cigarette stuck out horizontally. His body, stiffly upright on the metal chair, seemed to be smoking amidst involuntary chaos; some mere trifle, his prognathous jaw, his sweat-beaded forehead and perhaps his triangular eyes, was turning him into a prehistoric creature. It was as though he were perpetually climbing out of some muddy yellow water in the form of a lacustrine bird, its feathers flat against its skin and every tiny muscle in movement to raise it skywards. His voice rolled down over the terrestrial population, no longer particularly comprehensible, and carried him along on its waves like a kite. Above him, close to the ceiling, two blue globes were bumping together, the shock of their clashing curves reverberating in magnetic storms. It was like the idea of a God of destiny, a knot of mysteries and canonizations, born one day from the spark between two cog-wheels in a locomotive. Adam was turning into a sea. Unless he had fallen asleep, without the pose, owing to the magnetic influence of Julienne R.'s gaze or the hypnotic persuasion of a mere striped pyjama suit. In any case he was drifting backwards, soft, transparent, undulating, and the words were rattling together in his mouth like pebbles, with strange rumbling noises. A bubbling network had lined the cramped room, and the others were in danger of following it. When Adam stopped talking and began to emit feeble grunts, the doctor decided to intervene; but it was too late. He called out two or three times 'Hello! M. Pollo! M. Pollo! Hey!', shaking Adam by the shoulder. Then he noticed a kind of grin across Adam's bony face, sharpening his parchment-coloured features. It began high up, just below the cheekbones, and split the face in two without parting the lips or revealing even the tip of an incisor. At this he gave up all hope and sent for the nurse. Slowly, one by one, they left the cold room, while Adam was led away, tottering, down the corridor.

From the depths of his slumber, Adam felt them going; his lips moved and he almost whispered 'goodbye'. But not even a grunt came out of his throat. Somewhere or other a blue ball-point pen was squeaking slightly as it crossed the page of an exercise-book and wrote the one word: 'Aphasia.'

While Adam went round one corner of the passage and then another, leaning on the nurse's warm arm, he was entering a region of fable. He was thinking, perhaps, very softly, very tenuously, far ahead of his frozen vocal cords, that he was really in his proper place. That at last he had found the beautiful house of his dreams, cool and white, built amid the silence of a wonderful garden. He was telling himself that he was happy, all alone in his beige-painted room, with its single window through which the sounds of peace flowed in unbroken. He had no objection; it was to be his at last, that perennial repose, that boreal night with its midnight sun, with people to look after him; out-door walks and subterranean slumbers; even, now and then, a pretty nurse whom one could lead into a thicket at dusk. Letters. A visitor from time to time, and big parcels of chocolate and cigarettes. There would be the annual celebration on Founder's Day, April 25 or October 11. Christmas and Easter. Perhaps tomorrow the blonde girl would come to see him. Alone this time. He would take her by the hand and talk to her for a long time. He would write her a poem. After a couple of weeks, all being well, he would be allowed to write letters. Then, towards the late autumn, they'd be able to stroll in the garden together. He would say to her, I can stay here for another year, perhaps not so long; after that, when I leave, we'll go and live in the South, at Padua or Gibraltar. I'll work a bit, and in the evening we'll go to night-clubs or to a café. Now and then, when we feel like it, we'll come back here for a month or two. They'll be glad to see us and they'll give us the best room, the one that looks over the garden. Outside the dead leaves are crackling in the sun and the living leaves are rustling in the rain. One can hear a train. The corridors smell of vegetable broth, everything seems to be hollow, warm and yet cool. That's the moment to dig oneself a hole in the ground, pushing aside the twigs and crumbs of earth, and get into it, feet first, well hidden, to spend an invalid's winter. After that there'll be the cup of *tilleul* and then darkness, closing over the clouds of the Last Cigarette as though over Sinbad's magic smoke. At a pinch, a bell may ring. A mosquito is prowling round the lamp, making a noise like a marble-polishing machine. That's the moment to surrender the earth to the termites. The moment to escape backwards and pass through the stages of past time. One is caught in the torpor of the evenings of childhood, as though in bird-lime; one is smothering in the fog, after some meal or other, in front of a curiously empty holly-patterned plate with smears of soup left on it. Then comes the cradle period and one dies, suffocated in swaddling-clothes, choking with rage at being so small. But that's harmless. Because one has to go back even further, through blood and pus, to one's mother's womb and there, arms and legs curled into an egg-shape, with one's head against the rubber membrane, fall into a dark sleep, peopled by strange terrestrial nightmares.

Adam is all alone; he lies on his bed beneath strata of draughts, expecting nothing any more. He is enormously alive, staring up at the ceiling, at the spot where No. 17's hacmorrhage came through three years ago. He knows that everyone has gone away now, right away. He is going vaguely to sleep in the world allotted to him; opposite the high window, as though to counterbalance the six swastikas formed by the bars, a single cross hangs on the wall, mother-of-pearl and pink. He is inside the oyster, and the oyster is at the bottom of the sea. He still has a few bothers, of course; he will have to keep his room tidy, give samples of urine for analysis, answer test questions. And one is always at the mercy of being unexpectedly released. But with any luck he'll be here for a long time, attached to this bed, these walls, that garden, this harmony of bright metal and fresh paint.

While awaiting the worst, the story is over. But wait. You'll see. I (please note I haven't used that word too often) think we can count on them. It would be really strange if one of these days there were not something more to say about Adam or some other among him.

J.M.G. LE CLEZIO, WHO IS HALF ENGLISH AND HALF FRENCH, WAS BORN IN NICE IN 1940. THIS NOVEL, HIS FIRST, WON THE PRIX RENAUDOT, TIED FOR THE PRIX GONCOURT, AND CAUSED MORE COMMENT THAN ANY OTHER FIRST BOOK IN MANY YEARS.